TO NO END

SKORRAVIK TRILOGY: BOOK 1

Gaebrielle I. Wieck

Wandering Hope
Publication
LLC

TO NO END

Copyright © 2018 by Gaebrielle I. Wieck

For more information contact :

Wandering Hope Publication, LLC

www.wanderinghopepublicationllc.com

Book Formatting by Derek Murphy of Creativindie Design © 2018

Book Cover design by Damonza © 2018

Library of Congress Control Number : 2017919795

ISBN: 978-0-9997801-0-7 (paperback)

First Edition: March 2018

10 9 8 7 6 5 4 3 2 1

To No End

Sic Parvis Magna

"*Greatness from Small Beginnings.*"

Here's to 'To No End' being my small beginning to hopefully something spectacular.

"He who knows no hardships will know no hardihood. He who faces no calamity will need no courage. Mysterious though it is, the characteristics of human nature which we love best grow in a soil with a strong mixture of troubles."

Harry Emerson Fosdick

TO NO
END

CHAPTER 1

THE ROAD SEEMED TO WIND ON FOREVER. Alyx drove as fast as she could, but it seemed like she was barely moving. Her lip bled profusely, half-ass wiping her face off with the back of her hand. Her lip stung in objection. She glared down at her steering wheel and felt the rage creep within her heart. All she was doing was watching a matinee with her family for Christ's sake! They had the audacity to harass her in front of her own family? She couldn't get away from that place fast enough.

Her family had watched her run to her car, their mouths wide open. Memories of the bitch that hit her first replayed through her mind. She had blacked out through most of the fight but she could remember glimpses, particularly at the end.

———— ⊰❖⊱ ————

"Alyx, stop!" Why should she?

"She's not moving! Stop it!" The bitch is finally getting what she deserves. She could feel her fist connect with the girl's face, neck, anywhere that she could reach. She shouldn't have hit first.

She shouldn't have.

She could hear her internal voice saying, no hissing at her: "Punch the bitch."

Something didn't sit well with her then, as her fist connected with flesh once more. It wasn't her own voice, and for some unknown reason she couldn't control her reaction. It was like someone was controlling her actions, it wasn't Alyx anymore. She blinked, slowly drawing back at the crumpled body that was lying on the floor underneath her.

Suddenly, she felt two arms wrap around her stomach and pull her up, away from the girl who was lying on the disgusting theater lobby floor, blood pouring out of her nose and staining her purple shirt, some popcorn stuck in her now tangled hair, the onlookers gasping and whispering amongst one another. A few pulled out their phones and started recording the ordeal; she knew she would see the video on social media within the day. Alyx turned around and saw her older brother Duncan, who had reluctantly let go of her, probably fearing that she would start back up again.

"Alyx, stop! She's not worth it!" he shouted at her, his voice miles away, she could only hear her heart beating in her head, her rage was starting to subside but she knew she couldn't look at the girl, otherwise it would ignite all over again.

The girl who she thought was one of her best friends.

"Duncan." was all Alyx managed to gasp out before she began hurtling back to earth, realizing what she had just done. Her feet started to move on their own, and before she knew it she was in her car starting the ignition.

To No End

Alyx looked up from the steering wheel and slammed on her breaks, stopping inches behind a car at a stoplight. She exhaled and closed her eyes, trying to keep hold of her sanity. What had she done? Silence filled the car as she was trying to recount how it even started. The light turned green. She barely realized she had hit the gas as she was consumed within her own thoughts.

Kourtney had antagonized her, she should know better than that. She knew how to push Alyx's buttons, but she soon regretted it. But that voice, that voice that wasn't hers in her head. What was it? She had so much adrenaline prior that maybe she was just hyping herself more.

Alyx shook her head, it didn't matter anymore and she was done with Kourtney's bullshit. Her phone started to buzz in her purse beside her. She didn't want to answer, knowing it was either her mom, Duncan, or Cat, her best friend. She didn't want to talk to anyone right now. Alyx was good at

that, at running away from her problems, just like
she had run away from family just now, and just like
how she ran away from her dad.

Tears began to well up in her eyes. She was a
disappointment, she knew that, so how was she
going to face them now? Besides, could her dad even
hear what they were saying? She asked herself that
at least fifty times a day. She turned up her radio,
blaring drums and guitar's that almost rattled her
windows, praying that the music would also rattle
her bones enough to distract her.

It took about fifteen minutes for her to get
home, it would probably take about twenty minutes
for her family since everyone was trying to get out
of the parking lot after the movie. Even cutting
through the back roads, the traffic would be bad
around this time of day. She could remember coming
out of the bathroom and those girls had cornered
her, right as her mom, Maria, was searching for her.
Her home may be only a few minutes out of town,
but it was a sanctuary. The buildings started to turn
into trees, and the cement into grass. Alyx pulled up
her dirt driveway, starting to see her home. The

music no longer helping to keep her thoughts at bay, she sighed and turned it off. The late afternoon sun beamed down upon her, settling on the serene earth around her home. The open field nearby was bright green filled with wildflowers and wheat dancing around in the wind. A forest of trees bordered around and added some form of shelter, but there was more vegetation than anything. Some flowers her mom had added over the years, making it her own personal garden. Her mom loved her garden, her own sanctuary, almost as much as her family. Lord knows she needed it over these past few months.

Alyx parked in her usual spot and got out. She stood silently in front of the house, trying to keep herself together. The Colonial was anything but a mountain home, it had a walkway up to the front door that had more flowers bordering each side. Its cheery disposition stuck out like a sore thumb when most houses in Colorado were either stone, rustic or contemporary, with sleek, sharp edges. It has so much character to it. The flowers that adorn the walkway edges are wildflowers of all colors, some daisies, and some lilies; her mom practically being a wizard with plants. Alyx would always joke that she never inherited a green thumb like her, and her mom would of course smile in response, never saying anything but you always knew exactly what she meant. She would miss that smile after today.

After everything Alyx had done this had to be the last straw, even for her mom's forgiving heart. Her hand brushed against the soft petals as she walked up the path.

The large front porch was inviting as the sunlight warmed the old wood. The smell of flowers was greatly welcomed and soothed her nerves.

She walked up the steps, ignoring the creak of the wood and pulled out her house key. The door made a slight groan as she opened and closed it behind her. She stopped temporarily at the mirror that was hanging in the hallway. In her reflection she saw her long, dark hair, now in disarray, a few spots made thin due to the hair pulling that had happened earlier in the fight. At least what she could remember of it. Her wine-colored lipstick smudged across her lips and onto her cheeks. Her upturned nose was now bleeding, causing her to grab a tissue out of its box laying on the countertop nearby, and dabbing it against her face, sopping up the red liquid. Dumping her purse on the table in the entryway she made her way into the kitchen, grabbed an apple and moved upstairs, each step creaking in protest. Her room was closest to the stairs thankfully, so she could disappear as fast as she could.

She suddenly stopped. The door was open wide and she could feel the breeze gently blowing into the hallway from her room. Not how she left it. She looked around the hallway to see that the rest of her sibling's doors were shut and seemingly untouched.

Alyx slowly walked towards the entryway, she could hear papers fluttering from the breeze and a soft whisper, but she couldn't make out the words.

"Hello?" she said quietly, though her voice broke. She held up the apple ready to throw it at whomever would show themselves. The whisper stopped and the silence became overbearing. "I heard you, who are you?" she said again. This time a bit braver.

She came around the corner and gasped. Papers were strewn everywhere on her bed, the floor and some were tacked onto the wall. The place was trashed. She took a few steps in without thinking and grabbed at some of the papers closest to her. There were words like Death, Evil and Curse written in harsh and almost angry handwriting over every scrap of paper fluttering about around her. Could this be because she had gotten into that fight with Kourtney? That idea sounded ridiculous since this seemed to have happened so soon after. Or because of all the other things she had done? This had to be some sick prank. Alyx felt her face go pale as fear gripped her throat. What was going on?

She began to collect the paper and ball it up, afraid that if she didn't get rid of it, whoever had written the awful words would appear. Then she heard footsteps coming up the stairs.

"Alyx?" Duncan shouted, startling her. When did he get home? She tried to hide the paper as fast as she could but to no avail, he appeared in the doorway. He was just about to say something when he stopped, seeing her fists stuffed with wads of notes with the cruel words written on them. His mouth opened, not knowing what to say. He took a step inside. She looked at him, pleading that he wouldn't ask her any questions, a fool's hope of course.

"You're home earlier than expected," was all she managed to say. She continued to collect the paper.

"I went ahead of the others, I drove separately, remember?" he said slowly as he took another step towards her, testing her. He did just rip her off of another girl a few minutes ago. Not wanting to give him a chance to see them she grabbed the remaining paper and shoved past him, heading downstairs, Duncan closely behind her, out the back through the sun room and threw them away in one of the plastic trash cans by the backdoor. Feeling her heart in her throat she ran back up to her room and slammed the window shut, her light gray walls adding a sense of calm. Hopefully he didn't see what was written on the notes, but something in her gut told her otherwise. She wouldn't know how to explain, hell, she didn't know what to think in the first place. He followed her back upstairs, which only made her slam her door in his face before he had the chance to say anything. He was like a vulture.

"What were those?" he demanded through the door. She rolled her eyes, crossing her arms in annoyance. Once again, he just couldn't just ignore anything.

"Christ, Duncan give it a rest! Can you leave me alone for five seconds?" she demanded. He slammed his fist into the door.

"Seriously Alyx! What the hell just happened? What were those little pieces of paper about?" he yelled. She flinched from his sudden outburst, not being able to say anything to him was harder than she had thought. Especially when he stopped her. After what seemed to be an agonizingly long time of silence between the two of them, they both heard a car pull up into the driveway. Great, everyone was home now to demand answers. Duncan sighed heavily, but headed back downstairs, meeting up with the others. Would he say anything to them about the notes?

What were those whispers though? That couldn't have been her imagination. It was harsh and angry, and sounded like one person. A woman. She sounded so close to Alyx, almost as if, she was in her head? Alyx scoffed and shook her head. Okay, now she was losing her mind.

"Alyx? Where are you," Alyx's mom called from downstairs, a sharpness in her tone. Hesitantly, Alyx took a step and heard the whisper again, causing her to freeze in place. What was she saying? She wanted to talk to the woman, find out why she was trying to communicate with her. It sounded so much like the voice she heard earlier at the theater. But on the other hand, she watched enough movies to know that you don't mess with spirits, *if* that's what she was, but that had to have been what she was though, right? Had she died in this house? Strange that after all these years they had lived here that she would choose now to say something.

"Alyx, did you not hear me? Why did you ignore me? Your brother told me what happened." Her mom was suddenly standing in the entryway, a hand on her hip. Her voice a million miles away. Was she going crazy?

She could see her mom's lips moving, but another female voice caught her attention. The voice sounded but a soft whisper in the distance, slightly distorted and quiet, almost making her believe that she only imagined it. A cold sweat trickled down her temple. Christ, she needed a drink.

"Alyx! You will listen to me!" Maria shouted, causing Alyx to jump. She looked her in the eye this time, face full of emotion.

"Mom." She whispered. Everything didn't make sense, everything was different. It was all so wrong. The fight with her supposed best friend, that voice in her own mind. Her mom sighed and extended her arms for comfort. Alyx fell into her embrace and started to weep. The world seemed to shift.

Was she ready to change with it?

"Shh, it will be alright, I'm here," Maria comforted. Alyx couldn't speak, she could only stand there and cry. She didn't know anything anymore. "Are we going to talk about what happened, Alyx?" Maria asked, her voice still soothing but stern. She pulled Alyx back at arm's length, her eyes searching for answers. Taking a breath, she wiped her cheek with a hand.

"There's a lot you don't know," Alyx paused. "It's hard to explain. I know it looks bad."

"Looks bad? *That's* an understatement. That poor girl probably will get stitches because of you! How could you be so irresponsible? This could jeopardize everything for you!" her mom stopped in between breaths, trying to calm herself. A tinge of guilt struck Alyx like a hot poker, she never wanted her mom to feel like this. Once again, she was the screw up, always doing the wrong thing because she couldn't control her emotions. What's worse, she didn't care about her future, even though that's all her parents thought about. Still, she felt a sense of relief that Duncan didn't say anything to their mom about the notes.

"I wish your father was here." Her mom whispered, rubbing the bridge of her nose in agitation.

"Well he's not now is he!" she felt distressed, not wanting to talk about her dad. She could feel the helplessness start to seep in all over again. At a loss for words, Maria's jaw dropped in shock but quickly closed as she was starting to become visibly upset. Almost immediately Alyx bit her lip. Her mom took a step back, wrapping her arms around her shoulders and began to bite her own lip. A hereditary nervous habit no doubt. She gave one nod and backed out of the room.

Alyx opened her mouth to say something but stopped. She knew she was only going to screw things up more. She walked over to the bed and sat down, placing her head in her hands. Even though she was also to blame, she felt so much hatred for Kourtney and the others. They had backed her into a wall and practically spit on her. And that voice, it was so strange and out of place, and why appear after the fight? What did it all mean? Letting out a sigh she stopped short, something catching her eye.

One of the papers she had missed was laying halfway under the edge of the bed. The words Evil and Curse stuck out to her for some reason. Alyx grabbed the slightly wadded up paper and unfolded it, smoothing out the crinkles.

Death   Evil   Curse

Staring out of the window, she could only contemplate why those words held so much meaning. Her They were the first sign for answers since her father ended up in the hospital. Something that seemed to have a connection with him. It had to be, right?

Death, perhaps had to be connected with his near-death experience. The word Evil sent a chill up her spine, as it had so many unknown meanings regarding her father's situation. And Curse, it made sense. Alyx always thought that her family had a malevolent aura regarding how her family members had passed away. She had lost both grandfathers to some type of terminal cancer, and her great grandfathers had a rather violent end. One was killed in war, and the other was actually murdered in New York. Most of the men had a 'premature' death, none of them living to their potential age. She hadn't heard much about her great-great grandfathers but she knew they hadn't lived to be very old either.

As much as she tried to resist, her thoughts flashed to that horrendous day that changed her family's life.

———

Everything was a blur. The paramedics rushed Victor through the double doors of the hospital, the nurse cutting open his shirt revealing a graphic wound.

A stab wound.

"He's going into shock!" shouted one nurse.

Their mom, Alyx and Duncan rushed behind them. Maria frantically trying to keep her eyes on her husband.

To No End

"Mom? Why was dad stabbed?" Alyx shouted, in shock herself. She didn't understand why he would have been attacked and stabbed like that. He was never mean to anyone. Why did he have to suffer like this?

"I-I don't know!" her mom responded, her voice frantic, her thoughts clouded.

"Mom, you can't do this right now." Duncan tried to distract her, he was good at that. He narrowed his eyes at Alyx, silently telling her this was not okay. He placed a hand on the middle of Maria's back and led her to the waiting room.

"Are Emily and Josh on their way?" Alyx asked absent mindedly as she stared at the doors that her father had just disappeared behind. Sounds seemed distant, everyone was shouting and scurrying around as people were either sick or dying. She could hear someone moaning in pain in a room nearby, causing her to cover her ears like a child, shutting her eyes in the process. She couldn't take it anymore.

"Alyx!" Duncan's voice broke through as he grabbed her wrist and whirled her around to face him.

How was he so calm? Their father was just stabbed. Who would want to hurt him? His eyes were crazed.

"We don't know what's happening but I need you to at least try and hold it together. Mom needs you. Mom needs all of us right now." He gently tugged at her wrists, making her follow him. Alyx couldn't speak, she knew her brother was right, but she couldn't get the image out of her head.

Her father was lying on the ground a few feet away from the small gazebo out in the backyard. He was already covered in his own blood, as she screamed, dropping her book and running over to him. His blood stained the grass around him as he met her gaze. He looked so scared as he reached up towards her.

"Alyx, you must.... find.... her." he struggled with speaking as his breathing was sporadic and shallow. Weakly, he reached up to her, his hands in a fist, like he was holding something.

"Dad!? Wh-what's happening? She shouted, tears in her eyes. She took his hand and felt him place something on her palm. It had a slight weight to it and felt metallic, but was unusually warm, and...it

has a heartbeat. It must have been her adrenaline, she told herself.

Victor gave her a small, weak smile.

"I'm so sorry." He whispered and lost consciousness.

"Dad!" Alyx shouted, forgetting about the object he had placed in her hand a second ago. "Mom! Mom, call 911!" Alyx was frantic, shaking him. She checked his pulse, it was faint but there.

"Alyx, wh---?" her mom began to say as she ran over, but stopped after she saw her husband. Her eyes seemed to cloud over, unable to comprehend what was happening.

"Call an ambulance!" Alyx shouted again. Her mother jumped as her daughter's voice seemed to shock her back to reality. She frantically grabbed her cell out of the back pocket of her jean's--fumbling with dialing and pressed it to her ear, her eyes large and pleading.

"Hold on! Just hold on!" Tears were burning through her vision.

Alyx was suddenly pulled back to the waiting room as a baby started to cry. She was sitting on the edge of the cushion of the bench, her right leg tapping impatiently. She was sitting on her hands, not bearing to look at her blood-stained skin. She could feel the weight of the object in her jean pocket but she didn't dare take it out. In fact, she wanted to forget about everything she had just seen. She looked around, trying to distract herself. Her mom was leaning on the right arm of the chair, a hand by her mouth, nervously biting her nails. Her usual neat topknot bun was in disarray as a few long dark curls fell around her face. She was staring at a home décor magazine, pretending she was going to read it, but never bothering to pick it up.

Duncan was standing up by the double doors, waiting for their siblings to walk through the entrance. He has the same green colored eyes as her and their dad, Josh and Emily were more like their mom. Alyx had heard him talk on the phone with their sister, no doubt Josh and Emily were at another viewing, hoping to get their art showcase up and running. They haven't been around much lately, but then again neither had Alyx. As if on cue, Emily came bursting through the door, looking dressed up and chic as usual, her eyes wide with worry.

"Duncan! Where's mom?" Emily spoke loudly, making a few nurses stare at us with concern.

"Calm down, they're over there." Duncan raised his arms up in defense and pointed over towards Alyx and Maria. Duncan was most like their dad, Victor, with his endless patience and support, not to mention his lighter, messy, blonde hair. Their eyes met as Emily jogged over to them, Josh right behind her. Emily looked so much like their mom, except her blonde hair, but Josh could be Maria's twin. Alyx bolted up and greeted her sister with a hug.

"What's going on? Duncan called saying dad had an accident? What happened?" Emily asked after hugging Maria in greeting.

"We don't know what happened. Alyx had found him in the backyard, coming out of the forest." Maria explained after she hugged Josh in greeting. He glanced at Alyx but ignored her. She noticed his hands were still covered in paint. Red paint. She felt something crawl up her spine.

"The backyard? What? I-I don't get it, I thought he was working?" her eyes filled with confusion. She searched her sister's face for answers, then looked down at Alyx's hands, the blood clearly catching her eye. Instantly her face went pale. Alyx could only shake her head, not knowing what to say. She felt helpless.

"The doctors are with him right now," their mom said urgently. "He-he was attacked." Her voice grew faint on the last word. Josh looked shocked and lost, Emily had tears well up in her eyes.

"All we can do is wait." Duncan held his hands up again, trying to calm everyone down.

"How are you not freaking out right now, Duncan?" shouted Emily. Their mom let out a sigh.

"Please, not now." she whispered. Emily ignored her and tried to size up their brother. It would have been funny if the situation would have allowed it, the difference in size was vast.

"Because I can't lose hope that he will be fine. We don't know what's happening or what had happened, we have to be level-headed, for dad." With that, Duncan glanced at Alyx and sat down. Emily and

To No End

Duncan never got along much. Too different of personalities, always at odds. The room filled with silence as Emily sat in her own corner away from the family, the busyness of the hospital faded into the background. Their mom placed a hand on Josh's shoulder. The tension felt thick in the air. Duncan slammed through the double doors and disappeared with a huff, finally losing that excruciatingly long thread of patience.

Alyx slowly sat back down, unable to comprehend what was going on. She watched as the nurses walked by, carrying on about their business and attending to phone calls or assisting with patients. Everything was distant again. She only wanted to be as far away from this place as possible.

"Alyx? Can we talk?" a voice disturbed her thoughts. She snapped around and saw Duncan standing in the doorway. She rolled her eyes.

"I'm not really up for talking." She said with an annoyed tone in her voice. She stood up and started gathering her books that were scattered on her bed. Trying to look too busy to talk she pretended to clean up her room. Duncan sighed.

"Why did you get in a fight with Kourtney?"

"Because she deserved it." she challenged.

"How?"

"I don't need to explain, you're not dad."

"Yes you do and no, no I'm not. Also, while I have your attention, what the hell were those notes about?" He questioned her, unflinching.

"Then stop acting like him." Alyx shot him a glare, not wanting to answer his question. He looked at her, unaffected. He searched her face for answers, when he didn't find any, he pressed forward.

"Last time I checked, you wouldn't just attack someone, or lash out. You're smarter than that. Especially to assault someone I thought was your friend." He folded his arms.

"That right there. *Was*. Was my friend. Somehow people always end up showing their true colors to you." There was a slight pause, which made

Alyx turn around, using that moment of silence to tell her brother to leave, but stopping short as he looked at her, worry now filled his face.

"Alyx, seriously. I'm worried about you. You've changed since dad...," his voice faltered at the last bit. "You can't keep going on this destructive path. I know you go out and party every night. You smell like cheap beer and weed half the time. Mom doesn't know what to do about you. It's bad enough Emily won't talk to us most of the time. You can't keep doing this, and dragging Josh down as well."

"Josh is an adult, he can make his own decisions. As can I." she spat, offended.

"You're both lost. He just lost his full ride to college because of that charge, Alyx. If he hadn't of been at that party with you. But you insisted he went with, so now he's in this mess."

"But it's okay if I am though, right?" Alyx crossed her arms, anger started to consume her. "I'm the screw up. I do everything wrong so it should have been me that got arrested isn't it." She fumed.

He sighed again. She had no idea that could
be such an annoying sound.

"I didn't say that."

"I know that's what everyone's thinking. I'm
not stupid. It's my fault that I'm not there for our
family like I should be. It's my fault that Josh can't
go to the college that he wants to now and it's my
fault that I completely screwed up my future. You
want to add anything else to my list?" she
challenged. They stood in silence for a few minutes,
not knowing what to say.

A slight breeze came out of nowhere
suddenly, causing Alyx to look over at her window to
make sure she had shut it fully. And it was. There
was a soft rustling of paper as the note fell on the
floor at Duncan's feet. His eyes rested upon the old
parchment, the three words stuck out boldly like a
beacon against the tan.

"What is that you had found earlier?" he
mumbled, not knowing if he should let it go or
question further.

"Nothing." Alyx rolled her eyes and waved a
hand, dismissively.

Duncan clearly didn't buy it, but pressed no further.

"Clean the blood off your face." He threw a hand down, giving up for now as he walked back downstairs. She walked into her bathroom and shut the door. Looking into the mirror she saw how split her lip really was. Her lipstick hiding the real damage. She grabbed a few tissues and pressed them against the raw skin. She didn't realize how bad it hurt until now, her anger masking the pain.

Great, a swollen face is just what she needed. After she stopped the bleeding she grabbed some concealer and tried to cover up as much of the redness as she could. Running a hand through her hair a few times, trying to smooth out a few strands that always stood up from her cowlicks. Giving up, she walked back into her room and changed into a pair of distressed jeans and a cream-colored peasant blouse with lace. She zipped up a pair of olive peep-toed boots.

"Alyx!" her mom shouted from the foot of the stairs. "You have a guest!" Loudly bounding down the steps, Alyx gave them the fakest smile she could muster. Hopefully nobody noticed her poorly concealed busted lip.

"Alyx!" said a voice from around the corner. She turned to see Catherine, who was standing with her mom and had big ol' grin on her face. Cat's mom however looked less than pleased to see Alyx. Damn, word about the fight travelled fast in this town.

She excused herself and ended up nodding for Catherine to join her. She parted from her mother and walks over to Alyx, her face now only filled with worry. Catherine's long, blonde hair flowing behind her, made it seem like the entire room was watching her. Go figure, that always happened whenever she went anywhere, Alyx was always outshined. Catherine's mom and Maria began whispering as they headed for the kitchen, most likely going to grab the wine. Alyx heard her mom mention something about catching up as they were to 'absolutely finish the bottle off' in doing so.

Alyx ushered Catherine to follow.

"Mom I'll see you later, okay?" Catherine said in a rush as she bounded up the steps behind Alyx, leaving her mother before she could object.

"So, clearly we have some things to talk about." Catherine scoffed as she shut the door behind them once they walked into Alyx's room.

"You have no idea, Cat." Alyx flopped down on her bed and covered her eyes with an arm. She was already exhausted.

"Tell me! Why did you beat the shit out of Kourtney after the movie? Duncan texted me immediately. What did she say?" she urged. She sat down in the desk chair and began to spin around.

"Duncan's gossiping about me with you now?" Alyx groaned. Catherine rolled her eyes, but nodded her head, urging for her to continue. Alyx sighed. "She's dating him now."

"Wait, your ex?" This made her stop the chair immediately grabbing her attention. Her green eyes wide with surprise. Alyx nodded.

"Yeah. I hate myself for even getting pissed off--or even caring so much--but after everything they've done to me, I don't know, I guess, I just snapped." Alyx sat up.

"What did she say?" Cat asked.

"She told me that they were going to have a great summer together, blah blah blah, and then proceeded to say how he's *such* a good boyfriend, and how I had ruined things with *such* good people and bullshit basically," Alyx rolled her eyes, she could feel the pain in her knuckles the more she thought about it. There was a slight pause. "It was mainly taking a jab at me about what happened with the girls. They're mad at me, so I have to suffer. That's what I get for trying to be friends with them in the first place."

"That *bitch*," Cat scoffed. Alyx laughed but started to say something. Catherine held up a hand and objected. "She only enjoys sloppy seconds anyway. She's not worth your time or energy, girl." She allowed herself to smile a little, but felt a tinge of guilt in doing so. It wasn't even necessarily the fact that she was now dating her ex that made her so upset, it made her feel betrayed. It's not like she had a lot of people in her life anymore. Even if that was her own doing.

She didn't know that she chose a group of girls that treated her like shit, because it was most convenient to them at that time. For some reason, it was easy for them to backstab anyone they called their friend because it was entertaining. Those girls, had mentally drained her and almost made her go into hiding. She couldn't go to a party without one of them being there to somehow harass her. And her ex, that she thought she had deep feelings for, ended up being the biggest backstabber of all. He was all a beautiful lie.

Trusting him with secrets she had told him, she felt like an idiot. Now everyone knew things about her that she told him in confidence.

All of this had happened before her father's accident, but it had gotten progressively worse.

She felt like a big screw up, her relationship ended, she lost most of her friends, she got her brother arrested and now she could be facing assault charges and possibly not getting into college. Not that she even knew what she wanted to go to college for anyway. She felt so disconnected with who she was it made her sick. She felt trapped in this town. Trapped and unfulfilled, she had more to give, but she wasted it. Now she could be going to jail for all she knew.

"Why did you two break up by the way?" Cat interrupted her thoughts, making her blink and shake her head, it was time to move on.

"I didn't like who I was when I was with him. He, they, all of them made me a mean person. They just didn't want me to see the truth, I think mainly because they didn't want to accept that that's who they are. Mean people," Alyx sighed. "Although, I don't think I even knew who I was anymore. I was one of them." She confessed, feeling ashamed. Catherine looked at her, her eyes softened.

"Alyx, you're my best friend. I didn't like those girls but I would never abandon you. You are an amazing and caring person. You will see that in time." she comforted. Her expression changed to sadness as she looked at Alyx, which made her slightly uncomfortable.

"If you're my best friend, then will you please stop looking at me like I'm gonna break?"

"What else am I supposed to do? I know you're going through a lot, what with decisions about your future, and your dad-," Alyx cut her off immediately.

"Change of subject." Running a hand through her chestnut brown hair, she breathed in sharply. She didn't like to talk about her dad out loud, she dealt with the pain everyday silently in her head, if she couldn't find alcohol to drown it out first. Besides, he wouldn't want her to cry, not when she's been given a sign. Her mind drifted to the note she had found earlier. Even though she wanted to tell Catherine about it, she knew she couldn't. If this was the only way to save her dad, then she didn't want to involve anyone that might screw it up. His words echoed in her mind.

"You must--find her."

"He's going to be fine." Alyx finalized, sternly looking at her friend. Catherine paused, and then nodded once, her lips a straight line.

"Yeah. He will be." She replied. There were a few minutes of silence that followed between them. Uncomfortable, Catherine stood up and stretched.

"I've got to run home before the party tonight. Are you still coming?" she asked as she

made her way to the hallway. Alyx gave her a weak
smile.

"Hell yeah. Tell Eric to actually leave a few
bottles of beer for us this time." She tried to relieve
the tension, forcing herself to joke around for once.

"Will do," Cat began to walk down the stairs,
Alyx in tow, but stopped short on the first step.

She looked back up at Alyx. "My mom doesn't
hate you by the way. She doesn't know what all is
going on, I figured it wasn't any of her business
unless you all want everyone to know what's
happening--although I'm sure that's what both our
moms are doing at the present moment--but, if you
still want to be my best friend, please for the love of
god don't hit anybody else. Otherwise she will
'forbid' me. And you know how good I am with
authority. We might find ourselves sitting in a jail
cell together." And with a wink, she grinned all the
way out the front door.

Alyx returned to her room, shutting the door
behind her. Falling back on her bed with a groan,
she felt the weight of the day finally pressing down
on her. She was exhausted and all she wanted to do

was crawl up in her bed and hide from the world, but she knew she had to show up to the party tonight. Knowing full well that she must face the consequences of her actions sooner or later. She's bound to run into some of Kourtney's friends or maybe not, she couldn't just keep hiding forever.

Besides, it was Cat's going away party anyhow, and she would hate her for missing it.

Catherine was accepted to go to University of Colorado at Boulder this fall, majoring in business administration, focusing on marketing, with Tyler, their close friend, in tow of course majoring in mechanical engineering. Eric, their newest 'transfer friend,' was accepted to go to the University of Tennessee back where he was originally from before he moved to Colorado to finish up high school, in Chattanooga, majoring in chemical engineering, and Alyx had absolutely no idea what she was doing with her life. It seemed that everyone had everything figured out, while she had changed her mind at least eight times. All she knew was that she wanted more out of this life, she didn't want to stay in Boulder forever, but leaving clearly wasn't an option right now.

Looking at the clock she stood up and made her way to her closet. How could she possibly know what she wanted to do with the rest of her life when she didn't even know if her dad would be ending his? He had been in a coma for a month now. She flinched. Great, here comes the pain. Tears began to well in her eyes, she hated thinking about it. The urge to numb herself was almost unbearable.

It was 9:30, and the party didn't start for another two hours but she couldn't stay in her room any longer. She became dangerous alone with her own thoughts. She was probably more afraid that she wouldn't ever leave if she didn't go now. Changing out of the boots, she slid on some sandals, and grabbed a hoodie on her way out of her room. Sliding it over her head she grabbed her knapsack and car keys off her desk. She paused for a moment and saw the note lying folded on the surface next to where her car keys were just sitting.

Grabbing it, she stuffed it in the back pocket of her jeans. Opening the door, she slowly looked out in the hallway and down the stairs, checking for anyone around. Laughter came from the living room, which made her relax a bit. Carefully walking downstairs, she poked her head around the corner, making sure her family wasn't paying any attention to her. She saw the back of their heads, but Josh and Duncan were sprawled out on the sectional, as Emily was sitting on the floor using the ottoman as a desk for her laptop. The tv was blaring some singing contest show as Josh began to mock one of the judges.

Not wanting to be seen, Alyx quickly tiptoed back through the kitchen and out the back door.

The calm spring breeze was a welcome feeling as Alyx walked across the lawn to the detached garage. Duncan must have re-parked her car into the garage earlier. Lifting the door up, she cringed at the loud squealing of the wheels on their tracks as it opened. Thank god it wasn't attached to the house.

Her little four-door sat patiently in the faint light next to Duncan's truck. She could hear laughter from the house again from an open window. It was almost painful to listen to--she didn't feel like this is where she belonged anymore, no matter how bad she wanted to. Where did she belong? What did she want? She's felt more disconnection this past month than she ever had in the whole year.

Ever since she found her dad in the field, her world turned upside down. It felt wrong to laugh and smile, to feel any other kind of emotion other than sadness. Their dad should be there right now, telling them all about the day he had at work. But instead his life was almost completely stolen from him, from them.

She wrapped her arms around herself, gripping the car keys tight in her hand. She couldn't break down right now. She held herself until the shaking stopped, which did eventually but not without leaving an annoying headache behind as vengeance. Rubbing her forehead, Alyx climbed into her car and started it up. The last album she had in her car filled the empty space with guitars and drums. The eager and angst-filled melody began to calm her thoughts as she focused solely on the beat while backing out of the garage.

To No End

It was about a fifteen-minute drive to the school's parking lot, assuming she didn't speed the entire way there. Deciding to park nearest to the football field, she killed the engine and looked at her phone. No messages but it was only a little after ten. It had been almost two years since she had last been here, and as much as she hated it, it had a sense of familiarity that comforted her. All she had were questions anymore. With no one to answer them.

Damn it, too much time left. She sighed and went to the trunk, hopefully a little pre-gaming will help this whole waiting issue. Popping it open, she saw she still had a twelve pack of beer with four cans left inside. She grabbed one, ignoring the fact that it was warm and stuffed it in the front pocket of her hoodie, not caring how obvious it looked. She shut the trunk and locked it. It was the middle of summer so no one really cared to watch the school.

Besides, the only solo patrol cop used these nights to binge-watch his shows on TV.

Alyx walked to the fence of the field and felt for the weak spot in the chain links. Finding a small bent section Alyx began to pull at the metal, bending it enough to create an entryway big enough for her to get through. Closing it behind her, she walked toward the bleachers and carefully ducked under the tallest row to avoid the cameras on the outside of the commentator's box. She got to the ladder that led up to the roof of the small building and began to climb up. The weight of the beer bulged through her hoodie as she made her way up. Finally reaching the top, she sat down and looked out over the field, the moon present but not high above her yet, shone down brightly on the freshly mown grass.

Alyx cracked open the beer and took a sip. It wasn't the best but luke-warm beer it was. She would do anything right now to numb the pain, or numb her mind considering the million thoughts that ran through it every waking moment of the day. She wanted relief. She took a long swig and then another.

"Drinking, again are we?" chimed a voice. Alyx nearly spit out the last sip, surprised. She looked down behind her, standing next to the ladder, looking up at her was Duncan. Alyx rolled her eyes.

"Let me guess, you followed me, again." Duncan was becoming increasingly annoying about that. He climbed up the ladder and joined her, taking a seat beside her. He snatched the beer out of her hand and downed the rest of it.

"Seriously? I only grabbed one."

"What? I was thirsty? And you shouldn't be drinking. I'm twenty-three so I'm very legal. You on the other hand, not so much. What would dad think if--,"

"I'm not talking about dad." Alyx snapped. Duncan looked at her and furrowed his brow.

"Well it's about damn time you do. Would you even maybe try to see him more since we're talking about it? We're all gonna go visit him tomorrow, why don't you come with?"

"Sorry, but I have plans."

"What's that? Nursing a hangover?"

"You just think you're so freaking smart, don't you?" she scoffed, rolling her eyes.

"Sometimes, when I need to be, I am." he responded, smugly.

"Well now is definitely not the time."

Duncan laughed once, shaking his head in disbelief and slammed the empty beer can on the tin roof, crushing it.

"Why are you so goddamn selfish? That's our dad! He would come see us every day if something had happened to any of us! Let alone being attacked! Why can't you at least 'grace' him with your presence, more often?" he shouted, his control slipping away, an abnormal thing for her older brother. She had really pissed him off this time. She could feel the tears well up in her eyes, a familiar feeling now a days. Tears of guilt and embarrassment for being scolded by her brother. His words were true, she just didn't want to accept them because if she did, she would break this time. Duncan took a breath, calming himself once more. She used her hoodie's sleeve to wipe her face.

To No End

"Look, I know you've gone through some shit, and that you don't handle hospitals or frankly, any of this well. But we're fighting through this together because dad needs us. You're still part of this family, whether you want to be or not." Duncan rested a hand on his sister's shoulder.

"I hate crying." she grumbled.

"I know." he allowed himself to grin.

"I hate that all of this is happening and that dad has to go through this alone."

"He's not though. He has all of us by his side." Duncan replied consolingly.

Alyx sniffed and wiped her face again.

"I hate that you're right about me." Duncan chuckled and wrapped an arm around her shoulder, giving her a soft squeeze.

"I know."

CHAPTER 2

ALYX AND DUNCAN sat on the roof for a good forty-five minutes. They talked about life before everything happening prior, and of many other things, some hopefully in the nearby future.

"Are you going to go to college?" Duncan asked. Alyx could tell he was nervous with her answer due to the hesitation in his voice. She could only give him a weak smile and shrugged. She was just glad he wasn't going to ask her about the notes. He gave her a disappointed nod in response.

"I have no idea what I'm gonna do with my life period, Duncan."

"What about writing?"

"With everything going on I'd be lucky to even come up with anything. I'm running on empty."

"Maybe that's your problem. You think too much."

"You have to be *inspired* to write. Where can I get any inspiration knowing dad might not wake up? And seems like a lot of people hate me anyway so sorry if I'm lacking in the imagination department, that usually sucks a lot of fire out of you. Unfortunately, I'm no Poe." Although she felt like him.

"I don't hate you. Besides, just think how lucky you are that you're not arrested right now for that fight you were in. Especially since her family isn't going to charge you either." Duncan shook his head in disbelief. Alyx was surprised too.

"They're not?"

Duncan shook his head.

"Nope, mom had talked to Kourtney's mom and she said that it was all a big misunderstanding and as long as you steer clear from her, there's no ill will," Duncan paused. "What did she do to you exactly?" he questioned.

"Stupid drama. All I'm gonna say is that she made friends with people who hate me for stupid reasons, and she took their side because she probably didn't want to be targeted next. How those are friends, I'll never know. Plus, I just dated the wrong boy. I feel like I completely wasted my time and only hurt myself. I changed for a guy," she paused. "Remind me to thank mom later by the way."

"Will do. Did things get serious?" Duncan raised his eyebrows, questioning. Alyx nodded.

"Words were said that I did mean at the time but I didn't know they were only going to be used as ammunition later on. It makes me regret everything. I was just a stupid girl. I hated the person I became when I was with him."

"Dad never really liked Isaac you know," Duncan said bluntly. Alyx felt a pang in her chest. "I didn't really care much for the guy either to be honest. Why didn't you ever say anything to us?" She merely shrugged. Somehow, she had known all along that her family never really approved of him, perhaps that only helped fuel her to try and make things work with him. Just another expression of rebellion on her part, even if she didn't realize it at the time.

"I thought everything would be fine. I thought I could get through it on my own. I made a mistake, I know I'm not innocent either in all of this but it ended up sucking even more going through it all alone. I was lost, I still am. Finding dad like that, really screwed with me you know?" she admitted. Duncan closed his eyes, his brows furrowed. She could see his jaw clench, upset. She went on. "I didn't want anyone to fight my battle for me because I knew dad would want me to be strong. But when the one I always saw as the strongest person I knew, attacked and vulnerable like that, I spiraled out of control. Besides, dad is way more important than my petty drama with ex boyfriends and friends, why would I bother you all with that?" It was like word vomit, she couldn't stop. Alyx didn't realize how much she really needed to vent to Duncan. He was always a good listener, but she could see that her words were starting to affect him. That's his dad too.

Wordlessly, she leaned against her brother's shoulder. He could only sit in silence.

"Sorry if I upset you." Alyx spoke first. She could feel Duncan shake his head.

"Don't be. I just haven't taken enough time to fully process everything yet. It's all hard on us. I'm glad you told me though tonight, Alyx. I just wish you wouldn't run away from problems. Or from us. Family doesn't do that to each other." Alyx looked up at Duncan. He gave her a soft smile.

"To be honest, I wasn't planning on telling you all of that so consider yourself lucky. And I know," she sighed, even though his words stung, it was true. When was she going to face it? She tried to lighten the mood, the tension was too thick. Duncan chuckled and looked out at the field.

"She's dating him now." Alyx said nonchalantly. He scoffed.

"Seriously?"

"Relax, I think you're more upset than I am. I'm more sad about her siding with that hyena pack than her sudden interest in him." Alyx looked off into the distance, fixated on the breeze kicking up a bit that made a wind chime sing gently on the porch of a nearby home across the field, closest to the goal posts.

"Did you love him?" That question caught her off guard. She opened her mouth to say something but stopped short. Duncan waited patiently, not looking at her as she searched her feeling's. He's been in love before and had his heart broken as well. He of all people would know as much as you tried to hide it, those feelings never fully went away.

"It was a different kind of love. Not fully in love, but close. Really close." She was satisfied with her answer. Duncan sighed but didn't say any more about the subject.

A loud buzz came from the front pocket of her hoodie, making her jump. She pulled it out and pushed the side button, turning the screen on. A text from Catherine blared at her. It took a moment for her eyes to adjust to the sudden bright light.

Where are you? Are you still coming tonight?

"Ah shit. I forgot about the party." Alyx mumbled and stuffed her phone back in her pocket.

"Alyx, c'mon you still can't be serious about going." Duncan scoffed. Alyx shot him a look as she started to collect her things.

"Uh, duh."

"We want you to stop partying all together. I know you're hurting but this isn't the way to cope." He begged and followed her down the ladder.

"*Big brother*. If you want us to keep having these heart-to-hearts, you should probably calm down. I'm fine," She mocked and rolled her eyes. "And you mean you, not we. Mom has enough problems at the moment." She made her way back through the fence, and jogged down the hill, making her way towards her car. She could hear Duncan panting behind her, trying to keep up.

"I thought you were still working out!" she called back over her shoulder. Throwing the empty can into the passenger side floor she hopped into her driver's side. Duncan hit the window, wanting her to roll it down. Alyx jumped, but ignored his request, shrugging in apology as she started to back up, stopping short as she almost rear ended her brother's truck. Duncan only stood there, his arms slightly raised, his mouth open. The sight made her laugh, she didn't know why she felt a sudden rush of getting away. One of her favorite songs was playing on the radio, it lifted her spirits a little and got her pumped for the party. She rolled her windows down

and turned up the music. She felt a slight pang of
guilt as she looked in her rear-view mirror watching
her brother behind her, but he needed to stop being
so nosy and over-protective. She shook her head and
let the music seep in as she made it onto the main
road and was singing and moving along with the
beat. Her worries behind her, for the moment.

Alyx arrived at the party's location a few
minutes outside of town. It was hosted by a guy a
year younger than her and her friends who was
notorious for parties whenever his parents were out
of town. So luckily, private land meant no cops.
Usually. She found a parking spot near a few trucks
behind the house. As she got out she could see a
large bonfire and hear country music playing as
people were laughing and talking a little ways away.
She locked her car and made her way over. She felt a
little nervous as to who she would run into but she
knew she couldn't hide forever. She thought she
could hear a faint whisper off in the distance behind

her. She looked warily at her surroundings but saw nothing but darkness. She shook her head and hastily joined her friends.

"Alyx, you made it!" shouted an excited voice. As she got to the fire she saw Catherine who immediately jumped up off of Eric's lap. She could tell a few voices had stopped talking but she forced herself to ignore them. She greeted her with a hug and pulled her to a seat next to Eric. He gave Alyx a hug and a peck on the cheek.

"Sorry I'm late guys, where's Tyler?"

"Getting more booze for us. I'm not even buzzed yet." Eric complained, but pulled Catherine towards him. She giggled and playfully swatted him away. As if on cue, Tyler returned from inside the house with two full red cups. Nearly spilling, he spotted Alyx and raised them in greeting.

"Hey Alyx!" he jogged over and gave her a peck on the cheek too. He struggled to regain his balance and spilled anyway.

"Uhh, Ty I think you got some vodka on my shirt."

"Party foul, my bad!" he said nonchalantly and took a swig.

"I'm guessing some people are inside?" she asked looking at Catherine. Her friend looked at her with a slightly drunk, but worried expression.

"Well, uhh, see I was literally going to text you that Isaac's here with his friends. Kourtney is thankfully MIA." Her words were slurred but even drunk Catherine wouldn't lie to her. Alyx took a deep breath and exhaled, trying not to let the panic sink in.

"Okay, no big deal. I'll be fine. I'll just stay close to you guys out here," she reasoned. She was surprised at how under control she felt, maybe that talk with Duncan really did help things. Eric suddenly looked up, his gaze past Alyx.

"Well speak of the devil." Alyx allowed herself to peek around her shoulder. Of course, Isaac was suddenly standing in the doorway with a few of his friends. His sister peering out from behind him like a predator, hunting. So much for control.

She snatched one of Tyler's cups and downed the rest of it. She wanted to lose herself and fast, then maybe she could survive this whole ordeal. There were so many things that happened today that she wanted to forget.

"Slow down, Alyx." Eric said. She only ignored him, he didn't get how mean girls could be to each other. She wanted to feel numb, she wanted to forget everything. As soon as she saw her ex all of her problems began to flood back in. Her feeling of temporary bliss was fleeting indeed. He made her think of her dad. She took another cup near Tyler and drank the rest of that one too. Tyler threw up his hands in protest.

The drinks kept pouring and soon everything was becoming a blur. Isaac and the others seemed to leave her alone, mostly, but if they had shouted something at her she wouldn't have even noticed. She vaguely remembered making out with a random guy in the corner, though she did recall dancing most of the night.

She would refuse to stop dancing no matter if it was her favorite song or a song she hated. She couldn't stop dancing even when she felt like she was going to collapse from exhaustion.

She didn't stop dancing, not, at least, until she heard the voice, clear as day this time, almost as if someone was right in front of her, talking.

"Are you done? You look like a fool," a bored voice spoke in her mind. Alyx stopped and froze, people looked at her, confusion filled their drunken faces. "Do you not realize you can't dance the pain away? Or drink for that matter? You really should listen to that brother of yours more." The voice was a woman's, it was stern yet empathetic. There was a slight purr in her words, like she had known Alyx for years and was merely consoling her. The whispers from earlier, it sounded like this woman, but so much clearer. Her presence was overwhelming.

"Who are you?" The world was spinning, she had no idea which way was up or down. There was a melodic yet sultry laugh in response to her question. Her heart began to pound which only worsened her tolerance to the alcohol already in her system. She felt her face, a low burning especially in her cheeks.

"Who are you talking to, Alyx?" Catherine danced over to her, laughing hysterically, unable to control herself, she had more to drink then Alyx did.

"You're not alone anymore, darling. Also, good punch from earlier." Cooed the woman. Alyx began to walk, where she was going she had no idea, pushing past Catherine who fell against Tyler. She

just thought that maybe once she had gotten far
enough away she wouldn't hear the voice anymore.
It terrified her, first, because there was someone
inside her head and second, it scared her with the
familiarity, how warm and inviting the voice felt.
She shied away from it, not wanting anyone to be
kind or comforting to her.

She stopped walking and dizzyingly grabbed
onto a tree trunk, she must have been on the edge of
the woods nearby. Nausea started to creep up her
throat and she threw up a little on her shoes.

"Oh shit." Was all she managed to mumble.
Vodka never set well with her.

"Alyx? What are you doing out here?" said a
familiar voice. It made her heart sink, only after it
skipped a beat. Strange how her heart was a
confused mess, which only seemed to reflect herself.
In a drunken stupor, Alyx whirled around, nearly
falling until a hand wrapped around her arm,
catching her balance. She looked up, taking a second
for her to actually focus on the face.

"Ooh, such a handsome fellow." The woman's
voice murmured, fading into the background.

"Isaac?" Alyx croaked. She stumbled as the world began to spin again. He chuckled, holding her steady.

"I think it's time to cut you off." Alyx could only roll her eyes.

"No shit." Another wave of nausea rolled over and she doubled over, throwing up again, and just barely missing his shoes. He held her hair back as she slowly breathed and regained composure. He always took care of her at parties.

"We should head back, I wanted to talk to you about something." He said, he began to pull her back towards the party but she only resisted.

"I-I can't." she replied, fear gripping at her heart, she wanted that woman to go away, everything felt wrong. The laughter echoed in her head.

"Sweetie, I wish I could leave. We're in this together unfortunately," the woman sighed. Isaac looked at her, confusion and pain filled his eyes. The laughter continued.

"I just wanted to tell you how bad you hurt me," he suddenly said, letting go of her arm. "I didn't want everyone to be horrible to you, I just wanted you to know how bad I felt. They were only looking out for me." He started talking in a hurry. Everything was happening so fast; the world was spinning around her. She couldn't make sense of anything, why did he want to talk *now*, of all times?

"Looks like he wants you back, sweetheart." The woman taunted, she began to laugh.

"No, stop! Just shut up! Stop laughing!" Alyx couldn't stop the words from coming out. She thrashed around like a crazy person, feeling like she could shake the voice out of her head.

"Alyx! What the hell is wrong with you? I'm not laughing!" Isaac tried to grab at her, which only made her resist more. "Alyx! Let me help you!" he pleaded. "Please, talk to me!" She could feel a rage rise up within her. She didn't want to talk, she wanted to escape everything in her life, she wanted it all to just end and all everyone wanted to do was *talk.*

She wanted peace, but all that was shattered once she found her dad. She lost herself because of him. She felt sadness well up within her, *because of him?* How selfish was she? Even drunk she could feel the emotions build up inside, tears began to prick at her eyes and she stood still, maybe it was the alcohol, but she couldn't control her emotions anymore. Maybe she was crazy, maybe she had finally snapped. She must be, to even think about blaming her dad for anything.

"Leave me alone." She looked at Isaac, his blue eyes barely visible underneath his dark, shaggy hair. His face was twisted with pain which made her heart twinge with guilt.

"Look, I know we ended things badly but, that's in the past now. I still want to be with you, Alyx. I love you." He said softly, he moved closer to her. A giggle passed through her lips before she could stop herself.

"You're joking, right? You're dating my best friend! *Was* my best friend, and you claim you *love* me? Isaac, you have no idea what love is. Just leave me alone," She was hoping she didn't sound ridiculous through her slurred words so she could be taken seriously enough. If she had to be the bitch, she would be. If that made everyone go away, so be it. "Go let those *friends* and sister of yours manipulate you some more, okay? My dad is in the hospital at the moment and you want to talk about all of the things they've done to me? My dad might not wake up, do you understand that? I have no time to deal with this petty bullshit!" Alyx was sobbing now, god she was a ridiculous roller coaster of emotion. She probably sounded like a blubbering idiot but she was just glad that she told him how she felt.

"Ooh, good one, girl." The woman cheered. A chill crept up her spine, but followed with more agitation.

Even drunk, she was starting to get really tired of the voices shit.

"I didn't do anything, it was all them!" he argued, anger filled his voice.

"*Exactly!* You didn't do, anything! You let them treat me like I'm nothing! You let them harass me and insult me! How is that love? Don't go telling me you still loved me after you didn't do a damn thing to protect me!" Alyx was panting now, she had to leave; she needed to go somewhere, anywhere but here. She whirled around, breaking her arm free from Isaac's grasp. Which worsened her balance as the world around her spun around, things beginning to blur even worse.

"You can't always run away from everything," the woman hissed, irritated. Isaac could only stare after her, his mouth hung open in shock.

"Watch me." Alyx gritted between her teeth as she marched into the woods, nearly falling a couple of times, but steadied herself with a few tree branches along the way.

Alyx kept walking, she wanted as much distance from Isaac and the rest of them as she could make.

Panting and crying like a lunatic, she watched the moon above her poke through the trees as she traveled aimlessly. It was getting much later, she could tell but she could care less by knowing the time. The spring air caressed her face as her tears began to lessen, as if mother nature was trying to calm down a child. The leaves were turning green as the season progressed over time, which glistened in the moonlight from the rain they had gotten the night before. Alyx could feel herself shiver as the temperature cooled down around her. She didn't know where she was, or where she was going.

Alyx stopped at a small clearing that had a fallen tree trunk that was embedded in the earth.

She took a seat and wrapped her arms around herself, digging deeper into her own hoodie to stay warm. She knew she was being stupid, there could be bears or a mountain lion roaming around anywhere, but she didn't care anymore. She was just too tired to care.

"Tired and stupid." Whispered the voice disapprovingly. Alyx shook her head, momentarily forgetting about the woman. She grabbed both sides of her head and squeezed, hoping the pain would push her out.

"Who *are* you?" Alyx questioned to no one.

"In your state I don't think I should tell you quite yet." The voice replied, bored. She could *feel* something almost tugging on her brain and then, nothing.

The silence was almost deafening as she lowered her hands and breathed a sigh of relief.

"Just so tired." Alyx whispered, lowering her hands. Suddenly, the world began to spin and she, slowly, fell towards the earth, the stars began to dance and the moon greeted her as she lost consciousness.

To No End

The sunlight was blinding. Alyx slowly sat up and realized she was in her own bed. How she had gotten home was beyond her, but she was grateful. She looked around her room, the window was open near her, letting in the tranquil spring air that caressed her skin. Her room was the very epitome of relaxation, yet her mind and body were anything but. Her head was pounding and her body ached. Alyx looked down and saw that she was in her sweatpants and oversized t-shirt she normally wore to bed. She sighed. She could only wonder what her family was thinking. Once again, the troubled McOwen was home with a major hangover.

Alyx stood up and walked to her bathroom, looking in the mirror as soon as she flipped the lights on. She made a disapproving look, scrunching her face which only failed to help her appearance further.

Her hair was disheveled and matted, and still had a few leaves stuck in it. Her eyeliner was halfway smeared down her face and she reeked of vodka. Tears began to well up in her eyes, which only made them burn, as she grabbed a brush and began to pick through her hair. After twenty minutes of trying to detangle, she gave up, throwing the brush onto the fake marble countertop, which only made a container that held her bobby pins fall onto the cold laminate floor, but she didn't care. Nothing mattered anymore.

Alyx undressed and turned the faucet on the shower to hot. Throwing her pajamas in a heap next to her laundry basket.

She began to scrub the night before off of her skin, rubbing until she was lobster red all over.

What happened last night? She recalled running into Isaac and running into the woods, but what happened after? Or before that even?

She began to scrub her scalp with shampoo until it tingled. Dirt lazily swirled around the drain until the water made it surrender. She could remember something scaring her as well. Maybe she saw an animal that startled her?

Alyx turned off the water and grabbed a towel as she stepped out of the tub. She couldn't stress herself out more just trying to think. She had a thousand other things on her mind to do that already. Her thoughts instantly flew to her dad. If he only knew about what had happened last night she would be getting yelled at by now and receiving a rude awakening as well. She smiled to herself but quickly wiped it off her face with the towel in her hand. Walking back into her room she grabbed a flask out of her desk drawer, but was shocked to find it gone. She was way too sober to deal with this right now.

"God damnit." She muttered and threw on some clothes, grabbing a nearby pair of clean jeans and a loose tank top She ran a hand through her hair and sighed as she walked out of her room, twisting the knob and pulling open the door in anger as she did.

"Mom?" she called out as she bounded down the steps, the wood slightly creaking. There was no answer at first, then there were footsteps that came from the living room.

"Alyx?" asked Duncan. He came around the corner and greeted her with a furrowed brow. It looked like he had just gotten done with a shower as well as his wet hair was slicked back and he was wearing only a pair of basketball shorts. She looked past him at the clock in the living room.

1:52 pm.

"Holy shit it's seriously that late?" she gasped. He crossed his arms.

"We need to talk." He leaned against the door frame.

Alyx dismissed what he said and kept looking around the house, moving into the kitchen.

"Where is everyone?" she asked, grabbing an apple from a bowl on the counter. Leaning onto the cool marble she took a bite and gave Duncan a bored look as he followed her.

"Out. They went to go see dad." He refused to break eye contact, which was starting to annoy her.

"So why aren't you there?" she snapped, the ache of her hangover only fueling her irritation. Her brother paused for a moment, looking surprised by her question.

"Why aren't *you*?" he countered. "Besides, I was too tired from carrying your ass home last night." The anger began to rise in his voice. Alyx stopped mid-bite. So, it was Duncan that brought her home.

"Does mom know?" she lowered her hand, placing the apple on the counter.

"No," he started. "She has enough to worry about right now. I lied for you." He said venomously.

"Ah, I see, I'm just being brushed under the rug at the moment." She tossed the half-eaten apple back into the bowl and rolled her eyes. Alyx began to walk past her brother, toward the stairs, but Duncan stepped in front of her.

"No, I'm not allowing you to be selfish right now because you're better than that. You're acting out like a child and you need to knock it off."

"Gee thanks for the pep talk, bro." she gave Duncan a push, she just wanted to leave.

"Do you have any idea how serious this is, Alyx? I found you unconscious in the middle of the woods, drunk off your ass," Duncan stood his ground and stared his sister down. "You have a problem that you're not dealing with."

"You make me sound crazy."

"Not crazy, just handling things like an idiot." Duncan responded, rolling his eyes toward his sister.

"People grieve differently." Alyx spat and crossed her arms. Duncan looked shocked, but his expression quickly softened.

"He's not dead, Alyx."

"He might as well be. We haven't talked to him in over a month now." She looked down, staring at nothing in particular.

"Hey," he said, trying to capture her attention. "The doctors are doing everything they can."

"Clearly not enough otherwise dad would be the one standing here giving me a lecture."

"They don't exactly have a lot to go on you know. The stab wound is healing but for some reason he won't wake up." Alyx's mind instantly flew back to that horrific day of finding her blood-soaked father laying in the wild flowers, staining them as he reached out to her.

She shook her head, the urge of wanting alcohol was so strong that her throat began to burn. She wanted to forget everything again.

"You don't really want to know." She whispered, looking down again.

"Well, was there anything he had on him? A weapon or something?" he asked. Alyx's eyes fixated on a pool of light in the living room that flooded over a small patch on the dark hardwood floor, dust particles danced around lazily as everything became so quiet that the only sound was of the wall clock next to the TV. She searched her memories hesitantly, she couldn't quite recall any weapons. Then it dawned on her.

She remembered she had the necklace that her dad gave to her when she had found him. It was a whole sapphire jewel, the size of a one-dollar coin, with ornate gold on the outer bit of it. Off center there was another smaller sapphire gem connected. Along the edge, there was what looked like runes etched into the gold. She could recall seeing her reflection in it as she inspected it. She heard her father give a small agonized shout as he started to lose consciousness. She remembered he fought to keep his eyes open, panic in his face, but the loss of blood was probably too much. She could only wait for the ambulance to get there as she slipped the necklace into her back pocket and held her dads hand.

She had strangely thought nothing of it at the time. Until now.

Curiosity struck as she remembered the note, which he strangely still hadn't brought up, and now the necklace. Why was she just now remembering all of this? It's like a cloud had lifted.

"There wasn't any weapon, Duncan." Technically she didn't lie, she just reframed some truth.

Her brother looked disappointed. Shaking his head, he stormed off upstairs. She hadn't realized that she was holding her breath and exhaled. Maybe she should tell him, he had a right to know too. She closed her eyes and for once went with her gut. She jogged over to the end of the stairway.

"Duncan?" she called up the stairs. He glared down at her from at the top.

"What?"

"There was something else I found." His eyes got big, he motioned, urging her to tell him more.

"Come with me." She said as she bounded up the steps. She could hear his footsteps behind her. Walking into her room she looked around on the floor for her clothes. She had thrown the jeans she was wearing that day in a corner, not wanting to touch them again, so they were hidden under a large pile for the past month.

"I don't know if it means anything but--," she stopped short as she began to dig through the pile of clothes and quickly found them. The blood now dried onto the denim and the seeds from the field caught in the stitching, she cringed just looking at them let alone touching them. She reached into the back pocket and felt the cool metal against her fingertips. Ever so slowly she pulled the necklace out by its thick chain. Alyx held it up, letting the sunlight catch the facets of the jewel. It reflected the light against her face.

"Why did dad have a necklace?" Duncan asked, sitting on his knees beside her.

"I don't know, I found it in his shirt pocket," she lied. "I didn't think anything of it at the time, but I couldn't help but think this had something to do with what happened to him."

"What, like the necklace attacked him or something?" he scoffed. Alyx looked at him, rolling her eyes.

"Yeah, no. But this was no coincidence that he had this, I'm sure of it. He was on a dig which was a few miles away from here. Maybe he had a fight with one of his colleagues over this? He was stabbed, so the necklace wasn't the weapon, besides it's not covered in blood. It looks really valuable though."

"Why is it so important though? Why would dad go on a dig for this specifically?" Duncan questioned. Alyx paused for a moment. Wasn't there a legend their dad had told them about? She could vaguely remember him explaining one of the many stories he would occasionally tell them about. She wished she had paid more attention, or even cared more.

"I'm not entirely sure, but I think I know where we can find out," she said as she gathered the necklace up and stuck it in her pocket. "You'd better get dressed." She said and grabbed her bag, along with her car keys. Duncan clumsily got up and jogged to his room across the hallway. He returned in a plain t-shirt and cargo shorts. While he slipped on some sandals. Alyx grabbed a pair of her own sandals as they made their way downstairs, slipping them on as she opened the front door. Her brother walked past her.

Hopefully she would get some answers for once. A glimmer of hope flared up in her heart once again like it had when she found the note. She wasn't sure if she should tell Duncan about it until after she had gathered more information about the necklace first. This couldn't all be a coincidence, they both had to connect somehow. They climbed into her car and took off into the afternoon traffic.

CHAPTER 3

ALYX AND DUNCAN arrived at the University of
Colorado at Boulder, their father's 'office' so to
speak, pulling up along the deserted road, they
figured with the slow traffic they wouldn't have
their car towed. They parked on the farthest side on
the main campus. Alyx's eyes locked onto the
museum near one of the buildings for admission.

They knew that if they just walked in without
a pass or anyone aware then they would be thrown
out for sure. Even with barely anyone around, they
couldn't chance it. Get in and get out. The university
was generous enough to support the dig that Victor
and his partner, Bradley Christofferson was on, so

he made an office for himself. Whatever legend most caught his passionate eye he would even help fund it with his own money from time to time, so there was more motive for donations.

His main obsession and research was lost legends, mainly incorporating Scandinavian or Viking folklore, but he would branch out from time to time, researching rulers in various parts of the world. Malicious rulers that were sometimes barely known though their atrocities were very much real. He wanted to shed light on the ones that were so evil people didn't want to talk about them very much, aside from Adolf Hitler, Genghis Khan and the like. Her dad once told her that the only reason he would pick such horrible people was to show the world that evil exists, and that the only way to defeat said evil, was to unite and spread love and kindness. To show that good could always fight back.

She could remember him saying: 'Good dictators reminded their subjects how mortal they really are.' Something, however, stuck with her about one ruler that he had found. Noted as an 'evil' and 'malicious' queen that claimed to have had magic-like properties, also believed to have been 'immortal.'

Around 1000 A.D. there was a legend about two artifacts that were used as talismans by one of the rulers of that age. The necklace that she had been given by her dad, that day she had found him, made her realize that that legend seemed most unsettling. Especially due to the overwhelming evidence he had given her in just minutes.

Victor had written down his findings in a journal, which most likely would be back in his office, seeing as he hardly ever brought any of his research home. 'It's not good to bring my work home.' He would say to us as he would give their mother a peck on the cheek.

Alyx could only silently kick herself for not learning and especially not listening more to her father's passion when he *would* talk about it with the family. She was hoping that he would have more insight about the necklace he had given her.

Duncan opened the doors as Alyx followed closely behind, bounding up the cement steps to the admissions building. Walking into the familiar campus, they were a little unnerved at how quiet it was. They could hear phones ringing further down the hall and secretaries sighing and muttering to themselves that they don't get paid enough. The slaps of their sandals hitting the linoleum floor broke the women's concentration as they turned the corner.

"Excuse me, sweetheart can I help you?" a woman stopped Duncan as she held a phone away from her mouth and covered it with a hand. Her deep brown eyes looked at Duncan earnestly, hoping to catch his attention. She was probably in her late twenties and most likely not married due to her ridiculous amount of interest. Alyx rolled her eyes, just another girl infatuated with her brother, what else is new?

"No, thank you. My sister and I know where to go from here." He said nonchalantly, as they began to walk passed the desk. Looking somewhat disappointed, the woman spoke into the receiver to please hold and placed the phone down. She walked around the desk, to obviously try and show off her long legs, which she was probably silently praising herself for choosing a pencil skirt that morning.

Duncan gave Alyx a sideways glance, and followed with a cocky smirk.

"Are you sure? It's a big campus and some areas have been marked off for students." she questioned.

"Marked off?" Alyx questioned. The woman didn't bother to look at her, ignoring her existence, which made her fume silently.

"I'm sorry, but due to recent events, the campus was forced to close down specific areas."

"What if you tell us which areas, just so we don't run into them." Duncan said.

"I apologize sir, but I have just started working here a few weeks ago. I was informed not to allow anyone to just wander around."

"Well this is bullshit." Alyx snorted. The woman looked over at Alyx, like she was seeing her for the first time.

"Please, it's important." He gave her a pleading look. Oh lord, he was working his magic on her. Pretty soon she would be a puddle at his feet. Alyx began to giggle but stifled it with a cough. The woman began to light up like a Christmas tree at his attentiveness. She held out a hand.

"What are your names?" she glanced at Alyx, focusing her attention on Duncan.

"Uh, Adam. This is my sister Eve." Duncan said quickly. Alyx looked at him, her eyes almost popping out of her head. The woman stopped, her brows knitted together.

"Our parents have a weird sense of humor." Alyx quickly interjected. "Where are those areas if you don't mind me asking? We don't want to cause any trouble." The woman took a moment to process, her eyes glazing over as if contemplating if Alyx was a real threat or not, but blinked and then regained that annoyingly toothy smile towards Duncan.

"Well, I am Veronica, pleased to meet the both of you. I suppose if I show you the areas it will help, I can't disagree with that." She gave Duncan a wink and reached around her desk to pull out a small map of the campus. Taking a marker, she drew a large, black "X" on the exact location of their father's office, which was inside the Museum of Archaeological Discoveries, resting next door to their current location. Handing the map over to them she waved them on, returning to her desk once more.

Duncan coolly gave her a wave as they began to walk down the hall. He gave his sister a wink and smirked which Alyx responded with an over-dramatic throwing up gesture, and playfully nudged him. At least they made it in.

Once they disappeared around the corner Alyx quietly busted out laughing as Duncan shoved the map in his pocket.

"Are you serious? Adam and Eve? You should be so glad she's stupid." Alyx whispered. Duncan rolled his eyes and shrugged.

"I was thinking under pressure. You try and pull two names out of your ass."

"I would be better at it than you, that's for sure."

"Well, it still worked so shut the hell up." He mumbled as they continued walking.

Stepping outside they saw a few cyclists pass by, but it was still the same quiet atmosphere. They walked through the double doors of the museum and were greeted by the smell of whatever chemicals they had used in the water for mopping. Luckily, nobody was at the front desk which completely okay seeing as they still had a few more turns down the hallways. They passed relics of old items and talismans thought to be filled with magic, but were really only using certain powders to conjure fire and cause said fire to change its color. Illusions and cheap tricks that would have been seen as miracles back then. Sometimes Alyx thought that her dad just enjoyed debunking the rumors instead of learning more about the legends. If her dad was here, he would probably laugh and say that was only half right.

About five doors down they took a left turn and gasped. They had been to their dad's office for what seemed like a million times, but it looked completely different as soon as they arrived at a wall of police tape. It went over the door and small windows, not allowing anyone to get a good look inside.

"Jesus, it looks like a crime scene." Duncan remarked. Alyx could only nod in response, her heart was pounding. Did his coworkers think he was murdered here? Or that he had committed a crime himself? Her mind was racing, anything could be possible at this point, other than the likely-hood of him doing something awful was impossible, especially since he was the victim. She just knew it.

Duncan sighed and tore off the caution tape that barred the door. Alyx looked at him in shock, which he responded with a shrug. He pushed on the door, twisting the handle as he did.

"Damnit, of course it's locked." He took a step back looking around for another way inside. Alyx's eyes locked onto a small open window above the door, it was only a fraction open but it would be enough to push it open further with her fingers and climb through.

"Hey! There's a window up there." Alyx stated and pointed. Her brother investigated it a moment and then nodded.

"That should work. Here, I'll lift you up." He bent down and cupped his hands, his stance at the ready. She took the step and reached for the window as he lifted her up.

"A little higher, Duncan," She said with gritted teeth. Duncan grunted, but pushed her up further. She grabbed a hold of the frame and laced her fingers under the glass, sliding it up enough that she could lift herself up to stick her head through first.

It was unnervingly dark within the room itself, making her feel vulnerable as she was unable to move quick enough if something were to jump out. At least she could see a few inches away from her to make things out clear enough so she didn't fall, as her eyes adjusted.

She slid halfway in and looked around the room for something to climb down on. A chair sat next to the door which was conveniently tall enough for her to reach. It shook a little as her hands balanced her enough to lower herself down, only until she couldn't move.

"Are you in yet?" Duncan whispered through the door to her.

"Almost--my foot is stuck!" she insisted as she looked up. Her sandal was wedged in between the frame and the glass window, it must have gotten knocked shut as she got her legs through.

"Let me see if I can knock it through." He offered and she could hear a soft thud behind her, through the door.

"What are you doing? People are gonna hear you!" she warned. Suddenly, she felt pressure release from her foot and she began to tumble towards the floor, landing with a hard thud as she knocked the chair down with her. Spoke too soon.

"Son of a...," she grumbled as she sat up and rubbed her right shoulder in pain. Her attention was quickly grabbed by something else in the office however, it seemed like something moved on the other side of the desk. Hopefully it was just her imagination. It was dark as they had covered the windows with a sheet of thin fabric. Only a sliver of light cascaded through, highlighting a corner of a giant cherry wood desk. Dust particles took refuge in the only illuminated part of the room. Everything seemed to go silent as Alyx sat up on the floor. She didn't see anything move again. She was just overly creeped out.

"Alyx? Are you okay? Can you let me in if you're not bleeding out?" he whispered to her. She snapped out of the serene silence and turned around, reaching up to unlock the door. Duncan twisted the handle and with a soft click the door opened.

"Holy crap," he breathed. "What's going on?" He closed the door behind him, relocking it again.

"My thoughts exactly." She breathed and stood up.

Duncan walked over to the desk and began to search through the papers and notebooks stacked onto the cool wood. Alyx went onto the other side of her brother and began to help look. There was a ton of normal office work, which looked harmless and mundane until one specific notebook caught her eye.

"Hang on, I found something." She whispered. She flipped through the papers, reading her father's messy handwriting as he wrote down broken thoughts and rushed notes.

August 22nd, The Legend of the Necklaces of Iain

It took us ages to find the location of the necklaces, or talismans as they were so called, but we finally did it. You would think it would be fairly easy to find a really large Amethyst and Sapphire but the means to hide it... Bradley gets all the credit of course, he deserves it with his incessant research.

He led us straight to the dig site. Just a mile North of the Crimson Mountain's with its elevation between 8049 - 8080 ft, it was quite the climb. But we found a steep slope, too steep in fact, that the incline led to loose rock. Our curiosity was too much to write it off.

We of course had to dig through two tons of rubble to uncover the entrance. Bradley could barely contain his excitement, the poor guy. He was particularly infatuated with this dig. It took us around eight hours to reach the entrance, an actual entrance, the samples dating back to around 1,000 A.D., so the settlement was accurate.

Once we got inside I had an--unsettled feeling. Anyway, we got down to the king's quarters and my god--it was almost pristine inside. I swear to god, it was almost like someone was still living there. I noticed that Bradley kept staring at something behind the massive bed. We had found it.

The other piece, we had found the Sapphire necklace.

"Oh my god. They did find it after all." Duncan breathed. Victor had talked about the Necklaces of Iain every once in a while. Alyx looked at her brother gravely.

"If I have the sapphire with me now, where is the amethyst then?" she asked. She instinctively grabbed the necklace in her pocket, just to make sure it was there. Duncan followed her hand with his sharp gaze. She pulled the necklace out and put it on, feeling that she just needed to wear it. There was an unsettling weight about it. Within seconds, it began to have a silent drum to it, almost like it had a heartbeat. Alyx merely listened, wondering if Duncan could hear it to, but judging by the look on his face he was in deep thought about something else. She felt nervous as to why she wasn't even the least bit afraid.

"No idea, but I have a really bad feeling about all of this. Like there's something much bigger going on here." He said, his mouth dry.

Suddenly footsteps were coming down the hall, towards Victors office.

"Oh crap." Duncan whispered. The footsteps paused in front of the door.

"Hello? Who's in there." A woman's stern voice asked. Duncan shot Alyx a worried glance as they leaned up against the door, careful not to stand in front of the windows, not that there was a lot of light in the room to begin with, but they didn't want to risk it. The stern voice belonged to Mrs. Lowell, a bitter old woman who had worked in the campus's museum for years. She didn't like kids, and she was always particularly harsh with their dad whenever they came to visit him in his office. Of course, Victor would pay no mind, ignoring her insults or judgmental comments. Her brother, Josh had joked one time that once she died, she would haunt the halls here, screaming at kids for chewing their gum too loud or for falling asleep in class.

"I know someone's in there. I will call the police! There's caution tape on the door for a *reason*!" she shouted, anger rising in her voice.

"Don't put it past her." Duncan whispered to Alyx.

"Right! I'm going to call the authorities! You have no business being in Mr. McOwen's room when he is so gravely ill!"

Alyx felt anger rise in her throat. How dare this old hag talk about their dad at all!

"He's not dying!" Alyx hissed through the door. Duncan shushed her.

"Come out, *now!*" Mrs. Lowell shouted back, banging on the door.

"Come on, Alyx. Through the window!" Duncan whispered and started shoving her towards one of the large windows that almost touch the ceiling.

"Will it even open?" she asked. Duncan pulled off a corner of the fabric and tore it far enough over so they could fit through. He began to pull on the lock that held the window secure.

"Only from the inside," He managed to shove it open with a hard push. "Lucky for us."

"The police are on their way!" Mrs. Lowell screeched. She pounded on the door. Alyx was fed up, she took a step in front of the opaque window next to the door and pressed her middle finger against the cool glass.

"Excuse *me!*" Mrs. Lowell scoffed. A smirk slid across Alyx's face. She jogged towards the window, but paused, staring at the pile of research papers, she gathered them up and threw them into her bag, along with his notebook. Another book suddenly caught her eye, it was a relatively thick tome that was titled: Myths & Legends. Alyx snatched it out of a half open drawer and shoved it into her bag along with the papers

"Alyx, we need to go now!" he warned. She jogged over to the window, Duncan jumped down onto the lawn and motioned for her bag. It was a short drop down but enough that the bag would knock her off balance. She threw it down and sat on the sill, the five-foot drop beckoning her.

"Come on!" he shouted. Alyx couldn't resist looking behind her, searching around the room once more. It was still so peaceful even though its occupant could be dying.

Alyx shook her head. He's *not* dying. He's *not* going to die.

He can't be. He won't be.

With a determined jump, Alyx landed on the lawn beside her brother, a dull pain struck through the bottom of her feet, causing her to pause for a moment. By the time they had gotten to the car and made their getaway, two cop cars pulled into the parking lot, not even noticing Alyx and Duncan driving away.

CHAPTER 4

"THAT WAS STUPID." Duncan stated, matter-of-factly. They walked through the front door of their home and into the kitchen, placing their keys on the countertop.

"Shh." Alyx lifted a finger up to her lips. Looking around the corner, peering into the living room. She began to relax once she saw the room was empty, comforted by the sound of the ceiling fan that hummed throughout the silence. In a quiet tone, Duncan began again.

"That was *so* stupid. What if we had been caught by the police? What if Mrs. Lowell knew who we were?" He leaned against the island, burying his head in his hands.

"One, we were in dad's office, and two, she didn't see us, only a finger," Duncan looked up at her, still shocked that she had done that, which only made her smirk in response. "Relax bro. You focus too much on the what-ifs. Besides, we got what we needed. We know that there is quite a connection with these so-called 'Necklaces of Iain.'" Alyx began to rummage through her bag. Laying out the paper on the island, she automatically grabbed the necklace around her neck.

Meeting Duncan's gaze she noticed he glanced down repeatedly at the jewel. She gripped it tighter feeling a slight urge of protectiveness towards it. But why? She shook her head and slammed her hands down on the cool marble.

"Look, we now have a direction. I just knew something wasn't right, I mean, come on! I found him in our yard for Christ sake!" Alyx pleaded with him. He narrowed his gaze at her, in deep thought. A few minutes passed by in silence. Before it became unbearable, Duncan sighed and began to look through the stack of research papers.

"This all sounds ridiculous, you do realize that, right?" he raised his eyebrows. Alyx nodded and crossed her arms.

"This is the only bit of information that actually makes sense to me. Unless you know better, of course." She challenged. Duncan gave her an unenthusiastic look.

"Well, we can't go around telling people that he just magically appeared out of thin air in our backyard. And it's all because of jewelry." Duncan rolled his eyes, not convinced.

"Well, there's more. I found this too. Clearly it was much more to dad than just some pieces of jewelry. He must have kept it on hand for something." Alyx slipped the book out of her bag, ignoring her brother's comments.

"Alyx it's a book about myths and legends. Doesn't mean the story is real."

"*Duncan*, it's to at least try and understand why the necklaces are so important. We need something to go on. Why did dad and Bradley put so much time and money into finding them? Besides, they *did* find them! You seem to forget that part," she reached into her bag once more, revealing the note that she had found earlier in her room. "I also found this in my room, at least hundreds of them before I threw them out. You can't say that this has no connection to what's going on!" she held the note up to her brother's face, he looked at her, shocked that she finally decided to come clean about what she had tried to hide before. He leaned back and squinted, trying to read the words that suddenly appeared in front of him.

"Death, Evil, Curse." He recited. Alyx nodded.

"It's obviously a warning."

"But from who?"

"Still working that out." She huffed and snatched the note back. Duncan pointed to her necklace.

"You do realize that they only found one. The one *you're* wearing."

It was strange, she felt protective of the necklace even though she had only just remembered it a moment ago. It felt a part of her now, she didn't really feel it around her neck anymore, but she started to notice that she did seem to touch it a lot. She held it in her palm, investigating the jewel. It looked like any other gaudy piece, you'd find in an overly-priced jewelry store.

"Don't you find it super odd that dad had it with him the day he appeared out of the forest?" she pressed.

"Well, yeah. That's what makes me believe that it's a necklace from the legend! Why would he be carrying the exact same thing he and Bradley were looking for, only for it to be a fake?" she challenged. She looked back down at the sapphire again, seeing her own reflection. "Even more to it, I felt like something was *telling* me to take it." The sapphire seemed to glow slightly in response making her draw back.

"I just think that before we jump onto the crazy train here---,"

"Duncan. We're already on it," Alyx rolled her eyes and dropped the necklace. Did it weigh more? She thought so but shook her head. "I think the impossible is where we need to go with acceptance." Grabbing her bag, she slipped the book back in and headed upstairs to her room. She was relieved that Duncan didn't follow her this time.

Alyx sat on her bed, her bay window open to allow the slight breeze to creep into her room. The summer sun made her all white furniture glow. Her room was her sanctuary, next to the field that was apart of their backyard, until it was tainted. She wanted to do whatever she could to reclaim those positive vibes again.

She stretched, looking down at the pile of papers spread over her coral sheets. The book about myths and legends opened, the pages greeting her. She looked through the contents section in the front, her finger traced down the page. She skipped over the "Legends of the Western Islands" and "Giants" but decided to limit her search down by looking through the different stories about witches (there were many), and about rocks and stones that acted as talismans and a few about kings and queens, (that was never ending).

While flipping through she read a lot about changelings and possession through items cursed by witches. She flipped through some more but stopped suddenly when she came across a highlighted title.

Neena and the Vikings of Vinland.

In the upper right-hand corner, someone had written a note saying: "Connected with Sonja and Algot?" It looked like her dad's handwriting. Tucking a strand of hair behind her ear she began to read:

Never was there such a powerful and malicious being than this one that had plagued the lands of Vingland. Neena, half-Native American, believed to have been from a mostly unknown tribe, called--in rough translation. The Crimson Mountain Tribe, and half-Ostman (as they called themselves) or Viking, walked the earth searched for a purpose, or perhaps, vengeance. Some believed she wasn't entirely human herself, seeking possession of mortal men of noble birth.

"They did not know the half of it." Sighed a voice. Alyx froze, feeling her heart sink. She hadn't heard from the voice in a while. Now that she wasn't drunk off her ass, she felt a chill up her spine. This was really happening?

"Hello?" Alyx rasped out loud.

"Yes? Hello? Are you actually going to listen to me this time or are you going to abuse yourself with drinking so much that you pass out again?" The voice was female, and she had a slight accent, although she couldn't quite place where her accent was from.

"How do you---," Alyx stopped short. How did she know she had been drinking before? Her memories flashed to the bonfire, of what little she could remember of that night anyway.

"Holy shit, you *are* the voice. You're real." Alyx stated. She ran a hand through her hair. This *was* all actually happening.

"Of course I am, and I would like to request that you reframe from drinking so excessively if you don't mind. It takes me ages to get through to you again. Saps a lot out of me."

"Wait--are you inside my head?" Alyx grabbed either side of her head, squeezing it a fraction. A tremor of disgust wracked through her body as her mind drifted to something parasitic.

"Yes, you foolish girl. Though I'm particularly drained when you hit the rum."

"S-sorry?" It felt odd to apologize to a voice. She was officially crazy.

"I wish you were crazy," the woman sighed. "But unfortunately, my soul is connected to you at this present time."

"How?" Alyx breathed. She leaned back against her headboard, pulling her knees up to her chest.

"You are the lucky one who found my necklace," she purred. Her voice wasn't malicious but almost mesmerizing. Automatically, Alyx reached up to touch the sapphire. She heard the voice sigh.

"Oh, come on, you've done your research enough to know who I am. And don't confuse me with my sister, I'd take offense. I am also glad to know you had received my notes to you. That took a great deal of energy on my part, and you so rudely threw them away." she tsked.

"Sonja?" Alyx asked, hesitant. She could barely even hear her own voice. "Those notes were from you?"

"Bingo, is that what you children say now these days? I do get confused with all of your slang.

Especially with being, you know, asleep for centuries, I've had a lot to catch up on, Which I am learning quite a lot through your mind, believe it or not," Alyx had a feeling that Sonja would be rolling her eyes. "Yes, those notes were from me, to warn you about Neena. You are all in grave danger."

"How is it you're in a necklace exactly?" Ignoring her warning. This whole thing felt ridiculous to her, she was basically talking to herself.

"You should read on, history has always bored me enough that I would rather not talk about it." Now Alyx was rolling her eyes.

"This isn't exactly a history book. Myths and Legends and all."

"Where do you think 'myths and legends' come from?" Sonja scoffed. "They are birthed from a more well-known, if not real, representation. Thus, still history." Alyx sighed, she wasn't entirely wrong. She skimmed through the story until she reached the part about Sonja.

Sonja Armodottir was known as the Queen of Hope. Everyone bowed before her beauty and mercy, she had a kind soul and had put a stop to the Third War. She was married to King Algot in the month of Tvímánuður, or August, at the age of sixteen.

"Holy crap, sixteen? How does Neena play a role in this exactly?" Alyx breathed in surprise. She paused, trying to process the first few sentences.

"Of course, I had a duty to uphold, people depended upon me. My husband also needed a successor, that was also my duty. And my mother had found Neena, after her mother, whom was good friends with my own mother, was tragically murdered. My mother had a very kind heart, so she took the poor girl in," Sonja's voice seemed to fade with the last sentence, she started to sound like a hundred years old, so much responsibility for someone so young. "My mother also had an interest in Neena's gods as well. The certain, similarities between Odin and the Great Spirit, well that was my mom's passion. She was nothing without her faith, as she always put it."

Alyx skimmed through again and stopped, feeling a slight hesitation at her next question.

"You didn't have any kids?" There was a pause. Alyx immediately regretted asking that question.

"I was barren, yes, and yet somehow the fool loved me anyway." She couldn't be that insensitive. To ease the tension, she cleared her throat and kept on reading, praying to god that she could change the subject.

Her sister, Neena joined her council as Sonja continued to rule. Neena was often looked down on considering her heritage, being a half-breed. They often overlooked the Viking side in her, and only saw her mother's Native American culture. Posing as a medicine woman, Neena would aid those in need with Sonja. Time went on and people began to question Sonja's adopted sister, Neena. She would disappear, days or weeks at a time, more terrible with each return.

"I think you should read about the beginning, before me and Neena. It will make more sense then." Sonja offered.

"It's not in this book, is it?"

"Unfortunately, no. But perhaps your dear old daddy might have the answer, in his little book there." Alyx looked down at the well-used notebook her father wrote in. Grabbing his field journal, she opened it and began to skim through looking for anything that he may have uncovered during his research on the necklaces. Finally finding something she began to read, pointing a finger at the words.

We had realized that Vikings did indeed travel throughout North America. The items we found on the dig site were astonishing. Vikings, here in Colorado! Somewhere around 1000 A.D. The exact date is still undetermined. We had heard only rumors, and ended up finding two burial sites, it ended up being two men, perhaps brothers of noble birth buried side by side, possibly in late twenties, early thirties is my guess. Although, it was odd, two noble men, possibly Jarls or Kings and they were buried? I expected them to be burned, but perhaps due to the lack of bodies of water nearby we could make an exception. The amount of gold and weapons we had found were incredible. Of course, what on earth would bring Viking's so far inland? They were sailors and traders, but there were no routes marked or recorded to give evidence of them even traveling here. It's almost like they popped up out of nowhere.

Alyx turned the page to read the next entry:

Leif Eriksson did in fact have cousins that broke from his group, the runes that resided on a weathered piece of stone were proof enough, the translation saying:

Family of Eriksson, Family of Foolish Desires.
Seekers of Worlds, Founders of Power.
Only the god's favor the Brothers.

His own blood found more of North America than he himself was so idolized and famous for. Their names were Elof and Eero Brynjolfssen, along with his own brother, Thorvald Eriksson! We traced their journey which had shown they sailed across the North Atlantic from Greenland, and arrived at the coast of New Foundland. They named the region Vinland (after the wild grapes that grew in abundance and the general fertility of the land).

To No End

*We had found more of Eriksson's journey,
after reaching North America (Vinland), Thorvald
ended up breaking off and following their cousins
Eero and Elof, little is known as to their motives but
Bradley's theory was that they wanted to separate
from Christianity. The journey to Colorado was as if
they 'appeared' there or something. I made note to
study more into that later.*

*They settled and named the new land, the name
was unclear, of Vinland. They lived there for several
years, the exact time is unknown still, but it wasn't
long until the locals (Native Americans) began to
fight back. Coming down from the Crimson Mountain,
which influenced their tribal name of that region. The
Vikings were strong, but the Native Americans knew
the land and had the advantage. During an attack,
Thorvald was killed.*

*Eero and Elof, much known for their malice and
brutality, defeated the locals, and took them as
prisoners. It was in that moment that they became a
conquered people. Vikings overtook the land, there
were letters sent back to King Olaf in Norway to send
more people to settle in the new land, forcefully. I am
unsure what form of communication between the*

brother kings and their old home they used. Leif still
became the most famed European, receiving the title
of the first Scandinavian to find North America, 500
years before Christopher Columbus even dreamt of it.

Alyx stopped for a moment, taking in what
she had just read.

"What I just read was the real history? Not
just some legend my dad chased after?" Alyx
whispered.

"Yes. I was born shortly after my parents had
arrived. They were nobles who wanted to keep the
true Viking way alive, and so Eero and Elof granted
them rulership over the new land. My parents went
from simple nobles to Jarls due to their strong faith
in the gods. Eero and Elof always favored my father,
and I believe that Eero had some love for my mother
as well, but that's an entirely different story.
Continue reading." Sonja urged. Alyx sighed and
skimmed through some more, trying to find when
Neena came into all of this.

After we had followed the end of the journey

of Eero and Elof, that was when things started to fall into place with the legend. Of course, as time went on, there were more known births of 'mixing,' as they put it. Some Vikings had children with Native Americans, which apparently was not something the brothers wanted. That became banned by Jarl Armodottir at the time, who rose into power by the brothers, he had brought his wife Iain Armodottir, a Scottish woman he had met in Norway. She converted from Catholicism to the Nordic belief, best known as paganism. Iain gave birth to a daughter, Sonja Armodottir. They, however would bear no more children. Iain--in love with the Native American culture--hoped to bear a son by using their spiritual methods, which only caused great tension between the brothers and Jarl Armodottir.

She learned their ways from a local medicine woman, or the village Shaman, who had given birth not long after Iain, to a daughter named Neena. Sonja and Neena grew up together, especially once Neena's own mother was murdered, along with her father who was a Viking. Jarl Armodottir had ordered the couple to be executed. Strangely enough, however, Iain, whom had a strong relationship with Neena's mother, took her in as one of her own.

There were rumors that we had found, which is what my career is based off, of how Sonja and Neena grew up. Neena seems to have taken the place of her mother as the medicine woman, as Sonja became queen once her father had died unexpectedly, Iain stepping down from ruling because of grief, leaving Sonja, a sixteen-year-old to rule thousands. Eero and Elof apparently relinquished power as King's for unknown purposes. They were simply, less involved. Sonja's first act as queen was to establish Neena as a member of council. Many were outraged as Neena wasn't full Viking, and were disgusted by Sonja's lack of respect of the old ways that her father had so lovingly instated.

Now, my own opinion of course, I am very impressed by how a teenage girl could change so much history in so little of time. She educated her people, they were taught how to write and read, everyone was treated equally. She went on to marry Algot Grithsson, a noble from Iceland, a marriage to unite allies. Together, they put an end to the Third

War, a dispute between the local people who called themselves the Pale, and the Vikings.

Apparently as time went on, people started to go missing, particularly men. Neena also began to journey quite frequently, she would come back with a new form of medicine or more knowledge from her people, but was very much a recluse for being a member of the court. Very little is said about Neena's involvements in actual day to day community business. What is very vague is why Neena went ballistic out of nowhere at one point.

As time wore on, her condition only grew until she supposedly stopped responding all together. There was one sentence in the passage that always gave me the chills: 'She was very much changed.' Although simple, it seemed to hold so much magnitude.

Bradley began to believe that she had been ingesting a special hallucinogenic substance, for ceremonial purposes. With her knowledge of herbs, it seems reasonable. What her motives for that procedure were, we're not certain. All we know is that it wasn't good, as time wore on, it wasn't just Neena that was acting odd, her madness was contagious. It is said that odd behavior began to spread throughout the kingdom. It didn't take long until the King himself began to change. I constantly ask myself what this little girl went through, was it really magic or an insane amount of drug use? Perhaps this substance Bradley talked about prior caused an almost plague-like reaction. What started it? Where did Neena get this substance? Was she purposefully causing this to happen? Was it just because she was out of her mind?

Sonja found her dead husband, who was ill at the time, with Neena over his body.

"Those sadistic eyes she had when I found her." Sonja hissed. Alyx continued, not wanting to open old wounds just yet.

Sonja laid her husband to rest after detaining Neena. She was said to have become enraged, she wanted to destroy Neena. Something strange occurred, Neena disappeared.

Distraught by Neena's actions, Sonja became a ghost. She disappeared through most texts of the legend. These girls were natural escape artists, disappearing from history whenever they chose. Both sister's, gone. Where did they go? What were they doing?

As Sonja came back to society she was much colder, she was also expressed as very fragile both physically and emotionally. What I noticed through most of the legend is that Sonja was always depicted with a sapphire necklace. Her mother's. That's the story, but how do these pieces of jewelry come into play exactly? They are mentioned, but very little is elaborated. Merely that it was handed down within her family.

"I could never part from it." Sonja chimed in.

"But, the legend states that there are two necklaces. My dad is only talking about one." Alyx responded, lightly touching the necklace that rested upon her collarbone. Sonja's silence was her way of telling Alyx to continue reading.

It's mentioned quite frequently throughout the log. That must be one of the Necklaces of legend, her mother gave her and Neena two necklaces, one Sapphire for Sonja and one Amethyst for Neena. Mostly as a status symbol for the women.

115

Fear took over the people's hearts, they probably feared that their beloved Queen would end up like her ill-fated sister, so they acted, they no longer wanted rulers that were weak and easy to manipulate, so the villagers called upon the Pale to help, and I am very surprised that the Pale agreed after they were beaten and nearly destroyed during the Third War. But I assume desperate times and all.

There was a small rebellion, a treason that threatened the kingdom. It was a small, collective group, both Vikings and The Pale, fighting together, but it started to grow as the fear was stifling.

Sonja called upon the rebellion to talk peace, but she was actually waiting.

"What were you waiting for?" Alyx paused.

"Neena of course." Sonja said matter-of-factly.

Sonja fought with Neena. But then this is where it gets weird to the point that even I can't come up with an explanation for it. Legend spoke of a strange power that swallowed both young women.

They just, disappeared once more, but in front of everyone. Physically vanished.

"Talismans. I had an immense amount of help to track down the knowledge to train and gather enough energy to use the necklaces my mother had given to my sister and I as talismans."

"Wait, you're saying that this actually happened? You never tried to just kill her?" Alyx responded, slightly scoffing.

"After everything, I thought I could. But once I saw her, I couldn't. It's strange I know, but we were sisters, even if it wasn't by blood. So, I simply locked her away. However, Neena was always one step ahead. She knew I was planning something." The last words dropped off as Sonja was deep in thought.

"And she trapped you in return." Alyx finished her sentence.

Sonja paused.

"With our energy being depleted, our souls were being tormented. Neena's doing no doubt." Sonja responded disdainfully.

Bradley and I have had numerous discussions on this and it makes me feel crazy to say but I think the old man is onto something. Everything adds up, I don't believe that the 'magic' or power aspect is as real as everyone described in the story but it does have an almost supernatural characteristic to it. These two literally disappeared except the people that witnessed were almost driven mad, some were even killed after the ordeal.

What's even more odd is that after the two were disposed, there was a nameless fear that threatened the kingdom, Elof and Eero reemerged again and began to act mad, just like Neena had before. Then the trail goes cold. The legend in itself is vague and confusing with too many loose ends.

"Oh, my god." Alyx gasped, pulling herself away, she shut her mouth, realizing it was open the entire time. She looked up from the book, turning her gaze to the window, hoping to clear her head with the fresh air.

"An act of betrayal is all it takes, it was like a small rockslide that turned into an avalanche." Sonja sounded a million miles away.

"What happened to you when you went into hiding?" Alyx questioned, pity rose up in her. There was a moment of silence, which only caused irritation on Alyx's end, she needed to know more, and even the wind became a nuisance unless it had information behind it. There were too many holes.

"She had murdered my husband after she slept with him, there was nothing but madness in her heart, and I knew she was ill but she did something so unforgivable that I had to do *something*. She was not herself so I knew that I could not kill her, but I wanted to bring the *real* her back. She had done something to herself, but I hadn't a clue as to what. But when I saw her, something in me snapped. I had already planned on capturing her temporarily, but when I saw that she was gone," she paused, as if seeming to silently relive that moment. "I felt nothing but loathing for her, I exacted my revenge. She didn't deserve such an easy escape for her sins, the gods wanted me to destroy her, but I had a better plan in mind," the necklace suddenly became cold against Alyx's skin. "Everything she had ripped from me," Sonja hissed. "All for power. It's almost as if I couldn't control my anger once I saw her. Something else took over my senses."

The anger rising in her voice, Alyx swallowed.

"Affecting the necklace here." Alyx complained as she lifted the jewel from her skin, it was unbearable.

"Sorry," the necklace warmed back up to normal. "It is difficult sometimes to control my emotions now. We both became trapped into the necklaces. She cursed me to merely to be lost in darkness. Little did she know that I was reborn into darkness the minute she took my love away from me," she paused again. "Then I saw a light and I thought maybe I was dying after all, but then I heard your voice. You brought me out of that darkness, I can slowly feel my powers slowly returning." the necklace became slightly warmer.

"If only my dad could hear you right now. He would probably eat his words, he never thought that magic was real. Hell, I never actually thought magic was real, until now," Alyx couldn't help but find herself grinning. "Although, I can't deny that I hoped."

"Don't be too happy about it young one, all power has a cost. For us, our sanity," Sonja said gravely, pausing. "And our souls." She stated. Alyx's grin fell.

"It does make more sense now, there were so many things that happened without explanation, the curse really exists. Now how is it that my dad just ended up in the backyard, almost bleeding to death? Who would want to hurt him?"

"My guess would be that Neena is now awakening, I can feel her power growing as mine does, we are irrevocably connected. There is indeed a curse but it is not by my doing, nor directed at me. But, even trapped, she is still dangerous. Even cornered, a viper will still strike." Sonja sounded tired.

"Then what would the curse be for? And to who?" Alyx whispered. The wind picked up a little. There was another pause, followed by a sigh.

"I think it's your family that's cursed." Alyx felt the blood vanish from her face.

"Why *my* family?" her voice seemed to echo.

"Unfortunately, I don't know. It's only a feeling that I have, but the curse runs deep, that

121

much I can sense," she paused sensing Alyx's anxiety. "It is however just a theory."

"We are connected somehow. It does makes sense, that's why my father came out of nowhere, but the question is: where did he go?" she questioned, trying to place the whole curse thing to the side. She had so many things to worry about, she decided to address it later.

"I wonder if it had to do with our necklaces, it shouldn't be by mere coincidence that you or your father had found them. You were *meant* to find them. That must be the curses doing. That's why you wear mine now."

"It was with my father when I found him, I took it."

"If he went anywhere, there isn't enough power in mine alone to allow him to travel." Sonja denied.

"Well yours is the only one I had found, and he was out of state at the time, or was supposed to be." Alyx postulated.

"Perhaps he was near the other one. Say his partner for instance." Sonja questioned, thinking aloud.

"Bradley? Do you think he traveled like my dad? Where though? He could be anywhere in the world then." Alyx ran a hand through her hair feeling at a loss.

"Perhaps not anywhere, but *when*."

"Wait, you actually think that my dad was, sent back in time?"

"Not by my doing, surely. Neena on the other hand--,"

"Why though? Why send two archaeologists back in time?" Boy the irony.

"They could have known too much, or Neena had found a way to use them. There are too many possible explanations," she contemplated. "Knowing my sister."

"Oh god, we need to wake up my dad. This is getting much bigger than I can handle." Alyx sighed, standing up she began to pace.

"I don't think you quite understand the severity--waking your father up alone will not solve anything. You are quite correct it is much bigger than you. I feel pity that you were chosen to be dragged into our mess." Sonja stated, a hint of sadness in her voice.

"Yes, but waking him up will help with some things, he knows a lot more than I do, we can use his knowledge to get an upper hand on Neena. We just wake him up, clearly this isn't a medical issue anymore. I bet you could even do it." There was another pause.

"Alyxandra, it's not any power that makes him sleep. He's been poisoned, I could sense it on him when you took my necklace from him."

"Poisoned?" her voice grew small; did she say anything at all or was it her imagination?

"Your father is dying, little one and not entirely by the curses doing."

CHAPTER 5

THE WORDS HIT Alyx like a wall, causing her to double back, blinking rapidly, trying to make sense of the situation. Not only did she have to deal with a crazy feud between two ancient beings but now she had to face the realization that her dad was really, truly dying.

"Dying...?" her voice echoed inside her own mind. "He was asleep, he's not dying. Poisoned?" her thoughts were so rapid she couldn't quite comprehend which emotion to deal with first.

"Now, you had to have seen the signs, they're so clear." Sonja scoffed in disbelief, trying to take back her words, almost as if she was blaming Alyx for her own misfortune. She acted like Alyx's reaction was unreasonable.

"I didn't know, I didn't see." was all she managed to say. How did she feel? Numb, she felt numb, as if her brain was fried and she couldn't process any more information.

"Well how could you, I suppose. Always drinking everything away." she scolded. Alyx looked up in shock, even though there was no one in front of her. She sat on the floor, trying to make sense of everything. She's right, it *was* her fault, if she hadn't been partying the whole time and really tried to be there for her dad she would have noticed earlier, she wouldn't have wasted a whole month of him suffering because she couldn't handle the situation.

"I didn't mean to--," she began, tears started to well in her eyes.

"You mean, you didn't mean to forget about your father? You didn't just abandon him because you couldn't face what was happening to him? The one person who would most likely do anything to make sure you and your siblings were okay? It doesn't count that you were seeing him behind your families back either." she said bluntly. If Sonja was standing physically in front of her she would have been wagging a finger at her in disappointment. Alyx's mouth fell open in shock, tears streaming down her face, at least the sting of her words made her feel something.

"No, I didn't---," she choked out.

"Why don't you face it, little one? You were abandoning him. The truth is a cruel reality, but it is the truth regardless. Now, you can either cry about it and play victim, or, you can get up and do something about it. You decide." the last word faded to a whisper and an immense amount of pressure seemed to release itself from her mind. She looked around the room and breathed in wiping the tears off her face.

"Sonja?" she whispered to the empty room. No response. She truly was alone now.

Even after the cruel words Sonja had said, Alyx felt a sense of longing for her new 'friend' to return. If that was what she even was. The reality of it was Alyx was grateful for Sonja's blunt honesty. No one had ever just told her to toughen up and do something, they always pitied and walked around the sensitive topics with her--too uncomfortable to face them head on with her. What Sonja didn't know was that Alyx was seeing her dad just not when everyone was around.

Once Sonja had told her to change her life, and to do something about her dad, she started to believe things can be different.

Things will be different, because now, she had something she didn't have before.

Hope.

How Sonja gave that to her, she had no idea, but she would be forever grateful.

Getting up off the floor, she began to slip the journals and books back into her bag. It was time for her to do something about it.

⸻⟡⸻

"Where are you going?" Duncan asked as he bounded behind his sister as she made her way to the back door. She paused and looked at him like he had just asked her a stupid question.

"Outside. Bye." she said with an annoyed expression. She opened the door and bounded down the stone steps and started walking towards the field where she had found her dad, that seemed the most likely place to start.

"You're up to something." he accused her as he jogged to her side. Looking up at him she rolled her eyes. He forgot his shoes.

"Apparently--if you say so," she sighed and stopped at the edge of the forest. She placed her hands on her hips and slumped in frustration. "Now where to start." she asked to no one in particular.

"Are you still trying to figure out what happened to dad? What did you find in the journals?" Duncan prodded. She didn't have time for his annoying questions. She could tell he tried not to be too interested, but he could never help himself, he always loved to stick his nose into everything she did. "Fairy tree nymphs held him hostage?" he quickly added mockingly. Alyx shot him a look.

"Really? No, actually, I doubt tree nymphs even live around this area anyway." she countered.

"What really happened, Alyx?" Duncan grabbed her arm, forcing her to turn to look at him.

129

Her face grew serious. She inhaled, not wanting to tell him the truth but it wasn't just her dad either.

"He's been poisoned." Duncan looked at her like she just told him that she wanted to be a stripper. Surprised, but not entirely blindsided.

"That's it?" he scoffed, a grin spread across his face.

"What do you mean 'that's it?' He's dying, dummy!"

"Well, all we have to do is find the antidote then." he seemed almost elated that she had told him that.

"It's not that simple, Duncan. Don't you think the doctors would have cured him by now if it was?" she urged him.

"How is it not that simple? And I'm sure stuff like this happens all the time." Now he was the one losing it, she could tell he was just trying to convince himself.

"Because I don't think it belongs in this time. He's in an almost, magical coma. The poison slowly killing him through time." she said flustered, she pulled away from his grasp. " I know how crazy this all sounds, but the sooner you accept it the better."

"Alyx, it sounds hella crazy. 'This time?'" he held up his hands and made quotation marks in the air.

"Look, I don't know how to explain all of it but I just know. There are bigger things happening than just you and me!" Alyx started to walk over fallen trees and through thick underbrush.

"Is this because of Isaac?"

"What the hell? No! To hell with Isaac! It has nothing to do with him." she shouted, looking back at him with a scolding expression. She failed to see a fallen log that seemed to catch her foot just right, and she was sent tumbling down a steep hill, hitting some trees on the way down.

"Alyx!" she could barely hear her brothers call to her, was he that far away? She shouted in pain as her leg banged against a rock, and her left shoulder connected with a fallen log. She reached out, hoping to grab a hold of something, of anything.

Finally, her body tumbled once more and stopped in a clearing.

Banged up, Alyx slowly started to turn over, allowing a groan to escape and winced. She opened her eyes wide, trying to focus them. The sky was dancing above her, mocking her for falling. If this wasn't the universe telling her that she screwed up, she didn't know what it was then.

With significant effort, she pushed herself up off the ground, looking around, she noticed the air was still and a growing mist began to waft towards her. Standing up, she absent-mindedly brushed herself off as she stared at the mist, her brows narrowing in confusion.

"Odd," she whispered under her breath as she hesitantly pulled her gaze away to look up at the small drop off she had just fallen from. "Ah shit." she exhaled.

A sudden twig snapped, making Alyx jerk her head around in reaction. Her eyes darted around in a frenzy, her heart began to pound.

"H-hello?" she said weakly into the mist. The trees and thick brush around her began to lose their color, and the mist collected itself at her feet. She took a step back in apprehension. Another twig snapped.

"Girl--you better run." Sonja's voice spoke suddenly, almost too loudly in her mind, making Alyx jump.

"W-what?" she started to lose her voice. Why did she need to run? What was about to chase her? She hated being chased.

"*Run.*" Sonja hissed, fear gripping in her tone.

Without hesitation this time, Alyx jumped up onto the drop off, clawing her way up the hill. Sinking her fingers into anything she could grab whether it'd be dirt or a root sticking out. She had no idea who was chasing her or more importantly, *what*, but she knew with every fiber of her being that she had to get out of there. Hearing branches breaking and something running--no--*crawling* behind her only made her mindlessly tear at every sapling or root in front of her, pulling herself along as she ran. Her breathing was short and erratic but she didn't dare slow down as the feeling of being almost caught pushed her to her limit.

"Do not look back, keep going! You're almost there!" Sonja was deafening in her mind as she coached her through. She blinked and shook her head; the edge of the forest was right there!

"Jump, girl!" Sonja ordered and without question, Alyx obeyed.

She jumped. Throwing herself in the wildflowers she snapped around looking wildly at the edge of the forest she had just come out of. Her whole-body aching and screaming at her from the sudden abuse. There was complete silence at first, and then there was a deafening blow to what seemed like an invisible barrier that rippled, which distorted the *creature* that was pursuing her. Eyes widening, she could only watch desperately as the creature frantically clawed at the barrier, the distortion showing glimpses of its identity.

It had sickly pale skin, some patches of fur were spotted in bloody areas on its body. It seemed a mix of human and feline, moving in sharp fluid motions but stood, hunched like a Neanderthal. The main thing that really caught her attention were its eyes--its sickly yellow eyes that seemed to glow within the depths of the underbrush. It gave out a horrendous wail as it began to back away from the barrier, its eyes never leaving Alyx. Its long, thin limbs seemed to creek as it crawled back, a low growl reverberating from its chest.

Alyx could only sit there in terror, wide eyed at what she had just seen.

"You're safe now, girl," Sonja murmured. "You owe me." she added before she seemed to fade away once more, leaving Alyx to gawk at the now calm forest before her; the color and life coming back to the vegetation and the sun seemed to shine brighter than before.

"Alyx? Alyx!" Duncan's voice started to break through her trance. When did he get there? Alyx blinked and looked at her brother who had a hand on her shoulder shaking her gently, which made her wince slightly from her recent bruising. He lowered his hand, noticing her pain and proceeded to ask: "Your face is super pale, what happened to you?" His voice filled with worry. Alyx just shook her head. Now what was she supposed to say? They would lock her up in the loony bin for this one.

"Nothing. I thought I saw something is all." she whispered, not daring to take her eyes off the forest. Duncan gave her a confused look.

Standing up, she brushed off her shirt.

"Seriously, I'm fine. Do you always have to look at me like I'm a mental case or something?" she rolled her eyes, trying to play off the utter terror clutching at her heart. She was about two seconds away from passing out but she kept her calm, impressing even herself. Alyx began to walk up towards the house, allowing herself to glance back once more at the trees. She could feel something watching her, whether it was the creature or her brother, she didn't know.

⸺⬦⬦⸺

"Are you going to come downstairs and eat finally?" Duncan called from the other side of her bedroom door.

"In a bit." was all she managed to respond. Alyx had been sitting on her bed and staring out at the forest since her encounter earlier. Still shaken, she resorted to locking her door and shutting the world out, that's what she did best after all. Alyx heard a sigh as Duncan headed back downstairs in defeat, his footsteps hesitant and agitated. Slouching back against her headboard, she could see the sun setting in the distance, the sky marbling with oranges and pinks. The forest hadn't changed which seemed to only cause more unsettling within Alyx.

After something so--unreal--how could the world act like nothing had happened?

"You come across one Gvayras and you start contemplating the world? You would never make it where I'm from." Sonja mumbled. Alyx scoffed.

"You're joking, right? I almost *died*. Does that mean nothing to you?" she asked, fuming. There were a few minutes of silence.

"I'm stuck in your mind, girl. I'm obligated to care. But just saying, you face something like that every day at home."

"Gee thanks for your kind and compassionate words," Alyx retorted, sarcastically. Then something occurred to her. "You know what that creature is, and you saved me from it. I need answers. Now." she demanded. Sonja snorted once.

"I don't think you have quite the authority to demand answers about something you don't understand. You probably won't be able to handle it." Sonja challenged.

"Again--I almost died. I think I can demand anything at this point." Stubbornly, Alyx crossed her arms, as if Sonja was in front of her. She seemed to pause, as if measuring Alyx's sudden boldness. Finally, Sonja groaned and said:

"Sudden confidence from someone who had 'almost died.'" she mumbled. "Good gods, *fine*. The Gvayras is a wicked creature that my sister uses to track people. It is a merciless hunter that always finds its prey. It found you, girl."

"Why does it want me though? I haven't done anything to her."

"You have me. Also, my suspicions are once again clarified about the curse. But she needs both necklaces to regain not only her body but her full power as well," Alyx looked down at the sapphire dangling around her neck. "Once she finds you, she won't hesitate to kill you, especially if she deems you unworthy."

"How am I unworthy?"

"You are defying her, and keeping me away from her. That is proof enough." Sonja explained with a huff, as if Alyx should already know the answer.

"Neena's decision making is rather flawed, isn't it?"

"It makes no difference."

"At least you're not directly in her cross hairs," Alyx imagined Sonja holding up her hand, two fingers pointed straight out, and her thumb pointed to the sky, acting like she had a gun pointed exactly at Alyx. "Yet. Look, you have no idea what my sister has been through."

"She wants to kill you and yet you still defend her?"

"It's not that simple, little one." her voice was soft.

"Then help me understand."

Sonja paused, contemplating. Finally, she seemed to settle on: "In due time." she felt the voice fade away, and Alyx was alone once more. She looked through the window again and noticed night had finally set in. She made a move to close the blinds but stopped short once her hand grabbed the cord to pull them shut. Her eyes widened once they locked onto a shadowy figure standing on the edge of the forest. Alyx practically smashed her face against the window, trying to get a better look.

She couldn't see the full detail of the figure, but she could see a face slightly in the moonlight. The features were soft enough to show it was female, her lips curved into a chilling smirk, and her eyes were a terrifying shade of violet, due to its incredible illumination in the darkness. The violet that gave off a glint, a warning.

Neena had found Alyx.

━━━◦◦◇◦◦━━━

As Alyx walked through the automatic doors at the gas station, she looked around to see that it was barren, due to the hour no doubt. It was late at night, she couldn't remember what time she had left her house, but she didn't much care how late it was. The dark freaked her out slightly just by seeing Neena for the first time. But it made her realize just how much she needed to see her dad. Sonja kept telling her how much she had abandoned her father, and yet she wasn't quite ready for everyone to know that she was with him, almost every other night. Maybe it was time to tell *someone*, even if that someone was an ancient, magical being whom was unfortunately locked up in her mind for the time being.

"What are you buying?" Sonja faded in, curiosity overtaking her. Alyx walked up to the counter, greeted by a very tired, and cranky cashier. He looked up at her, his eyelids half closed, his head resting in his palm.

"Can I help you?" he asked in a not so customer-service way. Ignoring him, Alyx looked behind and bought the same thing she always did every other night.

"Can I get a pack of Marlboro's: Red's please?" The cashier nodded, turning around and grabbing the small pack of cigarettes. His eyes widen slightly and he nodded once her way.

"May I see your I.D. please?" She responded with a nod herself and grabbed her wallet, flashing her I.D. he acknowledged this and finished checking her out. Once she was done getting her change she walked out of the gas station, shoving the cigarettes in her back pocket, and she returned to her car. Hastily moving since everywhere she went now she felt like someone was watching her.

"What do you do with that?" Sonja piped up. Alyx turned her car on, the ignition humming to life.

"They're for a friend. You say I abandoned my dad, but you've only just appeared in my mind. You don't know everything." She replied out loud. The road was gently illuminated from the street lamps, the light reflecting off her windshield as she traveled under each one. Sonja didn't reply, allowing Alyx to show her the truth.

Alyx arrived around the back of St. Brethren, through the parking garage, winding its way up further and further. It was ghostly with very few, to no cars parked. Choosing a place closest to the door with the giant letter: B painted on the surface. She pulled out her phone and sent a quick text to her contact.

I'm here.

She sat in her car, waiting for a response. Nothing.

"Are we just waiting until sunrise?" Sonja questioned.

"You don't have much patience, do you?" Alyx replied. More silence. Finally, after a few minutes passed, the backdoor to the hospital opened. A man around his late fifties poked his head out. His balding head gleamed from the illumination. Alyx opened her door and made her way to the man.

"Hey, Jacoby." she greeted with a grin and gave him a nod. He replied with a wide, toothy smile. His face was kind but he looked a little rough around the edges. His small neck tattoo poked out slightly from his janitorial uniform, the collar pulled up as high as it could go.

"Got the usual?" his voice gruff, blocking the entrance into the hospital. She smirked.

"Always." She pulled the pack out and handed it over to Jacoby, who took it appreciatively. He slid one out and gave it a whiff.

"It smells heavenly." He exhaled a sigh of satisfaction, moving aside to let her pass. Alyx giggled and walked past him. They walked down the hallway which was softly lit by the buzzing fluorescents.

"Where are the nurses?" she whispered. Jacoby slipped the single cigarette behind an ear, dropping the pack in his pocket.

"There's only two on this floor tonight, your dad's level is not as filled now, so you shouldn't run into anyone. I'll send you a text if anything changes." He recited. Alyx gave him a kind smile and waved, making her way through the hallway, running her hand along the walls.

"Who was that?" Sonja questioned.

"Jacoby, he may seem rough but he's a big teddy bear." She replied in her mind.

"How did you meet him?"

"So many questions," Alyx laughed. "I snuck in one night and got caught, he agreed he'd let me return whenever as long as I didn't steal anything and brought him a pack of smokes. He's a good person, he just seems intimidating at first because he got out of prison a year ago." It was Sonja's turn to laugh now.

"You surprise me."

"Told you."

Alyx turned the corner, looking down both hallways and followed the numbers until she found 60B. She looked in, making sure a nurse wasn't checking in on him.

Once the coast was clear, she proceeded to open the door. The moonlight faintly pouring into the room. Everything was silent minus the whirring and clicking sounds the machines were making. She walked to his bed and took her usual seat next to him, the one she was sure her mom was using during the day.

In a way, she felt guilty that she wasn't telling the rest of her family, but she didn't feel the need to let them know. She wasn't sure why it was this big secret but it was easier to deceive than for her to tell the truth about this kind of stuff.

"You are indeed confusing." Sonja commented. Alyx sighed. She knew. Oh damn, she knew. As long as her father knew that she was there, that's all that mattered. As she pulled her legs up onto the chair, she leaned onto the armrest. She watched her dad breathe slowly, his hair was much too long for his liking now, but a haircut was on the last of their to-do list.

"You just sit here?" Sonja mentioned. Alyx nodded.

"Yup. I just enjoy his company. His breathing relaxes me." She replied, not taking her eyes off her dad.

"I see." Was all Sonja managed to say. It was silence for the next few hours before Alyx headed home.

CHAPTER 6

"ALYX? WHAT'S WRONG? You look like hell," Emily stated. She gave her sister a look. "What? Been out partying again?"

"As a matter of fact, no I haven't." And it was the truth, it had been a solid week since she had seen Neena that night. If anything, she hadn't been wanting to go out at all, which caused concern from her friends. The late-night visits with her dad were starting to wear her down as well.

"It's true actually." Her mom added as she walked into the kitchen. Emily was skimming through a magazine at the table, her legs crossed on the bench as Alyx washed out a bowl she had just used, in the sink. Maria set down two plastic bags on the island before joining Emily, kicking off her sandals in the process. She leaned back on Emily's lap, snuggling up to her second oldest child, Emily smiled in return and went back to reading her magazine. Alyx smiled too, their mom hadn't relaxed like that in a while, it was good to see some normalcy lately, considering how crazy everything had been lately. She silently shivered at the memory of the Gvayras.

"Alyx isn't lying though--really--she's been home for the past week. You would know if you were actually home too, Emily." Maria looked up at her daughter and smirked. Emily rolled her eyes and met her mother's gaze, her expression annoyed.

"Oh no, you're not going to guilt trip me, mom. Alyx is the one with the problem, not me," she narrowed her eyebrows, looking up at Alyx. "I've been out helping Josh, he needs me you know, and I'm trying to make sure his life is a *success*." she hissed the last word. Alyx sneered at her sister, god she could be such a bitch sometimes. Ignoring her,

Alyx turned and opened the refrigerator, hoping something would catch her eye.

"I'm not guilt tripping, merely trying to make sure all of my babies are home safe with me, and I miss my Joshie, you should send him home too you know," Maria sat up to give Emily a peck on the cheek. Emily sighed, trying to keep the annoyed facade up, but betrayed herself with a smile anyway. "Also, I think Alyx has learned her lesson, stop trying to torment her." Maria got up off the bench and began to put away the groceries.

"Oh yes, because we're gonna live here forever." Alyx said sarcastically, but she was genuinely glad her mom was defending her.

"No. Just until you're all married," she gave Alyx a wink and placed the bag of bread out onto the counter. "Unless your significant others want to live here too." she joked and raised her eyebrows, her lips spread into a smile.

Emily snorted from behind Alyx.

"Are you going to go back to see dad soon?" Emily added. Maria gave her daughter a small smile, nodding.

148

To No End

"Yeah, I just wanted to come home and shower, check up on you kids, also thought I should restock the fridge, since your brothers eat everything." she laughed, but it was less genuine. Alyx missed the real hearty laughs both her parents had, she also missed everyone together and getting along. When were things going to go back to normal?

Maria had been by her husband's side since day one, their relationship was everything Alyx strived for in her own life. They met when they were young, still in high school and were together ever since, a lot of the time, high school relationships didn't last, especially today, but her parents always said they fought for their love, against all the people that doubted them. They are romantics. For some reason society would always try to dictate their life, but married twenty-some years later, with four kids, they're still going strong.

If their dad pulled through, or more so, if Alyx found out what really was going on.

Alyx shook her head, clearing her thoughts. Her mom tucked a strand of hair behind her ear.

"Mom? Can I come with?" Alyx asked meekly. Maria looked at her in surprise. Deciding to see her dad during the day was something Sonja had been pushing Alyx to do the past week.

"Of course, you can," she said, happiness growing in her eyes. "Just let me shower and we'll go." Alyx nodded in response, a slight smile on her lips. She didn't know why she was so awkward about it, it was her dad after all. Maria left the room, leaving Emily and Alyx alone. Silence filled the air as her sister only stared at her in confusion.

"What?" Alyx asked.

"What are you doing?" she demanded. She tossed the magazine aside.

"Uh, going to see our dad?"

"You mean the one you abandoned because you couldn't take it?" she said venomously.

"Seriously, Em?" Alyx sighed, she didn't need to tell her sister the truth. Emily would forgive her in time.

"Don't 'Em' me. What game are you playing? Ever since dad got sick all you've done is beg for pity and make mom worry her ass off about you. Not only that but you majorly screwed Josh over. Your own brother. You're a selfish brat. You know that his court date is coming up soon. That whole charge for 'contributing to minors' bullshit? That could really screw him in life," Emily barely stopped to breathe. She stood up and got into Alyx's face. "So why now?" she added, narrowing her eyes at Alyx.

She could only look at Emily in shock. The truth was, she had to make up for lost time now. She knew she had screwed up majorly; Sonja had always been right, no need to sugar coat anything, she just didn't want to accept it at the time. She *was* just a selfish brat. But it was time to change that, to change all of it.

Emily snarled at Alyx and stomped away before giving her a shove on her way out of the kitchen. Alyx bit her lip, feeling hot tears prick at her eyes.

"You like to meet confrontation with submission, don't you?" Sonja suddenly chimed in. Alyx quickly wiped her eyes, acting like Sonja had physically seen them in the first place. Sniffing she swallowed, forcing the lump in her throat to disappear.

"It's just hitting me all at once is all." she choked. Alyx begged herself to keep it together.

"Uh-huh. People will *always* take silence as submission."

"I'm not submissive! People don't just walk all over me!" Alyx hissed, she was surprised that she was talking out loud.

"You keep telling yourself that, girl."

"Screw you."

"You don't want to be saying that to me, especially since my sister has found you," Alyx's eyes widened. "Oh, I know all about that." Sonja sighed.

"Why haven't you said anything about it? It's been a week!" Alyx scoffed.

"Why haven't *you*?" Sonja countered.

Alyx felt like a child, like she was caught doing something bad, and she hated it. She hadn't talked with Sonja in days, mainly because she tried to forget those eyes, but they were burned into her mind. Hearing Sonja's voice only reminded her of her sister. She would wake up in the middle of the night screaming, because of Neena and her 'pet', the Gvayras. It would constantly replay in her mind over and over what had happened that day. She was just barely acting normal enough for her family to believe her.

"Ignorantly, maybe I wanted it to go away."

"That's a very childish thing to say. Are you really that much of a child?"

"No." Alyx spat.

"Then grow up, girl." Sonja retorted.

"Why are you so mean to me all of the damn time?"

"Apparently not enough people have been mean to you."

"You don't know anything about me."

"But you know enough about me, and that should be enough for you to step back and reevaluate! Besides I'm stuck in your head, I at least know how you think!" Sonja snapped. Alyx could feel the necklace grow ice cold against her skin. She pulled it away, hissing under her breath.

"Do you mind? God, I wish you would just get out of my head already!" she shouted, and then paused hoping no one heard that.

"Alyx? Are you okay?" Maria jogged into the kitchen, her hair still wet from the shower, she was pulling down a blue t-shirt as she came around the corner. She could feel Sonja 'leave' in her mind-- conversation over for now.

"Yeah, I'm fine, ready?" Alyx asked in a huff. Maria nodded, concern written all over her face. Her eyebrows drawn as she looked down at the counter, her eyes searching for the car keys. She tucked a strand of damp hair behind her ear as she spotted them, grabbing her purse on the way as she snatched them up and headed out the door. Alyx sighed and followed suit, hoping her mom didn't ask any more questions.

———◈———

When they finally got to Saint Brethren hospital, it was very quiet as the summer breeze danced around their heads. She always hated going to visit in the hospital, they just wanted him to come home and wake up the next day to find this all had been a bad dream. But the reality of the situation was always too much for Alyx, hence why she drank so much. She always feared reality and tried to find ways to escape. Besides, it's always so different during the day than when she would visit her dad at night. Too many unwanted and pitiful eyes on her and her family.

Maybe she would get back into writing or pick up that last book she left off from someday.

They walked through the automatic doors and were instantly greeted by the smell of anti-bacterial soap and disinfectant spray. It smelled way too clean which made her nose burn.

It was always the same, the obvious health conscious nurses waddling past them in a frenzy as if they were a school of fish fueled by coffee. Once they made their way through the never-ending hallway, they made it to the front desk. A large woman wearing scrubs with cat prints and oversized glasses she probably kept from the eighties sneered down at them over the desk. It was one of those moments where everything began to grow and they shrunk down to the size of mice, like a cartoon or a bad acid trip.

"May I help you?" she asked with a gruff tone, obviously a smoker and annoyed at the visitors who were distracting her from finishing her paper work.

"Not now." Sonja chimed, if she was physically there she would be rolling her eyes, her arms crossed and probably an eyebrow raised. Alyx fought a smile, wanting to still be mad at her.

"Just checking back in to see my husband, Victor McOwen. I left about four hours ago, just picked up one of our kids." Maria said softly, intimidated by the woman. If the nurse hadn't been listening so intently like a vulture she probably would have never heard her.

"Ah yes, Mrs. McOwen go right ahead." she said short and turned her attention back to her computer screen. Maria motioned to Alyx to follow her.

They soon arrived at the elevator. Alyx could tell her mom was antsy, anxiously waiting to see her husband again, even knowing his state probably hadn't changed. They hastily stepped in, feeling more anxious as the metal doors slowly closed shut in front of them. They stood there for a few minutes in silence until Maria began to tap her foot impatiently.

"Mom, we're almost there."

"I know, the elevator just takes too long." she nodded and nervously bit a fingernail, staring up at the blaring red numbers on the screen as it began to count.

2.

Maria began to grab at her sleeves like a kid waiting impatiently for a ride.

3.

"I'm glad I came." Alyx chimed, hoping small talk would distract her anxiety. Her mom looked at her with a smile, visibly relaxing a little. She reached out to brush a strand of hair out of Alyx's face.

4.

"Me too, Alyx. It's a good thing for you to see him. He would want that." she murmured.

5.

The elevator shuttered to a halt before fully stopping to allow the doors to open. They walked out of the elevator and down the hallway, counting the numbers on the side of the doorways as they did.

Strangely, Alyx began to feel a pair of eyes, someone was watching her. She allowed herself to stop and look around behind her. At the last second, she swore she saw somebody sprint back into the elevator as the doors closed, a shadowy figure.

"Alyx?" her mom called, pulling her back to reality. She blinked twice, turning back to see Maria looking at her, her brows drawn down in confusion.

"What is it?" she asked.

"I thought I saw someone I knew. Never mind." she finalized and shook her head. No, it had to be her imagination. Alyx jogged after her mom, praying to God she was right. Maria found the room which had 60B in bold lettering on the door. Her mom knocked twice and opened the door, immediately setting her purse down on the nearest chair like she probably always did.

Hesitantly, Alyx walked in to see her once strong father, lying in bed, now thin and pale. Under his eyes were large dark circles and his face gaunt. His usual coppery colored hair was now lacking shine and a few grey strands were now starting to show, as patches began to fall out. He was hooked up to four different machines one in particular made Alyx gasp as it forced him to breathe.

Maria walked over to Victor and gave him a loving kiss. It was almost like she didn't notice the machines or his overall state. Alyx wrapped her arms around herself, begging that she wouldn't fall apart, seeing him like this, she couldn't do that to her mom.

Her mom took a seat next to him, a chair that looked well worn, that must be her main spot.

"Have they seen him lately?" Alyx couldn't take her eyes off her dad.

"Yeah. They were all here yesterday. I just know how you handle all this kind of stuff. I'm sorry none of us told you." Maria took Victor's hand but looked up at Alyx, asking for her forgiveness. Guilt flooded through her. She *was* just the selfish little girl that abandoned her dad, and the fact that her mom was apologizing to *her*? Well, that just solidified her feelings even further.

"Now you see the truth." murmured Sonja. Alyx's eyes widened, surprised. Alyx could only stand there watching her dad breathe, feeling helpless.

'I need to save him, Sonja.' she thought.

159

"You've always wanted to save him, but now this only solidifies everything, correct?"

"You can read my mind?" Alyx had only ever spoken out loud to her, this aspect could be much handier down the road.

"How else do I give you my witty one-liners? I am after all living in it."

'Duh.' Hopefully her mom wasn't seeing her many facial expressions changing like an old movie reel, otherwise she would be locked up. She felt a shiver crawl up her spine from the thought. Maria looked up at Alyx from the sudden violent movement.

"Are you cold?" she asked and handed her a black cardigan draped across the back of her chair. No matter what was going on her mom never stopped being a mom, it made Alyx smile. She couldn't think so harshly of her mom, she would never lock her up. Her sister on the other hand...

Thankful, she took it and gladly slipped it on.

"Do you mind if I go and step out into the hallway, mom?" Alyx asked, crossing her arms. Her mom nodded and turned her attention back to

Victor, pulling the blanket up a bit higher to keep him warm.

Alyx slipped out into the hallway, shutting the door behind her. She peeked into the small window and saw her mom brush a bit of Victor's hair back off his face. She gave a faint smile.

Turning around, she saw all the nurses walking around her going about their day holding spreadsheets and medical tablets. She looked down towards the elevators and stopped short.

A figure standing in the very middle--a hood erasing its features. The nurses oblivious to it. She squinted, hoping to make out its face. It didn't look like Neena, at least not from the back. Then the figure began to turn as it hid further in the elevator.

"Alyx?" Maria's voice made Alyx jump suddenly. "Are you okay? I didn't mean to scare you." she giggled slightly, poking her head out of the door. It seemed that that's all her mom asked her these days. She could feel the blood rush to her face.

"No, I just thought I saw someone again." Maria followed her gaze, but the elevators were shut.

"Well you must have just missed them."
Maria walked back into the room. Alyx began to
follow, but stopped to look back momentarily again.

"Neena is here, girl. She wants you. She's
waiting." Sonja warned.

"She's going to have to wait a little longer."
and Alyx rejoined her mom once again.

———✦◈✦———

They arrived home later that evening,
reluctantly leaving her dad at Saint Brethren. She
marched up the stairs and flopped down on her bed.
The springs squeaking at the sudden weight.
Sighing, she sat up and reached over to her desk,
grabbing something she hadn't touched since she
had found her dad. Her writing notebook.

She flipped open to a new, clean page,
grabbing her favorite pen and began to write. The
wonderful sound of the scribbling of pen onto paper
filled the silence of her room, the smell of ink
wafting in her nose was heavenly. For some reason,

her dad always inspired her to continue writing, and today was no exception.

The world is at a standstill
Delightful eyes gaze upon the stars
Lips so tender kiss the rain
Feet so forlorn that walk across the dunes
In somber unity

Feeling a certain amount of contentment, she closed the book shut and laid her head down onto her feather pillow. Looking out the window beside her bed, she had a clear view of the forest. The setting sun was casting shadows that darkened its features, but she could still make out the faint shape of the entrance where she was attacked by the Gvayras. The cool summer evening breeze sifted through the bottom half of the slightly opened window, causing the lightweight curtains to dance around in the air. Alyx sat up, shifting to sitting on her knees, trying to control the curtains that billowed around her, she shut the window with a soft thud. As she did so, she saw a faint shadow walk towards the forest. The same figure she saw at the hospital.

Neena.

She reopened the window and stuck her head out, trying to get a better view. Squinting, she leaned outside further, hoping not to fall out in the process. The figure stopped, and she could see a slight movement, turning to look up at Alyx. Her breath caught in her throat. She couldn't make out the face but it had to be Neena. Remembering those violet eyes that bored into her soul. She thought of her father and how frail he looked, and anger burst within her.

It was all Neena's fault.

"Now, Alyx I know how you're feeling." Sonja started.

"I don't give a shit how you 'think' I'm feeling! I don't care what your sister has gone through! My dad does not deserve to suffer because of your psycho ass family dispute!" Alyx yelled. For once, Sonja didn't respond, instead she left her mind almost immediately. Good maybe it was about time Alyx bit back. Passive aggressive her ass. Turning her attention back to Neena she was about to shout at her when she realized that the figure had vanished.

"Coward." Alyx sneered under her breath and ducked back into the house, slamming the window closed.

In a rush of anger, Alyx stripped and changed into an oversized t-shirt. She flopped onto the bed, flustered but exhausted, mentally it was draining. She had never hated someone so much before, even the hyena pack. She vowed to herself that she would stop Neena, she would stop the poison and save her father.

10:45 pm.

She yawned, trying to fight sleep but was losing. Something occurred to her then; she was losing time. There were starting to be gaps in her days that she had no idea what had happened. She would blink and it would be three hours later sometimes.

"Sleep, girl." whispered Sonja. She was screwing with her!

"You, what the f---!," Alyx struggled to say as exhaustion took her.

And everything went black.

CHAPTER 7

ALYX AWOKE WITH A START. Gasping, she knew she had slept, but it was a very restless night. Her mind was awake, but she couldn't move which was a terrifying experience.

"I apologize for what I had done but it was necessary." Sonja whispered. Anger flooded her body again.

"What is wrong with you!" Alyx jumped out of bed, afraid Sonja would 'chain' her to the bed again.

"I can't say it was a cordial thing to do but I can't have you attacking my sister." Sonja whispered.

"Why not?" Alyx began to get dressed, slipping on a pair of distressed boyfriend jeans, a black tank top and a pair of flip flops. For some reason, she felt her anger melt away. "Stop messing with my mind, Sonja." It was bad enough that she could basically turn her into a narcoleptic, she didn't need her to control her own emotions now.

"I'm just trying to calm you down so we can talk." she explained.

"Because it's still *my* mind. You're just unfortunately living in it temporarily." Alyx smoothed her hair down with a huff.

"You cannot take her head on. You will die and so will I. Call it self-preservation." she sighed. Unfortunately, it made sense.

"I don't know how powerful Neena is, but her powers have to tap-out at some point."

"Not exactly, as long as the earth is still alive, she will have a limitless amount of it. She siphons her strength through nature, through life."

"But she's not immortal. Maybe the books will explain more, also an antidote to save my dad. There must be *something*. I need more information," she said in a rush, she could feel herself start to panic. Forgiving Sonja for her actions in the process. Maybe she could research siphoning magic or something. She fell to her knees and poured the contents of her knapsack onto her bed. "I can't give up, not now, and you can't stop me forever. We can't stop her if we keep running away." she whispered.

"You're becoming quite obsessive."

"If I can do something, Sonja, I will." Alyx flipped through the many pages of notes and histories and began to read.

———⟡———

"Alyx? You're still in your room?" Duncan leaned against her door frame. Worry overcoming his features. "You do realize it's like, 1 in the afternoon." he said disapprovingly.

Alyx's head snapped up, blinking rapidly as the sun poured into her eyes from the window. Had she really been reading that long? She lost more time without realizing it.

"It is? But I just woke up." she claimed and stared, dumbfounded at her brother. He looked at her, surprised.

"Don't you remember? I came up and talked to you an hour ago," he paused, something catching his eye. "You still have the necklace on? Why are you still wearing it?"

Alyx looked down in a daze.

"I don't know." she held the sapphire up which reflected the sunlight, casting a glow across her walls. She smiled softly.

"Uh huh," he said unconvinced. "How about you text Catherine back by the way or call her, it's been weeks since you've talked to her and she won't stop blowing up my phone trying to talk to you, or Josh's." he rolled his eyes.

"I bet he enjoys that." Alyx said sarcastically, raising her brows, looking bored.

"He's not complaining but you know he's not gonna tell you." Duncan snorted.

"I know he wouldn't, he won't even look at me."

"Just give him time, he'll come around." Duncan, always the optimist. He gave a short knock

on the door frame and made his way downstairs.
Alyx sat back and stretched. Reaching for her phone
she realized it was dead so she plugged it into its
charger by her bed. Once it came back to life, her
phone immediately began to buzz as a tidal wave of
missed calls and text messages attacked her
notification box.

"Good lord." she scoffed.

Most--if not all--of the messages were from
Catherine, which started out nice but then began to
turn worried and then just plain mean as she began
to accuse Alyx of ignoring her on purpose. With a
sigh, she called Catherine, not looking forward to
their conversation.

"Um, so where the hell have you been?" she
shouted through the phone.

"Hi to you too, Cat."

"Don't you 'Cat' me! You just dropped off the
face of the earth! What happened? Decided to live
off the grid? I thought you were dead somewhere
until Duncan texted me back. But then you never
returned any of my calls or texts! Even though he
said you were home." Catherine said frantically, as
if Alyx didn't already have a mother.

"I'm sorry. I've been busy, with college coming up," a lie. "And with what's been going on with my dad." Not a lie.

"Alyx, you *know* I am here for you when it comes to your dad, and it's not like I can't help you look at different colleges either. Why would you just ignore me like that?" she asked, clearly hurt. Alyx felt guilty, she really didn't mean to ignore her, she honestly just forgot. It was strange, but she didn't realize that her phone had been blowing up on her the entire time she was practically running for her life.

"I swear I wasn't trying to, Cat." Alyx pleaded.

"Well, you did. What's done is done." she snapped and hung up the phone.

"Seriously, Cat?" Catherine had always had a flare for the dramatics. Tossing her phone down she sighed. First her ex, then her brother, now her best friend? Is there anyone she doesn't disappoint?

"I don't have time for this. Time is running out." she began to sift through the books again. Absent mindedly grabbing the necklace she twirled it around her fingers until something caught her eye.

Lifting the necklace up closer she saw a word that wasn't there before.

It was engraved, the words seemed to illuminate on the metal.

unna.

"What the---," she started and remembered her dad had a few notes on the language they had uncovered. Skimming through she tried to translate, but her frustration only grew.

"Sonja? I need your help. I know you know this word." she urged her in her mind. Nothing. Of course she was going to be choosy on how she helped.

"Find anything yet since you're a hermit now?" Duncan suddenly chimed and walked into her room.

"Did I invite you in?" she asked, annoyed but didn't look up at her brother.

"Alyx seriously? What is with the attitude? First off, I'm not a vampire, and secondly you're becoming a real bitch now." he reached over and snatched the notes from Alyx.

"What the hell, Duncan!" she shouted and reached over to try and grab them, but he only pulled them away.

"Is this about dad?"

"Of course, it is! I have to figure out what kind of poison it is." she said quickly.

"Alyx," he groaned. "If it were a poison, don't you think they would have found something by now?" he questioned. He looked at her like she was crazy, the look was starting to become normal for her now.

"It's not that simple. There's a curse behind it. Not just an everyday mundane poison." she said, looking at him dumbfounded.

"A curse." Duncan said flatly, clearly not believing her, he bit his lip trying not to laugh, but his grin gave his actions away.

"If you're not going to take me seriously then you can leave." Alyx hissed at him, glaring up at her brother.

"I am, but Alyx you have to know how this whole thing sounds."

"What else are we going to do? Kind of running out of options here and dad's running out of time." she pleaded with him. Duncan looked at her for a second.

"Alright, what were you looking at on the necklace?" that stopped her, what should she say? He already thought she was crazy, why seal her fate even more?

"I found something. Now will you please leave? I'm fine." she stated and held her hand out, motioning to the door. Duncan studied her for a moment. Sensing his anger rising he narrowed his eyes and tossed the notes that he had been holding at her. She scrambled to catch them midair but let the few drop to the floor. Duncan marched to the doorway and stopped, turning around he scowled at her.

"You're not the only one who wants to save dad you know. Maybe if you let someone help for once people wouldn't feel like you just want to blow them off. Dad certainly as hell wouldn't want you to go through this alone." he snapped and stomped across the hall to his own room and slammed the door making Alyx jump. Her brother never got mad so to see him like that really shook her up.

"Why do you do it?" Sonja whispered, like she was afraid to ask her anything. Alyx smoothed the notes out on the bed.

"Do what?" Alyx sighed, she was exhausted by all the questions.

"Push people away all of the time?"

Alyx paused, narrowing her eyebrows in confusion.

"What? No, I don't." she scoffed.

"You're a terrible liar. That's why you drank to forget." Sonja said matter-of-fact.

"I don't drink anymore. My dad needs me."

"He needed you before that, and that doesn't mean you're not still running away. The question is, what are you running from?" Sonja paused. Alyx looked down at the notes again trying to focus.

"Or more so, what are you running towards," Alyx looked up, her mouth hung open. "Just admit it, girl. Maybe you like all of this. Maybe this is what you were longing for." Alyx could swear she could picture Sonja smiling right now.

"Yeah, longing to save my dad." Alyx said flatly. Sonja laughed once.

"Oh, I don't doubt that part, but you shouldn't lie to yourself, especially since you're so bad at it in the first place. After all I am in your mind."

"Screw you," was the lame comeback Alyx could muster. Sonja laughed again as she slipped out of her mind, it had sounded a bit off but maybe Alyx was just imagining things. Wouldn't be the first time. Then she stopped, she needed Sonja to tell her about the word that had mysteriously shown itself on the necklace. "Sonja! Wait! What is this word? Please, just tell me!" she begged.

Again nothing.

Alyx grabbed the necklace again, her fingers caressed the strange word. Curious, she felt the word involuntarily slip through her lips.

"*Unna.*" she whispered. With a small rumble beginning to reverberate louder and louder, her whole room began to shake violently. Alyx screamed and crawled up to the foot of her bed, drawing her knees up to her chest. Her window slid open as the wind began to howl, blowing her papers everywhere. She covered her ears as the wind transformed into voices yelling from people she had never met or had heard from in her life. She snapped her eyes shut, hoping it would stop.

As quickly as it had started it did indeed end.

Alyx slowly lowered her hands and opened her eyes. Her light was off and the hallways too. The thing that was really alarming to her was the sudden change in the time of day. The wind was gone as the sun was setting. Alyx looked at her desk clock.

6:42 pm.

"What the hell?" she gasped as she ran a hand through her hair. Jumping off the bed she jogged over to her doorway.

"Duncan?" she called. His door was still shut. Had no one felt the earthquake? Suddenly, a blood curdling scream echoed in the distance making Alyx's blood run cold as she slowly turned around. She felt a presence standing behind her. Her blood left her face as the scream stayed ringing in her ears long after it was gone. What really caught her attention was the figure standing on her windowsill. She used the door frame to hold herself up as the cloaked stranger stood. Even with the sunset behind them there was a thick shadow cast over its face. It was the same figure she had been seeing, like the one at the hospital. Then, it looked as though it began to open its eyes.

The violet eyes that were imbedded in Alyx's mind since she first saw them. Neena.

Smoke began to billow around the woman. A slight cackle came from her, followed by a slight rumble of a growl. She was barely human to Alyx.

"We finally meet, little bird." Neena purred. Alyx froze. She called out to Sonja in her mind. Neena stepped down from the window gracefully, her features still covered in shadow but she walked across her bed and onto the floor, which sounded like soft clicks of heels again her wood floors. Neena towered over Alyx, even if she weren't already cowering. In fear, Alyx grabbed a book off her desk and threw it at her. Neena not even flinching, didn't stop the book, as it completely passed through her, her body turning into smoke where it had connected. Neena laughed.

"Oh, you really should see the look on your face, little bird. I'm not *really* here. At least, not physically." the accented voice was almost mesmerizing, maybe even slightly sensual, befitting an evil being who slept her way to the top and then murdered people in their sleep. Alyx could see her eyes narrow and the violet glow.

"Be careful with your thoughts, else they betray you," Alyx looked at Neena in horror. She laughed again. "You didn't think my sister was the only one with gifts, did you? I can read your mind, for a time. I'm aware my weak sister is trapped inside your head. All I ask is you release her to me, so we can finish what *she* started." Neena tried to sound sweet but only more smoke appeared at the end of her words. She was standing in the middle of her room now.

"Clearly I don't know how to." Alyx gritted. Anger filled her heart. Neena tsked.

"Little bird, so much hatred for one so young and small. That hatred could be the very thing to kill you," her eyes gleamed. "Oh, I see now. He's *your* father. Pity." she had no ounce of empathy on her face, only a smirk.

"Why are you doing all of this!" she had never wanted to punch somebody so much before, even more than Kourtney. Neena cackled, clearly entertained by Alyx's misfortune.

"Now if I tell you everything it would ruin the fun, wouldn't it?" she gave Alyx a wink.

"You're a sick bitch!" Alyx could feel hot tears running down her face. Neena stopped, her violet eyes radiated an emotion that didn't seem to belong on her face.

Sadness.

It flickered with it slightly, though was soon gone as she looked back at Alyx. She felt more anger as she witnessed a small glimpse of humanity in the woman.

"You think *I'm* sick? You have barely begun to live, little one," Neena hissed and seemed to *float* quickly towards Alyx who fell back against the wall. A purple substance seemed to secrete out of the corners of her eyes. Neena was inches from her face, the smoke still cloaking the rest of her features. She seemed to hiss at Alyx, a soft, threatening sound.

"Until you hear the screams of people you loved burn around you, until you've felt the blade of loss, then you will destroy that annoying light from within you. Choke it right out of you in fact," her hands flew up to Alyx's neck, but not quite touching her skin. Alyx's breath caught in her throat. "Until then," she slowly lowered her hands. "You must find me. *If* you want to save, *daddy dearest.* You opened the portal, you allowed our powers to begin to fully siphon again with the earth, now the rest is up to you." her voice started to echo as smoke began to billow around her, little by little Neena began to fade away. She cackled as her violet eyes seemed to reflect Alyx's terrified face until the smoke enveloped Neena entirely, and dissolved before Alyx.

And she was left alone in the dark.

CHAPTER 8

ALYX STOOD FOR a moment, her knees starting to shake, forcing her to slide down the wall, for fear of falling over, and sat on the wood floor.

"Alyx? Who were you talking to?" Duncan suddenly burst into her bedroom making her jump. She met his confused and frantic gaze. Tears streaming down her face, her mouth slightly opened.

"Don't tell him anything, he knows too much already. Do you really want Neena to target him too?" Sonja hissed. Her mouth snapped shut. Duncan knelt to look at his sister.

"Please, you know you can tell me anything. Don't shut me out, not like you did to everyone else. I won't let you." he stated and sat down, waiting for Alyx to speak. She blinked and shook her head, looking down at her hands.

"You have me." Sonja murmured shyly. For some reason, Alyx felt comfort, she didn't feel quite so alone. Duncan wouldn't believe her before, what would change now? Sonja did understand, she knew her sister better than anyone.

"To save my dad, will I have to kill Neena?" she asked Sonja, even though she already knew the answer.

"Yes."

"Where is she?"

"Not of this time." Alyx searched her brother's eyes, weighing Sonja's words in her mind.

"Fine." Alyx choked out loud, stating to both Duncan and Sonja. She knew she would have to push her brother away, to save him, their family and their father. She began to stand up, leaving Duncan staring up at her, confused.

"Leave." she said with a straight face, which even surprised Alyx herself, having no idea she had this much control. Duncan bolted upright, angry. He glowered at her.

"I'm not giving up!" he shouted and stormed out, stomping down the stairs. Alyx exhaled.

"Sonja? Can you tell me how to get there?" she paused. "How we can go back in time?"

She was definitely crazy, but she surprised herself as a feeling of excitement held onto her heart. She was terrified of Neena, of losing her family but also what she didn't realize was that she was also afraid of living without purpose. She sensed it now--to stop a madwoman and save her dad but to also venture to an unknown land. She wanted to test her own strength, and her ability to forgive herself.

"Do not take this lightly, Alyxandra. You don't know what you are signing up for." Sonja warned.

"I can't back out now. Neena wants me? She can sure as hell try." Alyx began to grab a knapsack and grabbed some of her father's notes, books and a flashlight that was sitting on her desk. If it wasn't for the encouragement and almost straight up excitement, she would still be scared shitless.

Instead, she felt a fire in her belly for making a difference now.

"Are you going somewhere, little bird?" Sonja chimed. Alyx paused, throwing the knapsack into her closet.

"Not you too." she groaned.

"What do you mean?" Sonja questioned.

"The whole 'little bird' bullshit. Neena calls me that, not you." Alyx hissed.

"Sorry," she paused. "But where *are* you going?" Sonja tries to redirect.

"I'll find it once everyone goes to bed," Alyx whispered as she shut her door, making sure no one was outside listening.

"I just need some information first." she finalized.

"Depends. I can only give you so many answers." Sonja said hesitantly.

"Why is that exactly?"

"That is one of them."

"Ugh, okay start by telling me how I can avoid the Gvayras then."

"Why are you going in to the forest?" Sonja seemed bewildered that Alyx was willing to try again.

"Everything points to that forest, I can't explain it but I just know that is has something to do with getting to Neena. I know you feel it too. That has to be where the portal opened." Alyx paced back and forth in her room waving her hands around in thought.

"You want to go towards danger like an idiot?" she scoffed.

"As far as I know, it's the only way to find out how to save my dad. Neena must have the antidote, right? Find her, find the antidote, come back and save my dad. Also, didn't you just give me shit early about running away from my problems?" she said it so matter-of-fact, like it was the simplest problem in the world to solve. She even started to believe herself a little.

"I meant running away from your father, not running purposefully to your death out of blind vengeance," she paused for a moment, contemplating. Finally, she spoke: "Hmmm. The only way is to mask your scent, it can only hunt you by its

nose, otherwise it has poor eyesight." Sonja
explained slowly, she was gaging Alyx's resolve no
doubt.

"Okay, so clearly I need to mask it then. But
the question is with what?" Alyx stopped short,
running a hand through her hair.

"Really anything that is very strong smelling
I suppose." Sonja shot out, clearly trying to half-ass
her answers. Little did she know a light bulb went
off in Alyx's mind, surprised she didn't see it.

"So maybe a gas bomb of some sort." Alyx
began to pace again, trying to put the plan together.

"You *are* crazy." Sonja finalized.

"Shh, let me think." Alyx sat down at her
desk and turned on her computer. All that went
through her mind was the horrible Gvayras that
haunted her dreams, with Neena's striking violet
eyes spying overhead. She began researching several
types of gas bombs. She could feel Sonja's
restlessness within her mind.

"My self-preservation is definitely not
looking good now." Sonja muttered.

To No End

Alyx wandered back upstairs with four plastic bags full of stuff. She had no idea what she was going to make exactly but she knew it was going to be revolting. Bounding up the steps, she was too busy talking with Sonja in her mind about modern day stores that she didn't notice Josh as she barreled into him at the top.

"Watch what the hell you're doing." Josh snarled and shoved past her, a canvas tucked under his arm. His shirt was covered in paint and he tried to hold what seemed like thousands of brushes in his pockets.

"So that's the brother you got arrested." Sonja cooed.

"Calm down." Alyx rolled her eyes. She walked into her room and began to unload everything, shutting the door behind her with a foot.

"It's not my fault you have *very* good genetics in your family."

"Are you sure that thing is even going to work?" Sonja asked, not impressed. Alyx sat in the middle of her room. She held a small cardboard tube with a fuse dangling out of the side, her eyes narrowed.

"Well, we're gonna find out now aren't we. Now hopefully my family doesn't think I'm making drugs." she whispered to herself. She looked down at the aluminum foil and the small electric stove they used when they went camping.

"That would be the least of their worries if this whole insane plan of yours doesn't work and they find you ripped to pieces."

"*So* comforting." Alyx rolled her eyes.

"I'm only being realistic."

"Try optimism next time."

"Noted."

Alyx stood up and carefully placed the bomb into her bag that was sitting in her closet. Looking at the clock she sighed and ran a hand through her hair. It was only two in the afternoon. She still had to wait seven hours before sundown and six more before she could sneak out without being caught. She felt anxious as she stood there, not knowing what to do.

"So, what do you do for fun? Besides poisoning your body?" Sonja scoffed, clearly trying to distract Alyx. She rolled her eyes again. Alyx began to dig through her desk, finding a piece of paper and a pen.

"It so happens I like to write." she sat down at her desk.

"Writing? What the hell do you have to write about?"

"Oh, you know, the usual 1,000 something year old sorceress who wants me and my family dead, a creature that wants to kill me, oh and my dad is also dying so there's that too." she responded sarcastically.

"Dually noted."

The only unusual thing was that, that wasn't what her muse was telling her to write about. Alyx kept going back to a feeling she had, the feeling that something big was about to happen that was both terrifying and exhilarating at the same time. It seemed like it was the first time in a while she could gather her thoughts and process everything that was happening. Her pen connected with paper as she poured out her heart.

Her dad was alone and probably scared in some sick nightmare created by this poison Neena had created. As much as Alyx hated her she still couldn't help wanting to know more about her. Was she born evil? Or did she become that way? Alyx surmised more so with the second reason.

"Some things are better left buried. She does not deserve pity, trust me." Sonja said, bitterness consuming her voice.

"Your emotions are making my head throb, and the necklace is giving me frost bite again." Alyx complained, and the pressure released, and the necklace returned to normal temperature. Her pen began scribbling again until she finally reached the last line. Reading it twice over she felt a slight feeling of peace wash over her as she leaned back in her chair. With everything going on she didn't realize how much she missed some of the mundane things in her life.

To No End

To live another day
Without redemption and fear
Is to live a life of peaceful prosperity
Or a dream
A human being cannot succumb to the addictive
features it so craves
Shall I venture forth to an unknown path?
To live my life without false wishes or dreams?
Or shall I hold onto normality with a lasting
embrace?
And greet reality like an old friend?

"Not bad." Sonja said flatly, acting more surprised than impressed but Alyx would take it. She clicked the penpoint closed dramatically and tossed it onto the surface of the desk.

"Well, good thing I'm not trying to impress you." she shoved the piece of paper into the drawer and began to walk about her room, slightly disappointed at Sonja's reaction, but shrugged, she was a bit rusty, she knew that already. Walking downstairs she saw her mom busying herself in the kitchen.

"Hey mom." Alyx greeted and leaned against the kitchen counter.

"Hey, hun." she replied with a smile and continued cleaning the counter tops.

"Are you going to visit dad today?" she knew at this point that was starting to become a dumb question.

"In a little while, yeah." Maria said, sounding tired as she placed a mixing bowl back up into the cabinet.

"Can I come with again?" Alyx asked.

"Why do you even ask? Of course, you can." she looked surprised at Alyx. Always surprising people around this house.

"I don't know why I keep asking first, but it's just a feeling I have that I need to." Alyx shrugged, tracing the grout lines on the kitchen island.

"What feeling is that?" Maria sat the bread down on the counter.

"Dad would hate me if he knew all of the things I've been doing, or have already done. He might not want to see me if he was awake." she said sheepishly. Maria looked as though someone had slapped her.

"Alyxandra Vrain. Don't you dare." she scolded, gritting her teeth.

"Why wouldn't he?" Alyx pleaded, genuinely questioning.

"Because he is your dad and loves all of you unconditionally. As do I. You should *never* worry about him 'hating you.'" she said the last part as if it was derogatory. Alyx bit her lip and shrugged. Now she just felt dumb for even saying anything.

"Even though I got Josh arrested and I got into a fight with Kourtney?" Alyx said slowly, weighing her words. Also, about leaving and fighting a crazed 1,000-year-old sorceress that has the antidote to save my dad? Better leave that part out.

"When he wakes up we'll figure it out," Maria said confidently. Alyx only nodded in response. "I'm just gonna go grab my keys and we'll go."

Maria ducked behind the corner to grab her purse from the bench in the entryway. Coming back around she stopped at the foot of the stairs.

"Duncan? Joshua? Alyx and I are going to go see dad." she called up to them.

"Okay mom." Josh called back down. Duncan appeared at the top of the steps.

194

"Say hi to dad for me, Alyx." was all he said but he was obviously trying to intimidate her now.

"By the gods, does he know about your little plan?" Sonja chimed in, her voice only half full of worry, the other half she was probably jumping up and down with happiness that he might stop Alyx. Fat chance. Alyx eyed him suspiciously. He looked at her with narrowed eyes. He knew something was up, but hopefully she would be gone before he knew what happened. She couldn't help but reach for the necklace, it was radiating a warm glow from within that made her feel a certain amount of peace. It would be okay, her family, especially her brother would forgive her for leaving, especially if they knew what she was doing.

She noticed his eyes flickered for a second towards her necklace which made her immediately drop her hand.

"Coming?" Maria asked, causing Alyx to look away from her brother. Good thing she did, she was tired of seeing the disapproval on his face. Maria had a hand on the door, beckoning for Alyx to join her.

"Yeah." Alyx said a little too quickly and jogged towards her mom, walking out of the front door and away from the daggers Duncan was sending her way.

———⊰❖⊱———

"Do you want something to drink?" her mom asked, breaking Alyx's gaze away from the tv. She looked at her mom and shrugged.

"A pop if they have any," her mom smiled and got up, sliding off the couch to do so. "I can do that, mom." she felt a tinge of guilt making her mom cater to her. Maria shook her head and smiled.

"It's fine. I wanted to get up and walk around anyway. Plus, it makes me feel useful," she gave Alyx a wink. "Be back soon." and she slipped out the door, greeting one of the nurses on her way. Alyx reached over for the remote and turned the tv off. She knelt beside the bed and looked at her dad. He was breathing slowly, thanks to the machine. He looked like he was sleeping if it weren't for all the heart monitors, breathing tube and I.V. drips. She took his hand and was shocked at how cold it was. She began to rub it between her hands for warmth.

"Dad? I doubt you can hear me but, I'm going to do something probably very dangerous and potentially stupid, and you'll be livid with me after you wake up. But I'm going to save you," she could feel a lump in her throat. "I need to save you. Mainly because the selfish part of me doesn't want to lose my dad but the other part is because your life is being stolen by someone who has no right to take it. You are supposed to live and be a father and a husband. I'm looking forward to the day when you yell at me again, because at least I'll know you are awake and really living again. Which is why I have to do this. For you. Because I know you would do it for anyone of us," she wiped a tear away, looking at him for a time she exhaled. "I love you, dad. I hope to see you soon."

Alyx stood and gave her dad a kiss on the cheek, slightly shaken by how gaunt his skin was now, and sat down again. Her mom came back in moments later, a pop in one hand.

"I hope I got you the right one. I usually get you and Duncan mixed up about what drinks you like," Alyx gave her a weak smile as she accepted the can. "Are you crying?" Maria asked, concern filled her eyes. Alyx laughed once and wiped the fresh tear away.

"It's nothing. I just miss him is all." She wasn't entirely lying. Maria gave her a soft smile.

"I miss him too." She laid a hand on her arm, caressing her skin with her thumb, comforting Alyx. They sat like that for a few minutes before she excused herself to go walk around.

Alyx slipped out and exhaled, it would be hard to leave, but it's something she had to do. Who else? She felt chosen by fate.

Walking down the hallway, occasionally giving a few nurses, some reassuring smiles and a curt nod, she ended up in the chapel not too far away from her dad's room. Quietly opening the door, she peeked in to make sure no one was there. Alyx was never a super religious person but at this point she needed all the help she could get.

She walked up to the front of the room which had a large, dark wood cross with Latin carved in the middle. The stained-glass window behind had the Virgin Mary and Jesus with a crown of thorns on it, allowing blues and greens and reds to pan across the floor and walls. Once she had shut the door behind her everything was quiet. Sitting down in the front pew she ran a hand through her hair and leaned forward, resting her arms on her knees.

"God? We haven't exactly talked a lot. I was hoping you would give me some help. So, I don't even know where to start," she paused.

"I'm going back in time, to save my dad," the words felt wrong as she said them. "I would really love it if I could get a warning or a sign, or even a friggen miracle at this point before I go do that." she waited a few minutes. She locked eyes with the glass Jesus who looked forlorn as always in every interpretation of him that she'd seen. She yearned for him to say something, especially now.

"Are ye lost, little one?" said a wispy voice. Alyx snapped her head around to see a small child back by the door. Confused at first as to why a child would call her 'little one' she froze. The child started to walk up the aisle towards her, the sun started to show her true appearance. She indeed had the body of a child, small and non-threatening, but had long white hair. However, her face was what really made her freeze.

The 'little girl' didn't have lips, her teeth were completely exposed but there was no blood or gore, just torn, pale skin that had been scarred over for years, but what was more frightening was that she had her eyes closed as if she was blind, but could still move freely without running into anything. Her hands weren't stretched out in front of her, she merely stood straight up, nothing seeming to phase her. The girl stopped a few feet in front of her. Alyx was unable to move at all, only looking at the poor creature in terror.

The eyelids twitched and rolled like her eyes were searching from underneath the veil but could still see Alyx through the darkness.

"You do not seem very intimidating. I wonder why Neena chose you for me to play with. Ye seem too young, and ye certainly not a threat that I'm sensing at least. Pity."

"P-play?" Alyx shouted in her mind.

"My sister actually sent a _bani_ after you?" Sonja whispered, clearly not knowing how to react.

"What do I do?" Alyx was frantic. The girl only scanned over her more, probably sensing the sheer panic.

"I would say run. Run right now!" Sonja shouted so loudly in her mind. Alyx immediately bolted to the right, jumping over the pews and nearly knocking over the holy water as she headed for the door.

Which wouldn't budge.

Alyx banged on the door, screaming for help. She could sense the girl coming closer towards her, taking her time. She allowed herself to start looking behind her when a searing pain in her brain made her double over, clutching her head in agony and snapping her eyes shut.

"Don't look her in the eyes! Once she opens them, you die!" Sonja bellowed. Keeping her eyes shut she slid to the floor. Well, this was how she was going to die after all.

"Look at me, little one." the girl cooed. Alyx could feel two small hands cup either side of her face. She felt light headed, but she kept pushing herself to not pass out. She also kept forcing her eyes to stay shut even though she had the most intense desire to open them.

"Open ye eyes, damn you!" the girl shouted, a slight hiss reverberated through her chest. Alyx shook her head. She could feel the hands start to add pressure against her skin, then they began to tremble, and the necklace began to grow almost unbearably warm.

"Why won't you obey me?" the little girl shouted, her voice building like she was about to throw a tantrum.

"Keep fighting, Alyxandra!" Sonja shouted with heavy breathing. Alyx still resisted trying to shake off the small hands. She could feel agitation radiating off the creature. Why hadn't she killed her yet?

Finally, with a high-pitched scream the girl pushed Alyx's face away, hard enough to make her smack the back of her head against the door which only added to her blurring vision. She felt a cold shiver crawl up her spine as she started to collapse, the floor meeting her face quickly. She could only hear her name being shouted by Sonja as she started to black out. The necklace regaining its normal temperature once more.

———⟡———

Alyx awoke to a sharp slap in the face. Her eyes snapped open in shock as she witnessed her brother Duncan kneeling in front of her, his hand still raised from striking her.

"What the hell?" she exclaimed, her hand flew to her face, gently rubbing her freshly bruised cheek.

"What do you mean 'what the hell?' I found you unconscious in here!" he scolded as he helped her to her feet. Realizing her surroundings, she froze, looking around the room frantically for the girl.

"Mom's looking for you." Duncan tried to ignore his sister's erratic behavior like it was normal.

"How long have I been in here?" she interjected quickly.

"I don't know, I got here about twenty minutes ago. Mom said you went for a walk." he looked at Alyx with concern. People were doing that so much now.

She pulled her phone out of her back pocket to check the time.

"Oh my god, I've been in here for forty-five minutes!" There she goes, losing more time.

"What happened?" Duncan urged but Alyx merely shook her head in response, turning towards the now open door. Duncan grabbed a hold of her arm.

"Alyx, enough of this bullshit and tell me what's going on!" he demanded. She pulled against him. Suddenly, she could hear soft whispers in the room, they weren't alone.

"You know you can't tell him. She can see us right now." Sonja chimed in. She was right, Duncan wouldn't understand. He didn't believe her when she first told him her theory and it's not like she had proof, besides the 1,000 something year old woman living inside her mind. Neena would know if Duncan was in on this and she would probably try to kill him too. She couldn't allow that to happen.

"Duncan, I really can't explain," not a lie. "This is something I have to do on my own." she went to walk out again but Duncan pulled her back into the chapel, shutting the door behind her. She looked around the dark room, hoping not to see the girl again. A shiver ran up her spine as the whispers started to become slightly louder around her, but it seemed that only Alyx could hear them, go figure.

"I need answers, Alyx, I'm your brother for Christ sake! We're family and you won't tell me anything! I've got enough to worry about, I can't worry about you too!" he paused, exhaling. He was starting to lose it too. Alyx stood in silence. His eyebrows furrowed in frustration.

"Most of the time you don't talk to anyone. You hole up in your room like some hermit. You've been ignoring your friends. You're always jumpy anymore, and become a zombie out of nowhere. I hear you talking to yourself and you look like you've seen a ghost half the time," he folded his arms as he paced back and forth in front of her, trying to make sense of everything. "When are you going to talk?" he met her gaze. She inhaled, wanting to tell him everything but exhaled when she heard the whispers pick up in intensity.

"When dad wakes up. When dad is awake and smiling again; then I will tell you everything." he leaned back, curiosity overtook his expression.

"You know something I don't," he studied her face, gaging the sincerity in her eyes. "You're serious about him being poisoned, aren't you?" She sighed with relief. Maybe he's finally understanding everything. She still felt the trepidation in her heart as Neena would soon target him merely because of his prying. Unfortunately for Alyx, her brother was too inquisitive for his own good.

"It makes sense at least more sense now," Alyx began. "Most people in comas last only a few weeks usually, dad has lasted almost two full months so far without being brain dead. He has enough brain activity still, he's not gone. Dad's still in there but he is slowly dying. The curse is assuring me of that." the words spewed out of her like word vomit. It was relieving to be able to explain some of what she'd found, even if it was a small fraction of the whole story.

"Except if it's poison, why wouldn't doctors be able to find that out and find the antidote? Also, why wouldn't it have just killed him?" Duncan prodded for more information.

"I already told you. The curse is what is slowly causing the poison to kill him. The poison itself isn't from here, it's not exactly even from *this* time."

"*This time*? There you go again with that word. You don't seriously still believe dad went back in time, do you?" he scoffed but stopped as he saw the serious look on her face.

Alyx couldn't help but fidget with the necklace around her neck. Duncan looked annoyed as he eyed the jewel.

"Okay what is so special about this damn thing?" he shouted and grabbed at the jewel. Alyx pulled away, only making her brother angrier. The rage building in his eyes, he snatched at it again, this time grabbing a hold of the gold chain. Alyx tried to pull away but the chain suddenly began to shrink, cutting off her airways as it began to choke her. She began to gasp for air but Duncan wouldn't let go. The whispers were now shouts all around her, almost sounded like chants. She looked at her brother, desperate for him to let go, but she only saw a dangerous look in his eyes. He was a stranger to her.

"Duncan..." she could only whisper, her throat burned as she was trying to breathe. The jewel itself began to glow as it became agonizingly hot against her skin, almost searing. Black spots started to pool onto the sides of her vision. She couldn't breathe, she had barely begun and had survived not one but three attacks on her life, this couldn't be it. Especially not by her own brother's hands.

Neena's eyes started to visualize in her mind, almost like an eerie beacon at night. A bad omen.

No, the *witch* was not going to get away with it.

This couldn't be it.

With all her strength she kneed her brother, which caused him to release the chain and fall to the floor. Immediately the chanting stopped. His eyes hazed over suddenly as he landed on his hands and knees in pain, breathing slowly so he wouldn't throw up. He looked up at her blinking rapidly as if now realizing what he had just done. She began to open the door, tears rolling down her face. She coughed, the air never tasted so sweet before.

"Alyx, wait! I'm so sorry!" he began but Alyx's raspy voice cut him off. She barreled through the door, gasping for air which caused a scene. The nurses looked at her with worry, their instincts kicking in.

"Miss are you alright?" one nurse asked, placing a hand on her shoulder. Recoiling from her touch, Alyx fell back in fear.

"Get away from me!" she kept gasping for more air. She ran down the hall, darting past her dad's room, she silently apologized to her mom as she made it to the elevators. Punching the buttons, she pleaded for the elevator to go faster. Cursing she gave up and ran towards the stairs. She slammed open the door and galloped down the cement steps, the sound echoing through the enclosed space. Once she had made it to the main floor she jogged through the lobby, pushing past a small group of interns.

Once she made it outside she looked for the bus stop which was allowing a small group of people to trickle inside the vehicle. She made it in as the doors closed behind her. Trying to catch her breath she handed the driver some money and told him her stop. He began to pull away from the bus stop as she made her way to the back row. As he drove away Alyx looked back down the road behind her. Duncan had just stopped at the bench by the bus stop, looking at the bus frantically. He shouted something at her, but looked nothing but ashamed. She then watched him disappear, to the parking lot no doubt.

She knew he was going to follow her, but she also knew she was going to make it home first. She was going to leave. Now.

"It serves him right. Trying to kill us like that." Sonja interjected. Alyx turned back around and tried to relax.

"That wasn't him back there. It was Neena's fault." Alyx hissed between her teeth. She would be home in a few minutes, hopefully she would get there in time. She couldn't help but grab hold of the necklace again.

It was still glowing.

CHAPTER 9

ALYX'S HOUSE WAS down the road from the bus stop; she began to sprint as soon as the doors opened for her. Her heart was pounding--this was it--she could feel it in her heart. She turned around the corner of the gate, sliding a bit from the gravel, almost losing her footing. She made her way across the stone pathway and up the steps to the house. The door was still unlocked drawing her attention to the cars still parked by the garage. Emily and Josh were still home.

Shutting the door behind her she made her way through the kitchen, hoping not to run into anyone. Heading up the stairs, she tried not to cause the wood to creek with each step. Alyx jogged into her room once she made it to the upper level, immediately grabbing her knapsack from out of the closet, she looked around the room making sure she collected everything and returned to her doorway. She felt uneasiness as she realized she wasn't sure when she would return, but none the less was thrilled as she knew adventure was awaiting her. Then she paused suddenly when she heard a soft voice amongst the wind. The window was opened suddenly, causing the drapes to dance around.

"Come find me, little one. It will be the end of you." Neena's voice was clear and soft, and yet she still had the same level of warning and malicious intent behind it. A chill crawled up her spine, but she felt anger rise in her heart. It was because of Neena that her dad was dying, it was her that possessed Duncan to try and harm Alyx. She needed to not just die, she needed to be destroyed. She wanted her very existence erased. She couldn't even imagine how many other lives she had taken because of her lust for power. The necklace began to grow ice cold, making Alyx suck in a breath and pulled the jewel away from her skin. As soon as it became cold it ended, almost like Sonja had no intention in the first place to affect the necklace. Alyx adjusted the strap on her knapsack and carried on, walking down the steps, praying that she wouldn't have to face any of her family before she left. Once she had gotten to the front door she inhaled, taking in the smell, the feel of the house; she didn't know what was going to happen, all she knew was that she had to go, she had to do this even if every fiber of her being was aching with fear. The hardest decisions were often the scariest.

Alyx made her way out the door, taking an immediate right, she was almost to the field when she heard a truck reeling up the driveway. Her heart began to race, she broke into a sprint towards the edge of the forest. She reached into her bag and got the gas bomb ready, knowing that the Gvayras would be waiting for her. She stopped about a foot away from the tree line when the truck's door slammed.

"Alyx!' Duncan called, searching for her. She swallowed once, getting the lighter out.

"Don't look back." Sonja murmured, trying to help Alyx focus. She felt a wave of peace wash over

her. For the first time in a long time she didn't feel
scared.

"At least you're with me." Alyx whispered out
loud.

"Not by my doing. But, I suppose things could
be worse." She replied.

"Sonja, which way do I go?" Alyx breathed,
realizing she had no idea where the portal had
opened.

"If you open your mind I will guide you. You
will remember everything, trust me." Sonja added,
feeling Alyx's hesitation.

"Alyx!" Duncan was getting closer now.

"Go now!" Sonja ordered. Alyx nodded and
began to run. As she ran over fallen branches and
moss-covered rocks she only focused on her
breathing, allowing that form of meditation to relax
her mind. Slowly she could *feel* Sonja start to peel
back the layers of her mental defense. She tried hard
not to fight the foreign intrusion, which proved
more challenging than anything she had ever done.
As Alyx ran she could feel the action becoming
something else entirely, she could feel that she was
no longer in control, almost an out of body

experience. Then she began to hear the threatening hissing she had nightmares so often about.

"It's time," Sonja warned, but Alyx didn't have to do anything, she only watched her hands ignite the fuse.

"We're almost to the cave, I can feel it." Sonja panted. It was probably taking a lot of energy to do this, even Alyx was starting to feel her own energy start to drain. Was she siphoning from her? The hisses turned into growls, and she could start to hear something closer behind her. Fear gripped her heart as Sonja began to weaken her control but she didn't dare break concentration or they could both die. The fuse began to pop and sizzle in her hand as she was still sprinting headlong through the forest. It seemed like she had been running for hours but she felt no physical sign of fatigue, which gave her a strange high. She felt invincible, minus her brain starting to feel a little numb.

"There it is!" Sonja called, relief obvious in her voice, bringing Alyx back to earth. The crawling was almost at her heels but Alyx felt her mind start to push back, causing her to regain control. With a hard throw, she released the gas bomb behind her, hearing it connect with flesh and bone with an almost wet plop. She heard an enraged growl as the crawling stopped. Alyx, however, did not. The cave was right there and she could feel the strange power that resonated from it. She began to slow down to a jog, ignoring the Gvayras' confused roars and snaps of its jaws as it wriggled through the hissing of the smoke that billowed around it. She allowed herself a quick look back as she stepped into the cave.

A cloud of white smoke obstructed most of her view, but she could see a long, gangly arm flash out here and there--and pieces of its iridescent skin flew out in chunks from the violent movements.

A loud scream filled the body of the cave suddenly, causing her head to snap back, considering the depths. What was strange was that the scream didn't echo or become drawn out, it ended quickly, almost like a life was snuffed out before it could gather enough breath to react.

Alyx swallowed and hesitated to move on. She wasn't sure how much longer the gas bomb would last, but she wasn't sure what was waiting for her at the end.

"Keep going, Alyxandra." Sonja said weakly. Alyx nodded once, and reached into her knapsack, fishing out a flashlight she had packed. Turning it on she began to walk, kicking up smells of the rocky floor that was wet from the dripping stalactites. It became colder as she descended further to god knows where, which made her wrap her arms around herself, wishing she had brought a jacket of some sort.

<hr />

It was about a fifteen-minute hike through the cave and yet there was still no sign of a victim anywhere. She knew it was the scream of a young girl, which only brought horrible images to her mind. There were a few different passageways she had come across but Sonja had allowed the necklace to be Alyx's GPS while she rested. There were no exact clues except the warmth from the necklace. She realized if she went a certain direction, the necklace would become either warm or cool.

217

Just like a game. Fitting. It didn't glow just yet either; Sonja had explained that the jewel would glow bright once she was at the portal. It felt like she had walked another twenty minutes before she began to hear something. It was a small, simple sound, but it didn't belong. It was the thick plopping of a liquid. Too thick to be just water.

Alyx had slowly kept walking, growing more and more afraid as the plopping noise was closer. She lowered her flashlight beam to the ground which had shown nothing but water at first, but then a glint of a black substance appeared, mixing with the clean minerals on the ground. It had grown as she walked on.

The light shook as it followed the path of the liquid. It raised higher as it began to drip from the ceiling of the cave. Her hand was uncontrollable. Alyx froze once the light connected with the victim. The white hair hung like moss to a rock, it was stained with black, almost like ink. It stuck to the girl's face.

The girl that had tried to kill her earlier at the hospital.

To No End

Alyx tried to fight the urge to scream--and also to vomit. Her face was twisted in a horrific paralyzed state. Her mouth was torn open, her jaw broken making it look like she was to scream forever in hell. Her eyeballs torn from their sockets and her thin, papery skin was lashed and torn. Her body seemed to be almost proudly, *decorated,* onto the cave ceiling like a mural, the proud artist using a stalactite to pin her up like a tack. Alyx fell to her knees, the beam still consistently illuminating the poor soul.

"What the *fuck* is this?" she could only whisper, her voice seemed a million miles away. She could feel Sonja begin to wake up within her mind.

"By the gods, now do you get it?" Sonja said weakly, her voice hoarse.

"Yeah, that bitch is psychotic!" Alyx breathed, forgetting that she hadn't been.

"She is unpredictable, and certainly not afraid to show you what she is capable of. Unfortunately, that is but a taste."

"How do we kill her?" she asked, Sonja paused.

"I don't know."

"You're lying." Alyx accused.

"If I was lying then why did I resort to only trying to capture her soul? Besides to torture her. If I knew how, I would have done so." she finalized. Without warning, there was a loud and heavy drop as a rock fell onto the ground, echoing through the darkness. Alyx scrambled to her feet and began to run, hoping the Gvayras didn't find her.

She kept slipping as she ran over the wet ground, which caused her anxiety to rise. Alyx tried to keep the flashlight steady but she couldn't control the panic causing the beam of light to flail around, worsening the visibility in front of her. Alyx then began to hear a low humming coming from a few feet in front of her.

"We made it!" Sonja said, bewildered. Alyx slowed down, but pointed the flashlight in a frenzy, because she only saw a dead end.

"This can't be!" she retorted, not convinced.

That was when the necklace began to glow.

It began to produce such a searing heat, Alyx had to move the jewel from her skin. It was illuminating so radiantly she had to look away. Alyx held the jewel up to each wall, and the necklace reacted as soon as it was near the cavern wall in front of her.

The light seemed to travel to the rock, the illumination flooding through every crevice and fissure until finally, it was cloaked in the brilliant light itself. Alyx could only look at it in wonder. Something made her feel like she had to come closer to the light, that she *needed* to come closer.

"You look with your eyes and yet you do not see." Sonja remarked.

"It's an invisible portal, a little difficult to find really." Alyx snapped.

She couldn't tear her eyes away from the glowing entryway, her hand began to extend out to touch it. A frigid air caressed her skin, making her lips crack into a slight smile. She should've dressed warmer.

"Alyx! Don't!" bellowed a voice, causing her to jump and crane her head around. She froze as Duncan stood behind her, his face white and sweating from exertion. His eyes were wide with terror and seemed almost frantic. Alyx gritted her teeth and could feel the pressure on her throat again where he had choked her. In her heart, she knew that her brother would never intentionally try to hurt her, but she couldn't see past what he had done. If he had stayed out of all of this, then Neena never would have targeted him.

"Leave, Duncan." Alyx managed to say as she could feel the emotional confusion in her mind take over. She turned her back to him.

"Alyx, you've gotta know that wasn't me!" he pleaded. She looked back at him. His eyes were begging for forgiveness but they were also darting back and forth between his sister and the glowing rock wall behind her.

"Are you really serious?" he added, making her scoff.

"You're friggen joking, aren't you?" her eyes wide.

"So, you weren't just bullshitting me. You're serious about this whole-time travel?"

"What gave it away? The giant night light of a portal in the end of a cave?" she could feel the anger rising within her. "You know what? I don't have time for this. Go home." she dismissed.

"And let you go, god knows where by yourself? I don't think so." he finalized.

"I don't need you. And if you didn't notice, you tried to kill me just a bit ago." she spat, making him cringe.

"You have to believe me. It wasn't me!" he pleaded. And she *did* believe him, but somehow, she was speaking without her control.

"I'll believe you, when you start believing me!" Alyx fumed. She couldn't control her emotions at all.

"Uh, Alyxandra. If you would be so kind as to carry on. We don't have much time left." Sonja interjected, causing her to refocus.

"Right. *If* you would leave now, Duncan. I've got to save dad." she turned to touch the wall.

"Alyx, wait!" Duncan shouted, his voice echoing through the cavern as she closed her eyes and touched the rocky surface. She felt his hand grab her shoulder as the white light began to wash over her like water.

It began to creep up her arm, her shoulder, her neck until finally it reached her face. The last thing she remembered was the warmth and a flash of light. Her brothers voice still ringing in her ears as she then lost consciousness.

CHAPTER 10

THEY SAY YOU SEE A FLASH OF LIGHT WHEN YOU DIE. Alyx never imagined it would happen so quickly and painlessly.

'I'm dead. I know I'm dead.' Alyx thought. She didn't feel trapped in her own mind, but she still felt paralyzed all the same. She couldn't move her arms or legs, and her eyelids, though they wouldn't budge, had a blinding white light that burned through... She had thought you wouldn't be afflicted with any diseases or disabilities after you died, so maybe she was only asleep?

"You are traveling, Alyxandra. You will wake up soon." Sonja whispered soothingly. She sounded like she was becoming stronger again, her voice filled with such affirmation.

Recollection washed over her as she remembered what had happened, what was happening to her. So, if she was traveling, then when was she going to wake the hell up?

⟶ ⋯⟐⋯ ⟵

Slowly, ever so slowly, Alyx could feel her body becoming more responsive as time passed. She felt her fingers twitch back to life as she regained full motor skills. Her eyes opened and squinted immediately as they adjusted to the light; it was the same blinding she had experienced prior. Blinking a couple of times, she soon realized that she was looking up at a bright, cloudy sky. It allowed just a sneak of blue hiding behind the puffy grey clouds. But what really struck her was the freezing cold snow.

Snow.

It was winter? Snow in June? How long was she out for? Panic gripped at her heart as she bolted upright. Looking around she wrapped her arms around herself, gasping as the cold bit into her flesh.

She was laying in the middle of a field, a forest upon the edge, ever so quiet. The snow was falling softly around her and melted as soon as it touched her skin. She shivered violently as she began to stand up, her body protesting after not moving for who knows how long.

Looking around there was nothing for miles. She then heard a soft groan behind her and then a gasp, which made her whirl around, almost slipping on the wet snow. Duncan was laying in the snow a few feet away.

"Duncan? What the hell are you doing here?" Alyx managed to say, teeth chattering. She felt the blood vanish from her face as it surrendered to the core of her body. He wasn't supposed to be here! Wherever "here" was.

"How did the boy follow?" Sonja started and then made a sound of self-realization. "Ahh, Neena allowed him too. It's not just you she wants now." she murmured groggily, clearly waking up as well. Alyx sighed and knelt, giving him a gentle shake.

"Duncan get up!" he immediately bolted upright, his eyes wide with fear.

"What the hell just happened?" he sounded in shock, or maybe he was just freezing as his voice shook.

"Well, I think we were sent back in time," she stated and stood up, wrapping her arms around herself again. "And you were not supposed to be. But of course, you can't just butt out." she searched the area some more, trying to figure out which direction to go. Duncan scrambled to stand up behind her.

"I didn't think this would happen." he interjected. She could only roll her eyes. They needed to get moving, otherwise they would freeze to death. She decided to walk towards the forest that was blanketed in snow.

"Where are you going?" he yelled after her.

"Will you please tell your brother to shut up? I'm sure Neena is well aware that we are here, she probably sent her trackers to come find us. He cannot lead them here. Besides, I'm trying to get my bearings." Sonja hissed. As Alyx began to walk through the forest, she noticed a lot of the once, probably huge trees, were starting to shrivel up and die. A pang of sadness filled her heart as she saw trees burnt, shriveled and dying of some sort of strange disease, a disease that caused a strange purple substance to ooze out of the bark. She sensed Duncan catching up behind her as she stopped to inspect one of the trunks.

"Do not touch. It is poison." Sonja warned.

"Poison? Was there some kind of battle here then with Neena?" Alyx questioned Sonja in her head.

"Looks that way, and from what it seems not that long ago either."

"You're sure it's Neena?"

"I'm sure." Sonja said flatly.

"You're sure." Alyx asked not convinced.

"Alyxandra, I've been asleep for over a thousand years. Give me a break."

"I figured you would at least have a sense of where we are." Alyx said aloud, forgetting about Duncan.

"Alyx? Who are you talking to?" Duncan questioned. Alyx merely dismissed him.

"Nothing--I can't say for certain but I think we've gone a thousand years back in the past." she murmured, in deep thought.

They walked for a few minutes longer until Sonja made a soft whistle.

"Hey--stop. I think someone's watching us." Alyx stopped walking immediately and crouched, looking around. Duncan clumsily stopped behind her and followed suit.

"Why did you stop?" he asked, frustrated.

"Shhh!' she scanned her surroundings. All she could see was dead trees and snow.

"Sonja there's nothing here."

"Keep going, but be cautious. I feel a village nearby." that took Alyx by surprise.

"A village?" she asked in her mind.

"You do realize you went back in time, yes? We didn't have your 'cities.' Well, not the type you have, at least there will be people, food and decent warm clothing." Sonja scoffed. Alyx hugged herself tighter, the thought of wearing warmer clothes was almost intoxicating. Still, she wished there was some discrepancy about what clothes she should be wearing beforehand.

229

"You could have at least warned me it was friggen snowing though!" as she thought this, she gritted her teeth.

"Alyxandra. Did you forget I was asleep? I had no idea it would be winter," she paused. "However, this doesn't seem...natural."

"Not natural?" Alyx questioned.

"No, it seems different. I know it's home, but it doesn't feel like it. Something's very wrong here."

"And what exactly is 'home' called?" Alyx inquired as she trudged through soggy roots that fell apart as soon as she stepped on them.

"Skorravik," Sonja breathed, which made Alyx smile slightly. The word gave her a sense of familiarity as she reached for a few branches to push away. "We're here."

As soon as she pulled back the branches she saw a clearing on the other side. From their vantage point, she had a decent view as they seemed to be slightly elevated enough to look down over a tall, wooden piked fencing, which surrounded a community to protect the people inside. A few yards away from the fence was indeed a small village. Alyx's mouth dropped as she saw people dressed in fur cloaks and worn woolen clothes, drenched in mud and snow. Smoke was rising from fires burning in each home.

She couldn't see as much as she wanted in the village, only the strong looking burly men with long beards and half shaven heads, their long hair braided down their backs. Their tattoos really stuck out as some had some interesting symbols on their necks.

"Oh my god, we're back with Vikings." Duncan breathed next to her. All Alyx could do was nod in agreement. They heard animals braying and mooing, and kids laughing and shouting. These were people *really* living off the land.

"Of course, it makes sense. Dad's notes were all about Leif Erickson's travels and how his cousins broke off from his voyage sometime after they landed in North America. This must be the encampment where Eero and Elof live." Alyx said, completely in awe.

"How did they get so far inland?" Duncan questioned to no one in particular. Alyx blinked, realizing that he had no knowledge of their dad's journal.

"There are other means of transportation, not just ships," Sonja mentioned in Alyx's mind. "More 'spiritual' methods. Us Norsemen, and women, are very intuitive beings, and I sense that in you as well. A true warrior, you merely doubt yourself. " she whispered as she faded out of Alyx's mind.

"Wait--what do you mean?" Alyx questioned, but she had no response.

It was strange that her words gave Alyx a strange sense of pride. She could hear the clangs of metal being hit repeatedly, and in synchronized patterns.

"Swords?" Alyx questioned, she felt a strange emotion wash over her, almost like this entire place was familiar to her. Almost like home. It also gave her a strong thrill, being this close to some of history's most profound settlements, a people rich in culture and language was...fascinating. Now she knew how her dad must have felt.

"Are you crying?" Duncan suddenly questioned. Alyx blinked and a fresh tear streamed down her face. Surprised, she wiped it away.

"It's nothing." she quickly said.

As they sat and watched the village Alyx could only think of one thing: How had Neena affected Skorravik? Everyone seemed in good spirits, had she really been in power this whole time? These people were laughing and living life like nothing had happened, they seemed perfectly content judging by what she was hearing.

"Do not judge anything that you cannot see for yourself. Just because it seems true, does not mean it is so." Sonja murmured, she sounded like she came straight out of a textbook.

"Uh, Alyx?" Duncan asked from beside her, his voice shaking.

"Hmm?" she responded in a daze. Her thoughts quickly shot back to earth as she saw a woman standing a few inches away holding a knife to Duncan's throat. The girl studied Alyx, her eyes were startling, an impossibly icy blue that seemed like clouded glass due to winter's chill. Alyx could almost see her own reflection in them. She was a petite woman with long white hair, which seemed to blend in perfectly with the snow. She glared at Alyx which seemed to cause her eyes to glow beneath her hood. She wore leather pants and a red woolen shirt that had a blade belt hooked across her chest where she carried two more daggers. The handles almost seemed to gleam from the brightness of the snow.

The metal looked so different, she didn't recognize what kind it was. However, what really caught her attention was the fact that she wasn't wearing any shoes. The woman looked down at Alyx, her nose tilted upward as her hips twisted with a look of distrust.

"*hverr ykkarr vera?*" the woman seemed to demand, making Alyx's eyes widen, helpless. How was she supposed to understand what the hell she was talking about? It sounded like a form of Danish or Old Norse--due to her dad's other obsession with ancient languages--but she spoke so fast she couldn't make it out to be certain.

"Whoops, that will be a problem." Sonja piped up and before she knew it, the woman's words began to change into English.

"Well, looks like I've got some wanderers peeking in on my village. What say you? Come to kill us? Is Neena bloodthirsty? Or is it Eero and Elof this time? I have already asked you. Who are you two?" she hissed, but it was slightly muffled as she wore a wrap around her mouth. *"illr gifr."* *Evil troll.* It threw her off a little, making her adjust to what she was hearing. The woman glared at Alyx. She pressed the blade closer to Duncan, who only gave a soft whimper. The woman's eyes never left Alyx.

Trying to size her up, Alyx never really liked girls that tried to intimidate her.

"How about you release my brother and I'll explain why we're here." she responded, slowly standing up.

"Be careful what you say, Alyxandra. This woman has seen her fair share of fights." Sonja warned. Alyx glanced at Duncan who looked at her, silently pleading for help. It looked like she had seen her fair share of death as well.

"Or you could tell me now otherwise I will kill him." she looked unfazed. Alyx believed her.

"Uh," was all she managed to say at first, not knowing what to do. "Well? Where to begin. We're here to save our father from a crazy psychotic ruler of yours." the girl looked at her interested at first, then raised her eyebrows as she looked Alyx over, as if realizing something.

To No End

"By the gods, it's true then. *Heimskr mær!*"
the woman hissed. *Foolish girl!* She reached for Alyx
and brought Duncan to his feet. Alyx tried to resist
but was surprised at how strong she was.

"Come!" she yelled and pushed the two to
walk, pointing a blade at their backs.

Duncan and Alyx trudged through the snow,
miserable and shivering and now being taken to a
Viking village with no idea whether this girl would
kill them.

Great start.

As they walked on, the men of the village
stared at the two, mostly Alyx, as much to the men's
delight, she was basically wearing nothing.

"Kaia! Now what are you doing with those
people?" a burly man with the biggest smile Alyx
had ever seen came jogging over to them.

"Begone, Torsten. Where is my *bróðir*?" she
hissed. *Brother.* She said the word protectively. The
man named Torsten scratched his beard in wonder,
unfazed by her venom. He had hazel eyes and blonde
hair braided down his back, one side shaved and
adorned with symbols like some of the other men.
He gave 'Kaia' a smile.

"I think he's with the *ierl*," *Earl*. "He will be done soon."

"I need to see him, now."

"So impatient as always. Who are these people? And why do they wear such strange clothing?" Torsten let out a chuckle and patted Alyx's head. "Such a small thing." he gave her a smile. If she wasn't so frightened at the moment, Alyx would've responded with a grin at his kindness. Kaia gave Alyx a push to keep her moving, then Duncan. People continued to stare at both of them, whispered worries with each other and gossiping about who they might be. Torsten came up next to Kaia's brooding frame and shrugged.

"If you won't tell me then fine, I will join you to talk with your *bróðir* and find out for myself." Kaia opened her mouth to protest but was cut off by another girl who pushed through a group of people nearby. She was Native American with long raven black hair braided down her back. Her eyes were unusually two-colored, one brown and the other, green. And they were studying Alyx as she walked towards her. She had a certain air about her that just screamed wisdom, but her age surprised Alyx, she looked much too young to hold herself with such regal defiance.

She was also not wearing shoes.

"Calm yourself, Torsten." she moved fluidly and almost feline like.

"Chenoa, where is my *bróðir*?" Kaia asked again, slightly relieved at the sight of her.

"He just talked to *ierl* Sigurd. I had told him you were back. Although, I didn't know you had company. Who are these people?" Chenoa asked in a calm manner. She pulled her hood up further.

"By the gods--I need to talk with Viggo first. Follow me." Kaia huffed and pushed the two on. They passed more homes that had carvings upon the walls and doors depicting a few of the gods, particularly Odin. Her dad would've had a hay day. She shivered as they walked passed what looked like a well and then a stable, and both had some wary eyes watching from them, mixed with curiosity.

They had finally reached a larger home on the top of a small hill. Alyx could feel the warmth from a fire within and relished in it. Kaia forced the two to stop and wait.

"Viggo?" Kaia called into the home. A few minutes had passed by until finally a young man maybe in his early twenties walked out into the snow. He was just putting his fur cloak on when he paused to greet his sister, but instead saw Duncan and Alyx held by her.

Alyx's breath caught in her throat.

He was the most beautiful man she had ever seen.

His hair was almost as white as Kaia's, and shaven on either side, the same symbols tattooed along the shaved hairline, and was braided down his back like most men she had seen here. He had soft stubble growing around his slightly curved lips which were pressed into a thin line. His eyes were the same brilliant icy blue as his sister's but his ears that she could see clearly were slightly pointed. His brows furrowed which made his eyes cloud over. His broad shoulders tensed as he walked down the wooden steps, his gaze fixed on Alyx. She got this feeling that he was trying so hard to fit in but still stood out so much. She could feel her face go crimson which helped a bit with the cold. He studied her.

People were doing that a lot lately.

"Kaia, *hvat ykkarr gera*?" he asked with a gravelly but tired voice, a shiver ran up her spine, but to her surprise, it wasn't out of fear. *What are you doing?* Now that she was paying more attention, they all seemed to have strange accents.

"They, meaning me as well, do not speak your language, so I made sure you understood us." Sonja explained.

"So, I'm the only one that understands all of you talking?" Then it occurred to her, Alyx looked at her brother, confusion never left his face. "How can they understand me then?" she asked in her mind, yet somehow, she already knew the answer.

"I'm giving you the ability. You can speak fluently." Sonja seemed somewhat impressed with herself.

"You made me a walking translator?" Alyx couldn't deny that she was mildly impressed with Sonja as well.

Mildly.

"Viggo, these two are the ones Fjola had seen." Kaia pleaded for her brother to understand, matter of factly. He looked at her confused, then the same face of realization washed over him, like his sister had. His eyes darted around behind them, noticing that they had an audience.

"Follow me." His voice lowered and threatening. Kaia shoved Duncan and Alyx, forcing them to follow her brother behind homes until finally reaching a small clearing on the edge of the village. The fence had a small door that blended in almost perfectly. Viggo went in first, then Alyx, then Duncan and finally Kaia. Torsten and Chenoa stayed outside to guard, although Torsten didn't look very pleased.

Once Alyx was inside the sudden warmth from a fire made her fall to her knees, like she had melted into a puddle. She reached out, wanting to be closer to its warmth, almost wanting to wrap the flames around herself like a blanket. Just as she almost touched the hearth, Viggo took rope and began to tie her hands together. He looked at her intently as he did so, never leaving her gaze, but he looked at her quizzically, almost like he was trying to figure her out, which bothered her more than she liked. She noticed she was checking him out more than she should in a more civilized society, but unusual times after all. His very masculine features were really the only thing that explained how different he was from his sister, his natural aura that he gave off just screamed power. The white hair didn't mask any of them for that matter, he had a very strong, wide set jaw that clenched when he noticed that she was staring at his lips. Her lips parted slightly in wonder, what was it about him that she couldn't look away? She could feel it was something much more than vanity, something deeper.

Kaia tied rope around Duncan's wrists, but she only focused on what she was doing as Alyx's brother stared at Kaia's face, practically drooling in a dumbfounded state. Alyx rolled her eyes. Viggo stood up and began to pace slightly, pinching the bridge of his nose in thought. His jaw was clenched and his eyes shut too tightly to be comfortable. He opened his eyes and exhaled, walking over to the fire as he did. He stood with his back to them.

Alyx knew she should be scared but all she could think about was looking into those eyes of his again.

"Pull yourself together." Sonja stated, disgusted.

"What are we going to do, *bróðir*?" Kaia whispered. *Brother.* She leaned against a small windowsill that allowed only a bit of sunlight to come through making her already brilliant hair illuminate. Alyx looked around to see that this was where the siblings lived, away from the village, but still close enough to guard or protect. Or maybe monitor, someone or *something*.

"Are you so sure they are the ones?" he murmured. Not looking away from the fire.

"*Bróðir*, do you not see the way they are dressed? Also, the girl said she is looking to save her father and hopefully help us destroy Neena! I had found them once I returned. This all means something! This will give us our chance!" Kaia pleaded.

"We cannot be so certain! She could be telling you lies!" he suddenly cut her off, turning to meet her desperate gaze. His eyes narrowed in frustration. "We cannot be fools to hope! I refuse to lose anyone else to that witch!"

Feeling awkward, Alyx cleared her throat, drawing attention towards her. Kaia glared at her intrusion.

"Uh, so I think I need to explain some more." she said meekly.

"You will speak when spoken to, little one!" Kaia pointed a finger at Alyx, warning her with dagger-like eyes. With Alyx's own wide open, she drew back, but didn't back down.

"Little girl? I doubt *you're* much older there, honey." Alyx snapped.

Kaia looked her up and down and sneered, rolling her eyes.

"Your words are nothing to me because you *know* nothing. You *are* nothing." she emphasized.

"Am I to stand here and listen to petty bickering? If so I will waste my time somewhere else," Viggo fumed, his jaw clenched in annoyance. Kaia gave Alyx a look before she turned her attention back to her brother. He looked down at Alyx, his eyes searching her soul.

"Now, what is your reasoning?" he kept his eyes narrowed but his voice was far less harsh this time. Alyx swallowed once, taken aback by the softness in his voice. She shook her head, he only wanted information, she told herself.

"I don't know if either of you will believe us, let alone help us but my brother and I were sent here to save our father. My own personal goal would be to end Neena as well." she added. His brows shot up.

"Where from exactly?" Viggo questioned. Alyx hesitated.

"Well, that's the part I don't think you'll believe." Viggo bent down, face to face with Alyx.

"Try me." He replied. She felt chills up her arms.

"We're from the future?" she said weakly, pausing, realizing just how cliché that sounded, but for whatever reason Viggo didn't flinch, he didn't really react in any way other than by studying her for reassurance in the truth she had just told him.

"Now do you believe me, bróðir?" Kaia asked. Viggo blinked as if remembering his sister was there. He straightened his back and turned to look at her.

"Yes, but now you know who we have to find to confirm." he gritted his teeth.

"Unfortunately, *vér nauðsyn fljóð*," *We need the woman*. "He's the only one who knows where *she* is." Kaia argued. Alyx then realized they weren't talking about her now.

"I'm sorry who is this person you're looking for? I feel like I'm missing something," Alyx suddenly remembered Duncan beside her, his jaw hanging open in disbelief. "Oh, I'm sorry, am I asking too many questions for your liking?" Duncan shook his head.

"Honestly, I didn't even know you were asking questions. Alyx, since when do you know how to speak Danish?" he spat out in disbelief.

"Long story," she stated and rolled her eyes. "And it's Old Norse actually." she added. Alyx closed her eyes to process, then turned her attention back to Viggo and Kaia who were staring dumbfounded at their exchange.

"I told you that you could understand everyone now." Sonja chimed in her head, pleased with herself.

"Yeah except Duncan's out of the loop." she responded, obviously frustrated.

Viggo ended up clearing his throat, bringing Alyx back.

"Maybe we should tell you what's going on." he said, annoyed, he gave his sister a look.

"Are you sure, Viggo?" Kaia questioned. "We don't even know these people!" She shot Alyx a glance. Viggo looked at his sister with no expression.

"This is all much bigger than you and I. If she can help us, then by the gods tell her everything. Especially if Fjola's vision is right. That is proof enough for me. Besides, where are they going to go? We have them captured." His face was hard as stone, unwavering. Kaia nodded once, agreeing. Viggo began to walk out.

"Wait, where are you going?" Kaia asked.

"I never said I was going to be the one to explain. Besides I have better things to do with my time then to tell history lessons all day." he gave Kaia a smirk and walked out. Kaia fumed, but strangely Alyx was disappointed.

"Uh, so tell us I guess." Alyx said, trying to refocus her. Kaia glared at Alyx.

"Look, I do not like you and I personally think we do not need you, but my brother believes otherwise, as does Fjola," she sat down in front of them. "You were sent to us for a reason, it was foreseen. You can help us in some way, but we do not need you, just know that. Usually Fjola's visions are correct, no matter how vague they might be sometimes, so we cannot ignore this. We must find her to confirm that you are the ones. You and your *bróðir* are to help us destroy Neena, and her puppets that are ruling over Skorravik falsely."

"Wait, hold up here," Alyx held up her bound hands. "I need to save my dad first! Neena comes second."

"This is much bigger than any of us. We are the only ones who can destroy her. You are a part of a lengthy list who wishes for Neena's end."

"Weren't you just saying how you don't think we're needed?" Alyx said causing Kaia to pause. "Besides what can we even do to help? I wasn't even sure where to begin myself."

"You know secrets, your ancestor was the one that helped capture Neena in the first place. Fjola had seen it so." Kaia said it like Alyx should have just automatically known about that, which caught Alyx off guard.

248

"I had no idea it was *your* ancestor that helped me! Now it makes sense!" Sonja breathed.

"Wait, my ancestor helped you how?" Alyx questioned in her mind.

"A man of knowledge came to me and told me of the use of talismans, so I could use the Necklaces of Iain to capture her soul within." Sonja explained.

"What was he like? What did he look like?" Alyx couldn't stop the questions pouring out of her.

"I never saw him, he would hide in shadow, never showing me his face. He was very discreet, I do not blame him, my sister caught onto his trail rather quickly. We had to work fast." Sonja responded calmly.

"He also helped my father fight against her forces, even though he knew my father would not win," Kaia's voice quieted as she continued. "He did what he could."

"What was his name? Where is he now?" Alyx spat out questions.

"Isleif Abisson. He was known here as a very strange, but knowledgeable man. He knew much about Shaman-ism, the gods, everything."

"When you say 'was'..." Alyx trailed off, afraid of the answer. 'That has to be the same Isleif my dad was talking about!" Alyx thought.

"He was killed a few years ago, by a poisoned blade." Alyx stopped, her mouth gone dry.

"A poisoned blade?" she repeated, her voice a million miles away.

"Is this familiar?" Kaia questioned. Alyx nodded.

"That's what happened to our father."

"Are you so sure?" Kaia looked at her with hesitation. Alyx was surprised that Kaia had told her this much, due to her icy welcome wagon earlier.

"What else could it be?"

"Well, it is believed that Neena had laid a curse on him as he died."

Alyx's brows drew together. "But I thought she was captured?"

"She was, but her 'puppets,' Eero and Elof, got to him. Neena must have given them some power or something, no one is certain. We just know she has an immense amount of power. If you question too much you are executed. Dooming anyone to reach Valhalla." she spat the last sentence out.

"How do you know all of this?"

"We have many spies." Kaia merely stated, straight forward.

"Who are you all exactly?"

"We are merely a group of people that seek only one thing: revenge."

"Well, we have almost opposite goals. I do want to get rid of Neena but my dad comes first. Surely you understand." Alyx pleaded.

"I do. But if you want to save him, you will need to save us first." she said blankly.

CHAPTER 11

"NEENA IS WITHOUT MERCY," Kaia began. "She kills any who defy her, and in horrific ways. Some ways we have never seen before. We've witnessed her tear a person's skin off for refusing to bow to her." Kaia closed her eyes, shaking her head as if to erase the horrible memories. Once she opened them again, they were filled with a pain Alyx had never seen before. A drop that started to ripple in the lake. It was deep and full of such sorrow that she would probably never understand, it seemed that if something wasn't done and Neena was left unchecked, then the ripple would only spread across the region. Or perhaps worse.

"What happened to your family?" Alyx hesitantly asked. Kaia looked at her, furrowing her brows but not entirely angry.

"I will not go into full detail. All you need to know is that Neena has taken almost everything away from Viggo and I. If we had lost our mother too--." She drifted off, emotions filling her eyes, but she quickly stuffed them down, not wanting to seem weak. Alyx's eyes widened.

"She killed your dad didn't she." Alyx said matter-of-factly. Kaia looked at her, eyes filled with pain. Even though it was obvious that they both did not like each other, Alyx couldn't help but feel for Kaia's predicament. She had already lost her dad, she didn't want to see another girl lose her's too, even if it was someone like Alyx.

"She will take yours too if you do not help us. This is a mad woman we are dealing with."

What Kaia said gave Alyx goosebumps. She was right, and that scared her even more. Still, she couldn't reason her involvement in the war against Neena. She knew she was a dangerous ruler, but how could Alyx and her brother stop someone with so much power? She was just an over-emotional young woman, and Duncan well, he's more of a lover than a fighter.

"What do we need to know?" Alyx questioned.

"Even locked away she still had control over her puppets. We know we could potentially blind her by taking them out, but no one has been able to get close enough to do so. That's why we've called upon the help of an... unfortunate group." she said, disgusted. All evidence of her past emotions now gone.

"What do they call themselves?"

"The Band of Eight." Kaia mocked.

"Sounds like a boy band to me." Alyx joked out loud with a smirk. Kaia gave her a look.

"A--what?"

"Never mind. So, it looks like you guys have your hands full, I wouldn't want to gum anything up by being so heavily involved, so if you just want to tell us who to talk to about poisons that would be great." Alyx babbled, holding up her hands to be untied.

Kaia raised an eyebrow and gave her a bored look.

"Damn. The sass is strong with this one."
Alyx thought. Kaia grabbed her wrists and pulled
Alyx intimidatingly close, the blasé look passed.

"Or, you shut the hell up and do exactly as I
say or so help me, *meyla*," *Little girl.* "Or by the
gods..." she began to threaten.

"Kaia, are you done threatening her?" a voice
chuckled as Torsten walked in with a smirk on his
face. Kaia's eyes widened slightly as she looked
over, her hands not letting go.

"Don't get involved, Torsten."

"Luckily, I am very bad with getting involved.
In fact, I make it a hobby of mine." he said, a gleam
in his eye. He was very charming to Alyx's surprise.
He leaned against the wood frame of the hut,
crossing his arms. Alyx could tell they were close
just by how they looked at each other, although he
had a kind face, he had an intimidating demeanor
that just screamed 'don't mess with me.' Kaia's
white hair fell around her face, which had been
exposed for quite some time now. How Alyx hadn't
realized it was beyond her, but she must have taken
it off when they arrived in the hut for questioning,

maybe giving the appearance of her relaxing, but the grip on Alyx's wrist said otherwise.

"Will you just let the poor girl go, Kaia? She had only just arrived and you are trying to force her into a war she barely knows anything about." Torsten said almost in a bored tone.

"She won't take anything seriously. She acts like none of this affects her." Kaia lashed out. Duncan could only watch helplessly, not understanding from the corner.

"How the hell does it?" Alyx yelled, she glanced at her brother. "Sure, I want my own revenge for what Neena has done to me, but I don't live here. I wasn't born here in Skorravik. You all are, so how does this affect me?"

"Alyx! What are they saying? What do they want?" Duncan urged her to tell him. Kaia shook her once, regaining her attention.

"You *will* help us." she growled, although she could tell this girl was not used to asking for assistance for anything.

"Just because my ancestor meddled in something he shouldn't have, doesn't mean my brother and I have to clean up after him. Although the information on the blade helps, we really don't have much to go off of to help our dad." Alyx huffed, this was getting ridiculous, she wanted straight answers for once.

"Neena's infamous poison has met your father? How very unfortunate indeed," Torsten's voice was filled with sarcasm, he looked down at his hands, a grin spread across his face. "I recall a certain mother of a certain woman who possessed the knowledge of special herbs--and poisons." he looked at Kaia, who was fuming. Her impossibly blue-colored eyes glinted in anger.

"Funny how this is just *now* being brought up. You threaten us to help you and keep the truth hidden from us. Classy." Alyx began to stare Kaia down. Kaia opened her mouth to say something but stopped herself, instead she shoved Alyx away, glaring at her.

"We have an idea, but I'm afraid you are not going to like it," Kaia grumbled. "But, if you want the help from my mother to save your father, you and your *bróðir* must help us first." Kaia's grimace slowly melted away to an arrogant smirk, crossing her arms. Pausing, Alyx turned her attention to

Duncan whose eyes were large and doe-like. She sighed, feeling almost sorry for the mess she put him in, but it evaporated as soon as she could still feel his hands around her neck. Still, she knew she had to tell him what was going on, and she knew deep down that it wasn't Duncan's fault. Her hands were tied, they were forced to be a part of something that she didn't prepare him, let alone herself, for.

She looked back at Kaia who gave her an annoyed look. Clearly patience was not a strong suit of hers. Finally, she narrowed her eyes and nodded.

"Okay, fine. You get your way, but first let me talk to my brother, bring him up to speed and all that. But I don't want him involved, this isn't his to bear." Alyx explained, pointing to Duncan, she could almost hear his heart pounding. Kaia looked over at Duncan with a bland look, not impressed with his emotional state. Waving a hand, she replied:

"Alright. I'll give you some time. After that, we leave." Alyx nodded and watched as Kaia ordered Torsten to leave the hut with her. He merely gave her a playful smirk and a wink, giving Alyx a cocky wave and throwing an arm around Kaia's shoulders, who proceeded to turn bright crimson. As soon as they closed the wooden door behind them, she whirled around to face her brother.

"What the *fuck* just happened, Alyx?" Duncan's voice broke as he stared at the door. She gritted her teeth and knelt in between him and the door, blocking his view. It was almost comedic to see her once fierce and protective brother kind of melt into a little boy puddle, filled with confusion and fear. It was harsh of her, she knew, but she still couldn't help but have some satisfaction from it.

"We only have a few minutes before we leave."

"Leave? Where are we going? With them?" he was frantic, it made it difficult not to slap him to his senses, among other reasons. "Also, how can you speak a different language all of a sudden, and perfectly!" he looked at her like she was a ghost. "You couldn't even pass one semester of Spanish!" Alyx rolled her eyes.

"There's a lot to explain and not enough time. Look, all you really need to know right now is that I just agreed for us to help Kaia and Viggo. In exchange they will let us talk to their mom, she specializes in poisons and herbs. She will give us the antidote to save dad! But I also told her that you don't need to be involved in anything that they need me to do, this isn't your fault that you were brought into all of this. It was just supposed to be me." she explained in a rush. Duncan blinked rapidly, trying to process everything Alyx had just told him.

"Wait, so Kaia is that white-haired girl, right? And Viggo was that one douchey-looking guy before? They both have the creepy eyes?" he fluttered his fingers near his own eyes, dramatizing. Alyx nodded, she wouldn't have quite put it that way though. "And we're really back in time? This isn't some weird-ass cosplay convention?"

"Unfortunately, no," she sighed, this was taking too long and Kaia would be back soon. "Focus, Duncan. Yes, we were sent back in time. I'm going to help these people with whatever, uprising, *whatever*. We are going to get the antidote, get back home, save dad. Boom." she finalized.

"You make it sound so easy." Duncan snorted, unconvinced.

"Indeed." Sonja chimed in, her tone mocking. Alyx groaned out loud.

"It will be!" Duncan looked surprised at her sudden outburst.

"Look, as long as you do exactly what they say, and let me do the talking and negotiating, we won't be killed." Alyx glanced towards the door, she could hear people coming closer and they did not sound happy.

"That's the difficult part, Alyx. I don't really understand a damn thing they're saying!" he hissed. Damn it, he's right.

"I could help you know." Sonja cooed. Alyx straightened up.

"Wait, how?" Alyx thought, Sonja giggled.

"Sweetie, if I gave you the gift of our language, I can give your neurotic brother the gift as well."

"What's the catch?" Alyx asked hesitantly.

"Nothing, believe it or not. If doing this will only help our chances of not being killed because of his naivety, then fine. However, it will have a slight side-affect." she added softly.

"What side-affect?" Alyx urged. Duncan was looking at Alyx strangely as they both sat in sudden silence. Behind her, she could hear Kaia returning, almost to the door.

"You will lose time and consciousness for a bit. All magic pays a price and I must siphon from your energy. Seeing as I don't have a direct link to the earth's energy anymore." she quickly explained in a huff. So *that's* why Alyx kept losing time! Every time Sonja used her powers she was siphoning directly from Alyx.

"Alyx? Whatever you're thinking make it fast because they're almost back." Duncan warned.

"Deal?" Sonja urged. Without hesitation Alyx blurted out:

"Deal!"

"Touch your brother, now!" Sonja shouted. Alyx reached out and basically smacked Duncan across the face, just as Kaia walked in. With a burst of energy Alyx could feel at first the power move through her, bubbling through her veins, then she could see the glow of it more through her arm and into her brother's face. Then after a shout, Alyx could see her vision go blurry, and everything went black.

To No End

Awakening to the sound of a horse neighing, Alyx felt a painful jab in her temples. She was traveling, her body swaying left to right in a lazy, rhythmic sort of way. She opened her eyes to find that she was laying on top of a shorter, black horse, perhaps more pony than a horse, with a light blonde mane. A rope that was tied around her waist kept her from falling out of a fur-made saddle. She leaned up on her elbows, pleasantly surprised that there was a thick, fur cloak wrapped around her and her hands were no longer bound. Sitting up, she saw that she was among a group of about twenty men, slightly relieved that she didn't see Kaia anywhere in sight.

They were on a dirt path, most of the men walked on foot while there were only a select few on horseback. Duncan was traveling next to her on another short, brown horse, and her eyes widened in shock to find him in an enthusiastic conversation with Chenoa, who seemed somewhat taken by him, listening to his words intently while she patted her spotted animal on the neck lovingly. Confused, she looked over the men's heads to see three horses two rows in front of her. Although she could only see their backs she knew exactly which one was Viggo.

He had an air about him that she could pick out in a crowd. He tried to intimidate, tried to deflect but she could sense something else about him, what that was she didn't know for sure but she knew he got shit done. The hood of his cloak was down, his long white braid hung at his back and against the snow his tattoos stuck out like a sore thumb. Damn, he was beautiful.

Alyx shook her head, seriously? He's an asshole. She thought to herself. Trying to distract herself, she saw a slightly smaller figure on his right. The world came crashing down on her once again when she realized that that was Kaia. Her cloak was up, but she could tell by the arrogance of how she carried herself on horseback. Also, there was the fact that the girl didn't know about damn shoes.

Annoyed, she looked over to Viggo's left. There was a man that she hadn't seen before, he was slightly taller than Viggo but stockier. He had broad shoulders and looked to be much older than the siblings. He had long dark hair braided back, which seemed to be the custom here. With his hood down, she could spot some tattoos of words she didn't know that ran up his neck. The man was looking at Viggo intently, furiously talking, but keeping his voice low enough so that others couldn't hear him. He had a brooding look about him which made her look away, worried that he could sense her staring at him.

"Hey! You're finally awake!" Suddenly Torsten came galloping up next to Alyx, his horse whinnied in surprise as he yanked the reigns back, slowing the animal down to match her speed. He gave her a huge grin and waved to her. She pulled her hood up and laughed nervously.

"Yeah." was all she managed to say. She forgot what had happened for a second.

"Hey, Sonja? You okay?" she asked in her mind. There wasn't an answer. Maybe that had taken more out of Sonja than it did Alyx.

"Well that's good. We're almost to our temporary settlement. We'll camp here for a few days." he said cheerfully. Alyx gave him a weird smile, not sure how to react to his kindness.

"Uh, thanks for letting me know." she replied. He laughed and urged his horse to carry on up through the group.

"Hey, Alyx! How are you feeling?" Duncan called over to her. He said something to Chenoa who nodded once and moved closer to his sister. Alyx shrugged in response. Their horses whinnied at the close quarters.

"Could be better. I see you're doing just fine." she said, slightly annoyed. He could make friends wherever he went, and apparently no matter *when*. He laughed once and glanced over to Chenoa who was looking around, probably scouting the surroundings.

"Yeah. Chenoa is really cool to talk to. She knows so much about the land it's insane," He gave her a goofy grin. "She could teach us more about the cultures too. We could learn so much more than dad ever did."

"It looks like my little slap to the face helped your language barrier problem." Alyx said, looking at her nails sarcastically. Duncan instinctively rubbed the side of his face and furrowed his eyebrows, the grin not leaving his face.

"Yeah, ow by the way. Did you really have to slap the shit out of me for it?" he complained.

"Yes. Yes, I did," she looked over at Viggo and the two on either side of him again.

"So, I see we're just following blindly behind the three Musketeers here?" she questioned.

"Yeah, he said something about we follow the 'Band of Eight' or something like that, then we 'find our end goal.'" he said with air quotations.

"Let's just hope we're not going to our death." Sonja suddenly chimed in her mind. Alyx softly gasped.

"Hey are you okay?" Alyx questioned in a rush in her mind.

"Yeah. Just knocked a lot out of me. I'll be better in no time, just need to rest." she replied, obviously still exhausted.

"I thought you siphoned from me though. Knocked me on my ass." Sonja laughed once.

"Yes, I had to transfer energy, that isn't exactly an easy thing to do, you know. That's like throwing another human being across a room," she explained. "With one hand." she exhaled loudly in her mind.

"Well, just rest up. Torsten said we're almost there anyway. I guess we'll just have to see what this Band of Eight wants from us."

"Hopefully not our deaths."

"Agreed."

They traveled on another hour it seemed before they started to gather into a small clearing that was just on the edge of a copse. The road completely disappeared, the area was already carved out and tents set up, people were getting a fire started and laughing here and there as moods were lighter now that they all were getting a chance to relax.

"Hey, could I get a little help here?" Alyx asked Duncan, pointing at her rope that was tied tightly into a knot. He threw a leg over, dismounting his horse. He laughed and tightened his black furred cloak around his shoulders more. Chenoa took his horses reigns and eyed Alyx questioningly with her big chocolate colored eyes. She looked so innocent, and yet she seemed to look around Duncan's age. Alyx returned the gaze by looking down at the woman's bare feet. She hoped she would find out soon why these two did not like shoes.

"Yeah, hold on a second," he said and jogged over. Duncan began to fumble with the knots, cursing out loud, but the knot was too stubborn. "Damn, whoever tied this is hella good. They must have been in boy scouts or something." Alyx rolled her eyes at the comment. Then, Duncan froze and eyed something behind her, making her go rigid, slowly turning her head to look back. She hated surprises anymore. Viggo walked around the back of her horse, his hand sliding across the animals back and up to her waist, grabbing at the rope. He shortly messed with it before swiftly untying and pulling it from around her. He wrapped it around his palm and elbow, rounding it up, his eyes were gleaming, she could see her own reflection. His gaze never left hers as he didn't say anything, just merely handed Duncan the rope and turned away, moving back over to his sister. Alyx was speechless, she didn't even realize that Duncan was waving a hand in front of her face as she was so transfixed with watching Viggo walk away.

"Uh, did you break?" he asked with a chuckle and gave her leg a slight shove. She shook her head and swung her leg over her horse, dropping down onto the ground. They guided their horses over to the posts where Kaia and Viggo had tied them up as well and looked around, not knowing what to do next.

"Hey, Viggo wants you two to follow him." Torsten said cheerfully.

"Wait, so we have a choice now?" Alyx mocked. Torsten grinned.

"Not really, but it is highly recommended that you follow Viggo's orders still." he nodded for them to follow, and they did. Trudging through ankle deep snow that had freshly fallen, they made their way to a larger tent that had a fur pelt as a rug at the opening, slowly becoming soggy as they marched forward inside. They ducked through and saw that there were more furs laid out on the ground, clearly someone of nobility was staying here. She lowered her hood and ran a hand through her hair, trying to smooth out her crazy strands. Torsten made his way over to Kaia who only had a look of annoyance as she pulled off her hood in a huff and sat down on a bench, her legs on either side, her bare feet covered in mud and snow. Viggo turned to look at Alyx and Duncan, his facial expression unreadable. Alyx barely noticed the same man he was conversing with earlier standing behind Viggo. He had deep green eyes, and a bushy dark beard. Now that she could see his face properly he looked to be about in his late twenties.

"Trygg, these are the two I was telling you about." Viggo stated and nodded towards Alyx and Duncan. Trygg looked Alyx up and down, making her cringe. He didn't smile but merely rubbed his face in thought. He sat down in a large chair, adorned with deer antlers.

"They are not very impressive I must say," he said in a gruff tone. "How could these two be the ones to help my sister?" he questioned, holding a hand out towards Alyx, giving Viggo a look. Viggo looked blandly at Trygg.

"Your sister was the one who had the vision of them." he stated. Trygg laughed as if it was an inside joke. He looked down, sighing.

"Well, my sister *is* the gifted one in my family." he stated softly, a grin spread on his face.

Viggo gave him a slight grin in return, the most reaction she had seen from him ever, it was almost a bit unnerving.

"So, we carry on with the plan then?" Viggo urged. Trygg looked at them both.

"I suppose we do. *Hvat mega vér gera?*" he asked. *What else can we do?*

"Um, so what *are* we doing?" Alyx piped up. Viggo looked at her, his eyebrows raised in surprise.

"You already agreed to help us, so you are going to ask questions? I do not think that is wise." he mildly threatened. Her eyes narrowed.

"If my life is on the line, I definitely get a say. I owe none of you." she spat. Trygg suddenly erupted in laughter, slapping his legs.

"These are definitely the ones my sister had seen. So defiant!" he spat out in mid laughter. Duncan gave Alyx a look. Viggo looked less than thrilled.

"I take it none of you are used to being told no." she said. Torsten laughed once and motioned towards Viggo.

"Especially by a woman of your standing." he whispered dramatically towards Alyx. Viggo shot

272

him a look, which Torsten only laughed off but backed down never the less.

"I agree we should tell her, *lítt* Viggo." *Little.* Trygg wiped a tear away as his laughter subsided. Viggo glared at him for the 'little Viggo' comment but exhaled, trying to control his temper.

"A few days ago, before you two arrived, Fjola, Trygg's little sister had a vision of two outsiders wandering throughout Skorravik. She claimed that you would arrive out of a cloud, and extend your hand as a sign of help." he explains. Trygg cut him off:

"Supposedly, my sister saw that you two who are 'travelers of time' are to end the reign of Neena and the idiot Kings that rule by her order, Eero and Elof. The two original founders who had taken over this land and made it the *Östman* way," *Viking or man.* "You had the power to restore balance and to vanquish that witch back into whatever hellish void she had crawled out of. How, we're not sure," he said with gritted teeth, all traces of laughter gone. "Shortly after she had told us of her vision, Neena had sent troops to take her. I was out scouting with my men when I was told she was abducted. We need to save her." he said finally. A cloud seemed to draw a shadow over his features. His anger was visible through his already intimidating demeanor.

"How am I supposed to save her exactly?" Alyx asked, incredulous.

"Not just you, your brother as well." Viggo stated. Alyx scoffed and shook her head violently.

"No. He is not a part of this, you have only me to help. He's not getting involved." she finalized. Duncan looked taken a back.

"And you didn't bother asking me first before making that decision?" he asked. She looked at him, her eyes pleading.

"Duncan, you weren't supposed to come here with me in the first place, why the hell would I have you go do something dangerous?"

"Uh, maybe because I'm the big brother here?" he said, he looked at her like she was stupid, and in that moment, she felt like it. He had always protected her, and unfortunately, they were both just as stubborn. Viggo shrugged.

"The boy can decide whatever he wants to do. He is a man, girl."

"My name is not *girl*," Alyx spat. She looked at Trygg who looked at her amusingly. "My brother is not coming with me, he can help here. I go in alone." she stated. Trygg studied her. Duncan rolled his eyes and sighed.

"Have you ever killed anyone before, girl?" Trygg asked, his lips curving into a smirk.

CHAPTER 12

ALYX LOOKED AT TRYGG IN SHOCK.

"Wait, killed anyone? I'm gonna have to kill someone?" She was hoping the only one she would bring down was Neena, but not necessarily her doing the dirty work in the process either. "No, never." she breathed. Trygg's smirk stretched into a toothy smile, his eyes gleaming.

"Looks like you're a virgin then." he joked.

"I'm sorry that I don't go around killing people. Where my brother and I are from, that's pretty frowned upon." she explained. Viggo looked at her, his eyes narrowed menacingly.

"I figured you two never had to actually do anything to survive, probably had everything handed to you." Viggo spat. Alyx gave him a look, taken a back. What did she do to him?

"Things are different in our time. Surely your sister had mentioned that." she pleaded. Trygg's smile disappeared as he shook his head.

"Her visions are never really completely clear. She receives more shadows and whispers than anything. Just vague and infuriating," he practically spat the last word out, flicking his hand outwards in annoyance. "The point is, you two were in it. Ykkarr *munu* ásjá." Alyx sighed and narrowed her brows at Trygg. *You will help us.*

"What do you need me to do?" she finalized and crossed her arms. She could see out of the corner of her eye, Viggo was watching her, trying to figure her out.

"One of my men scouted the surrounding area of the mead hall. Although what we had found was that the false kings had tripled it in size. They worked the men day and night to finish it. Why, I could not say but they seem to be hiding something there. We must get inside and find my sister."

"And find out what they are hiding." Viggo interrupted. Trygg nodded once.

"Yes, but my sister will be rescued first." he stated. It was Viggo's turn to nod.

"So how do I get inside?" Alyx questioned. Trygg looked at her with a blank face.

"We are going to turn you in."

"Wait, what?" she took a step back. Duncan began to size Trygg up, who only looked bored.

"Oh, hell no! We're not just going to offer my sister up for yours!" he disagreed. Trygg didn't even flinch.

"We will get her out, do not worry. But we need someone on the inside first before we just go running in. There are guards at every post. We should think this all through, otherwise believe me, if my men and I could have done this on our own we would have. There is much more than just guards in there I'm sure, also we have the right bait."

"Like what?" Duncan spat, ignoring the 'bait' comment.

"You do realize that a very powerful, and very much enraged woman dwells within those walls. If my experience with women has taught me

278

anything over the years is that you never piss one of them off. You give them, *abilities,* then that is certainly a recipe for disaster." his eyes wide open. Alyx gave him a faint grin.

"He's not entirely wrong." Sonja whispered in her mind, mildly impressed. Growing more serious, Trygg stood up out of his chair.

"Now then, let's begin the specifics on how we are going to do this." he began and they moved over to a table that had a large yellowed map swept over the wooden surface, a single candle was lit next to it. On the parchment was a rough hand drawn blueprint of what looked like the mead hall.

"There are three distinct levels. My men found that Eero and Elof are residing on the top. My sister is most likely down in the cellar." Trygg explained as his fingers brushed over the tan parchment. His eyes looked focused yet filled with anger. Alyx swallowed. So, three floors and probably a shit ton of guards protecting each level. Lovely.

Something also bothered her. She leaned over towards Duncan.

"I don't recall mead halls having three floors, let alone a cellar. It's not like they had the machinery to dig underneath a building." she mumbled. Duncan looked at her, bewildered.

"I guess I never thought about that. How do you suppose Neena made it happen?" he questioned. Alyx shrugged, the two men ignoring them as Trygg said something to Viggo about him having to most likely carry his sister out with them.

"My guess is her use of energy. There isn't anything powerful enough to create multiple levels of rock. Except my sister." Sonja said in Alyx's mind, her voice full of contemplation.

"How do you expect to go in unseen?" Alyx questioned, silently agreeing with Sonja. Trygg looked up at her, confused. "Well, do you plan to sneak in after I'm caught or do you just run in like a bat out of hell?" He didn't answer her right away. Viggo stepped forward.

"Never mind what we are planning on doing, I suggest you focus on your part. You will be the bait, and distract the guards. Then after we have successfully obtained Fjola, then we will rescue you." he stated. Somehow, she didn't fully trust him.

"I need insurance on this." she said.

"Insurance?" Trygg asked slowly, the word foreign to him. She sighed.

"I need to make sure that what you're saying is true and that you won't just leave me in that dungeon to rot." she said matter-of-factly. Viggo looked over at Trygg, stone faced.

"You just trust. You do your part, we help you. You have my word." Viggo gave her a piercing gaze, his eyes gleamed. She kept wondering what went on behind those eyes, what he was thinking. Duncan stepped towards them, clearing his throat.

"The only question I have is how do we let you know that we have her?" Trygg looked at him, surprised that he could even talk.

"We have someone on the inside helping, he is one of my men. He will seek you out, he will help you escape as we deal with the rest of the guards." Trygg explained. Alyx scoffed. It was like pulling teeth for her to get any information out of them, but it was so easy for Duncan to talk to them. The men ignored her. Was it really because she was a woman? She thought women were treated as equals in Viking culture.

"They do not see you as one of them. Because you are not." Sonja said, annoyed. Alyx bit the inside of her cheek, her cheeks beginning to burn. Well then.

"Great. When do we do this then?" Duncan persisted. Alyx grabbed his shoulder, turning him to face her.

"I told you you're not going." she said. Duncan rolled his eyes.

"I'm a big boy, Alyx. I think I can do this." he mocked.

"You're not a part of this." He glared at her.

"He's my dad too. I'm involved if it means saving his life." he said venomously. She let her hand fall as he turned back to look at Trygg.

"We leave at dusk. The mead hall is *rôst* from here." *A mile.* With that, he gave them a wave of his hand to leave. Alyx and Duncan followed Viggo and Kaia out of the tent. Kaia stomped away without a word, but Viggo lingered behind, turning to face Alyx.

"Just so you are aware for future interactions, make sure you watch that mouth of yours, *meyla*." he said flatly. *Little girl.* His eyes

282

gleamed with intimidation. Alyx gritted her teeth and tried to size him up, putting her face just inches away from his, which was no easy task considering how much taller he was to her.

"And just so *you* are aware, that name is not *little girl* for the thousandth time, it's Alyx. *Alyxandra*. Secondly, I'm not from this time so I'll just let you know how things go back home for me. The women, say whatever they want. We don't bow down to men. So, I'll feel comfortable saying what I feel, okay, *boy*?" the words rushed out before she could reign them in. Viggo looked like he was about to explode, his eyes were practically trying to set her on fire.

And it was kind of working.

Too late to apologize, Alyx held her ground. His upper lip twitched as he tried to control his anger. Somehow, Viggo managed to step away from her, and grabbed the nearest item to throw, which happened to be an iron pot. He chucked it towards her, but it flew past her right side, making her exhale in relief. He gave her a loud roar, his anger building. Still he didn't say anything to her, only stared at her in a frenzy, trying to work up his words. Kaia ran up to her brother, trying to calm him, stepping in between Alyx and Viggo. She whispered a few inaudible words to him and he visibly started to calm down. He straightened up and adjusted his cloak, but his eyes still never left Alyx. She bit her lip and started to regret her outburst. Maybe she really did need to rethink her whole defiant attitude in this time.

He began to walk away then, his anger melting away. Kaia however was not having it. She glared at Alyx, as if she needed another reason to hate her.

"You are such a spoiled little brat aren't you." Kaia hissed. Alyx noticed the many eyes on them.

"I don't handle orders very well." she technically wasn't lying. Kaia sneered.

"Well in this *time,* you need too. Otherwise, you die. Not just by us, but by others. There are many people in this world that would love to kill you, do not forget that. With that little stunt you pulled back there I'm surprised my brother left you standing. We have limitations, girl. Make sure you do not find them. Otherwise it will be the end of you." she threatened, pointing a finger at Alyx. She forced herself to shut up, as Kaia lowered her hand. Giving her one last glare, she stormed off, going in the same direction of her brother.

Duncan jogged up to Alyx.

"Alyx, you have *got* to friggen keep your shit together," he said. "He looked like he wanted to just slice you right then and there." His eyes were wide. Alyx sighed.

"Maybe it wasn't your brother we should be worried about after all." Sonja slowly added in her mind.

"No shit." Alyx said out loud, her eyes were locked onto where Viggo had been standing.

Night had arrived quicker then she anticipated. You would think she would be used to it by now, given that she's lived in the mountains her entire life.

Alyx had spent most of her time talking with Chenoa and Torsten. Of course, Chenoa was more

interested in whatever Duncan was saying but
Torsten explained briefly about Skorravik to Alyx.

"Skorravik is the country as a whole?" she
questioned. Torsten bit into the leg of meat he had
in his hand, shaking his head with a grin.

"No. Skorravik is more the small region in
which the false King's rule. The whole country is
Vinland. The village that we just left, the one which
we all live in, is called *Eyjara*. Viggo, Kaia and I
were all born there. Chenoa here, is from a tribe
that is up in the mountains," he gave her a nod,
Chenoa returned a kind grin. "Her whole family was
killed a couple years ago by the false kings and the
little *witch* that lives in that mead hall with them."
He lowered his voice so Chenoa couldn't quite hear
them. Alyx looked at the girl, her heart swelled with
sadness for her. To lose your whole family was
something she couldn't possibly comprehend.
Duncan was talking with her animatedly, causing
Chenoa to burst into laughter.

"I'm guessing that everyone here had lost
someone because of Neena." Alyx finalized. Torsten
nodded solemnly. Her eyes searched the men, until
they rested upon Viggo and Kaia, their backs turned

to her, looking intently at a piece of parchment with Trygg. She nodded towards them.

"So, I've gotta ask then. What happened to Viggo and Kaia?" she questioned. Torsten hesitated, his eyes looked slightly pained. "Kaia mentioned that they had lost their father due to Neena."

"I don't know if I'm the right person to tell you their story, Alyxandra." Torsten replied gravely.

"You don't have to call me that."

"By your name?"

"Not my full name at least, it's so formal. Just Alyx is fine. How did you even know my full name anyways?" she gave Torsten a look. He grinned and motioned towards Duncan. Alyx rolled her eyes and laughed.

"Of course, he would." she said as she poked the fire that popped in front of them, the light slowly snuffing out, as they were letting the fires die out to not be spotted from a distance. The darkness that was settling upon them created an ideal camouflage.

Suddenly, there was movement that began to buzz around the camp. Trygg moved to the main fire in front of a group of men. He stepped up onto a tree stump, trying to get everyone's attention, the silence that followed was almost immediate.

"Men, we are moving out. The plan remains unaltered, we shall see victory within the night, this I am confident!" he bellowed and the crowd cheered, punching the air. "We will see justice soon, the light that shines from the gods will envelope us all and welcome us to *Valhalla* if they see fit! For you my men, you will dine with Odin and dance among the stars! We will bring this *witch* and her puppets down!" he clamored, and for some reason Alyx could feel a strange swell of excitement and adrenaline in her heart. Trygg's passion was contagious, he was a good motivator that's for sure a true leader. She looked over to see her brother's reaction which was of pure admiration and strength, she had never seen him look like that before.

The men gathered their things and moved out. Alyx stood, not knowing where to go exactly among the chatter and banging of axes against shields, readying for battle. Duncan stood by her side, Chenoa close by. Then, Kaia jogged over, saying something to Chenoa, who nodded and ran over to her horse. Then Kaia made her way over to Alyx, her expression like stone.

"Follow me." was all she said and began to walk towards Viggo. Alyx obeyed and followed suit. Duncan was close behind, but Torsten laid a hand on his chest.

"Better just let her go on her own. You will stick close with me, okay?" he said kindly. Duncan nodded, but watched Alyx nervously as she stood in front of Viggo. Their eyes glancing over the men in the encampment, arms at the ready. Torsten gave Alyx and Duncan a grin. "Don't worry, they are back up in case the rescue doesn't go as smooth as we all hope."

Viggo towered over her, his eyes still gleamed from earlier.

"You will ride with me. I will be the one that gives you up to the false Kings." he explained, his voice monotone. Alyx nodded, trying not to say anything at this point, she didn't want to make him even more upset, otherwise he probably wouldn't rescue her after all. She followed him over to his horse. Out of one of the saddle bags he fished out a short piece of rope, he motioned for her to hold up her wrists, which she did, and began to tie them together. Once her hands were bound again--a feeling she wasn't very fond of--he gave her a nod to climb up on his horse. She struggled, wrapping her hands around one of the ropes on the fur saddle she tried to pull herself up. Then she felt a hand push up one of her feet so she could swing a leg over. Once she was on she pulled the cloak back around her, not wanting her legs to show. She silently cursed herself for wearing such skimpy clothing.

"It's not like you told me what I should be wearing though." Alyx mumbled to Sonja in her mind. Sonja scoffed.

"Just another thing on my already long list of things I should have done. Besides, would you have even listened to me?" she said.

"You're probably right about that."

Viggo pulled himself up with ease behind her, she felt her face burn. She hadn't had a man so close to her for a while, so this was a little much for her to handle. He wrapped his arms around her to grab the reigns, making her just sit there awkwardly, not knowing what to do besides grab a hold of the horse's hair and hope she wouldn't fall off. Viggo cleared his throat and, not intentionally, whispered in her ear.

"The man that will come find you, his name is Bjorn. He is Trygg's cousin. He can be trusted." Viggo explained softly, but all Alyx could think of was how close Viggo was to her. She felt stupid, he hated her, so why was she getting all flustered? Alyx nodded so he didn't think she was just stupid, or a mute suddenly.

Kaia brought her horse over to them.

"We won't be too far behind, Viggo. Please be careful." she begged.

"Always am." he responded as he pulled up the hood of his cloak. He gave the reigns a slight snap and his horse began to trot away. The men began to spill out of the camp behind them, trying to keep a fair distance away.

Viggo began to move up farther away so they wouldn't be spotted as they approached the mead hall. Pretty soon, it was just the two of them. The moonlight was now visible above their heads, peeking through some of the naked trees, and allowing the snow to illuminate underneath them. Alyx wanted to say something to him, but didn't know what. To her surprise, it was Viggo that spoke first.

"I wanted to apologize for my behavior earlier." he spat out. Alyx turned her head slightly to look at him, moving her hood out of her way in the process. He didn't look at her directly this time, almost like he was embarrassed to be apologizing in the first place. That must have been something he clearly didn't do often.

"I was just going to say I'm sorry for being a brat. I just don't take well to any authority. It wasn't personal. But I do need to relax on my attitude." she explained. She was telling the truth, she felt like a total ass earlier and things could have gotten out of hand because of her. She had to be more careful. She would have died and her father would have probably too because of her.

"Things have not been easy for us, Alyxandra. Please remember that." The use of her name almost made her faint. But it was more in the way he had said it. There wasn't any hate or venom behind it. He was genuine and kind, something she hadn't seen from him before.

"I will, Viggo." she responded and she thought she could feel him physically flinch out of surprise, once she used his name.

As she tried to clear her head, a rather large village came into sight. There were lights from torches and a community fire pit roaring to life. It was large, almost too large to call it a village, but in her mind, cities were filled with skyscrapers and huge office buildings.

"When we arrive, please, let me do all the talking. I don't know what will happen, but we will make sure you get out of there alive, okay?" he whispered as they came through the entrance. The tall wooden walls were spiked at the top. People were laughing and drinking, and so only a few were not distracted by the two of them on horseback. There was one thing that seemed strange to her though. The only ones that were laughing were guards, the others seemed to be the townspeople, who were either begging for food or passed out in the streets. Her eyes widened in horror as there were women and children who looked like skeletons, starving and no one would give them anything, not even scraps. She could feel the necklace beneath the cloak grow ice cold, colder than the snow around her.

"How could she do this to my people?" Sonja cried in her mind. She could feel the anger rising within her.

"This is why we are doing this, Sonja. Because these people are clearly suffering and Neena is not fit to rule. Nor is Eero and Elof. Now I can see why the others call them the false kings." Alyx mocked, but her mind was filled with so much disdain she couldn't see any humor left. To see these people helpless and no one reaching out to help them was ridiculous. It was crazy to think how similar her time period was with this. There were still corrupt rulers who thirsted for power and stomped on the weak on their way to the top. It was disgusting.

"Why is Neena doing this? What does she want out of all this? Power?" Alyx questioned Sonja. There was silence for a few minutes. Alyx focused on a little girl with blonde hair, her ringlets cascading down around her gaunt face. She held up her small hands towards Viggo and Alyx as they rode by, making her heart wrench as her big eyes pleaded.

"She is sickened by people. She had always claimed that they are nothing but parasites and are only capable of destruction and chaos." Sonja hissed. Alyx felt sickened by Neena's beliefs as she looked upon the innocent.

"How ironic that she would do the same thing she vowed to destroy." Alyx spat. They moved closer to the mead hall. Looking up at the unusually illuminated windows, she could've sworn she had seen a shadow move across the top. She squinted but there was nothing there. However, there was a feeling of bad energy all around her, the entire place just felt off. She looked around, the guards seemed no longer humorous, and began to follow them, eyeing them closely.

Once they had arrived at the front of the mead hall, she looked at the large stone steps leading up to the double-wooden doors. Viggo swung a leg over and landed down onto the ground, his eyes fixed on the door. He led them up the steps, the horse neighing as it made its way up, trying not to slip on some loose pieces of rock. She could hear merriment through the wooden doors, and the flicker of fire danced underneath the small opening above the floor the men stood upon.

"I wish to call upon the Kings!" Viggo called up to the door. Two guards were standing post, eyeing him suspiciously.

"What do you wish to present to the Kings?" one guard questioned as he leaned down, from the steps. Viggo moved up towards Alyx, fully removing her hood.

"I have the mortal woman who is family of Isleif Abisson, the traitor." he said. The guard stopped, taken by surprise as he stared down at Alyx, who felt slightly vulnerable. The guard then motioned towards someone inside and the doors began to open. The sound of laughter and the warmth from a large fire pit greeted them. Viggo held out his arms for Alyx to fall into as she got off of the horse. Another guard walked over, holding out a hand to take the reins.

"I have only come to drop her off. I will still need my horse." Viggo explained. The guard shook his head.

"The Kings have been long awaiting for her head. They would like to congratulate you and reward you for your service in giving her to them. Stay and drink." he stated and stood behind Viggo so he was forced to walk inside the hall. Viggo wrapped an arm around Alyx and pulled her with him as they walked on. The light wrapped them up as the doors shut out the darkness behind them.

CHAPTER 13

THE MEAD HALL was something out of a movie. There were tall rafters and beams that made even modern-day architecture look stale and cold. There were wooden carvings of the gods, no doubt, etched on balusters along with runes. Fur pelts were decorated on the walls and floors. But what really stood out was the immense fire pit that stood in the center of the room. A large boar was skewered over it, being turned slowly to create a decadent marbling on the skin. Men all around them were cheering and drinking what looked to be a deep brown liquid. On impulse, Alyx fidgeted with the necklace.

"Mead." Sonja commented, answering Alyx's unasked question. Now that she was inside, it seemed more like a palace with all the ornate decor than a mead hall, then again this could be normal since she'd never been in a real mead hall before. It was warm and cozy inside and she only felt guiltier knowing that the rest of the people were begging and freezing to death outside. Anger filled her heart as she silently cursed Neena in her head, her inhumane and twisted actions fueling Alyx's anger. Men were cheering and toasting, some women were dancing and celebrating. What, she didn't know exactly, but this didn't seem like the typical Viking gathering that she had read about or seen in movies, everyone was invited, community based.

She tried to remember the different statuses between people among the Viking culture. Looking around, she didn't see any marks or examples of wealth or nobility, no crowns or authoritative demeanor, just drunken men groping over giggling women. Why would they allow the rest of their people to starve or freeze to death?

"Some probably did not have a choice. Neena would make it for them," Sonja piped up. "She wanted division, better control and manipulation. A people divided is easier to rule over." Sonja spat with as much venom as she could muster.

"You two wait here." One of the guards said. Viggo pulled Alyx to a stop, his arm still around her. Strangely, he made her feel safe. A huge change from his previous demeanor. They waited as men danced and cheered around them. She couldn't help but think that maybe she looked that stupid when she was at parties.

"You were." Sonja chimed in, interrupting her thoughts.

"Gee, thanks." Alyx responded sarcastically.

After a few moments had passed, the energy began to shift again in the hall. The men began to quiet down as a shadow was casted over the top of the large stairway. Alyx swallowed, suddenly feeling nervous.

Two men appeared then, they seemed huge. Large builds with long arms. They had long brown beards and their heads shaved. They had tattoos visible as well except there was something *carved* into their foreheads. It was a rudimentary marking that was scarred now. What looked like a chain or a lasso was evident. What did it mean?

"It is the symbol for captivity," Sonja whispered, sounding a bit unnerved. "Pray that it does not happen to you as well."

The two men stopped on the last stair, facing Viggo and Alyx but keeping a safe distance. They looked at her with a sort of, *possessive* intent which made her skin crawl. Both seemed so familiar to her. She eyed them suspiciously. Who they reminded her of she couldn't quite recall.

"My brother and I wanted to welcome you to our home," the slightly younger looking brother spoke first. She was taken a back at how, *old,* they sounded. He spoke slowly and calculated. His tone was raspy and weathered, almost like he was constantly exhausted by just speaking. But there was an undertone that threw her off, it seemed to almost have an echo to it, like a second person was speaking with him. "I am Elof, and this is my brother Eero. We thank you young half-Pale for bringing us this girl, she's associated with a traitor." he explained. He held a hand up, acknowledging Viggo who stiffened next to her. Eero gave her a

frightful glare, like she was the bane of
his existence. "Half-Pale?" Alyx mentally asked.
Sonja didn't answer, she merely listened.

"You, girl, will account for your crimes.
Guard, take her to the cellars." Eero spoke slowly.
Her heart leapt knowing that she would indeed get
to find Fjola. The guard came over and grabbed Alyx
by her wrists, Viggo hesitantly allowed him to take
her. The guard escorted her down the steps, she
turned to look back at Viggo who was trying to not
look her way. The guard opened the large wooden
door with a heavy looking iron key and shoved her
through. She tumbled slightly but regained her
balance, glaring at the man's roughness. She walked
on in front of him as he directed her towards a cell
in the middle. She couldn't see into the other cells
very easily but she could hear weak coughs and
moans. He shoved her into the cell and slammed the
door shut behind her. She caught her balance and
leaned against the door, looking out, trying to find
any faces. It was very dark down in the dungeons
but down the hall she could hear women chattering
in a busy manner, followed by iron pots and pans
clanging and a fire popping. There seemed to be

kitchens nearby. She saw there was a guard standing at the bottom of the steps, stiff and aware. As she searched she wondered when this Bjorn guy would show himself. Deciding not to wait on him she proceeded to gather other prisoner's attentions.

"Psst. Hello?" she whispered, hoping the guard was too far away to hear her. Silence. "Is there anyone in here?" she questioned. There was a scoff that followed. She tried to look down the hall, but the bars limited her vision.

"You asking for a death wish, girl? The guards will end your talking if you don't shut it." a man piped up.

"I'm looking for someone."

"Aren't we all." the man laughed gruffly, he sounded young, maybe around her age. He seemed close by, maybe just two cells down from hers on her right.

"I'm looking for a girl named Fjola." she said slightly louder. There was a pause.

"Fjola? By the gods, Fjola! There's someone here for you." He whispered, sounding more energetic. Suddenly there was a slight rustle a few cells down.

"What?" a girl responded, she sounded completely out of it.

"By the gods did they give you that concoction again? I don't think your body can handle much more of that stuff." he said, worry evident in his voice. What stuff was he talking about?

"Oh gods, they're drugging her." Sonja piped up in her mind.

"Drugging her? Why?" Alyx questioned.

"To suppress her visions, I assume. Only Neena wants full control of her sight." Sonja explained.

"We have to help her! How the hell do we get to her?"

"Hopefully this Bjorn will show up soon." Sonja stated and Alyx nodded in agreement.

Time went by and Bjorn never showed up. The guard started to doze, allowing Alyx to speak a little more loudly as she settled onto a pile of hay.

"What is your name?" she asked the man near her, trying to kill time.

"Ezhno." he said curtly.

"What are you in here for?" she asked.

"What are *you* in here for?" he responded and laughed once, but began to cough erratically almost immediately after.

"I see. So, you're a traitor too?" she scoffed.

"In a sense. I just know more than the *kings* would like. They also don't appreciate my opinion on tyranny," he explained. "They see me as a rebel, not a rather opinionated traveler unfortunately." he laughed once.

"How do you suppose we stop them?" she questioned. He laughed again.

"If we knew that do you not think we wouldn't have stopped them?" he said. She laughed once.

"True."

She nestled further into the hay, sensing that she would be there awhile, she might as well get comfortable, wrapping her cloak around herself protectively. Where was Bjorn?

Something was wrong, very wrong.

"I can sense it too." Sonja said in her mind.

Suddenly, there was a loud bang and a shout.

"Let me go!" roared a voice.

"Viggo?" Alyx shouted and stood up, pressing her face to the bars.

Viggo came down the steps, thrashing around as the guards held axes and swords near him, prodding him to move on with threats and iron. What was going on!? They shoved him forward and into the cell next to Alyx, slamming the door shut behind him. Viggo whirled around and threw himself at the cell door, reaching to grab one of the guards.

"By the gods!" Viggo warned, gritting his teeth, but the guards merely laughed, not allowing him to finish his threat. They walked up the steps, not a care in the world.

"Viggo!" Alyx called and tried to see him. He pressed his face to the bars, trying to make eye contact.

"You *are* safe! Good. It was a trap the whole time." he hissed and spat on the ground. She heard him lash out, kicking the cells door. The creak and groan of the metal refused to submit under his outburst.

"Damn it! How are we going to get out of here?" she asked, hitting the cell door. There was a loud bang as Viggo kicked the wall in anger.

"This was not part of the plan. Bjorn was caught and is taken too." he paused, waiting for Alyx to say something, when she didn't he added. "Don't worry he can take care of himself, I've seen him in worse situations." Viggo said.

"That must have been why they brought Fjola up so soon." Ezhno suddenly breathed.

"What do you mean?" Alyx questioned.

"Just an hour or so before you arrived, they brought Fjola up. When they brought her back down she was completely hysterical and kept shouting about blood being spilled on a trap."

"By the gods, who knows what they had done to her." Viggo breathed in response. Alyx wished that Fjola would say something, but it only followed with silence.

"She should consider herself lucky for still being alive." Sonja added. Alyx scoffed out loud.

"Except they could kill her at any minute since they probably don't need her sight anymore. They have me." Alyx spat in her mind.

"Ah, but they do not have your brother. He is key in this as well. They need both of you." she murmured.

"How do you know this? And need both of us for what?" Alyx urged. Sonja didn't answer. "Seriously? You're going to go quiet now?" she said out loud.

"What do you mean?" Viggo asked.

"Never mind." Alyx hissed and plopped down onto the hay in a huff. This wasn't supposed to happen! How was she supposed to save her dad being locked up?

"I'm sure Trygg has a plan for this. He has to." Alyx said optimistically.

"Alyxandra. This was the *only* plan." Viggo finalized.

"Not helping." she countered.

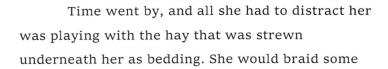

Time went by, and all she had to distract her was playing with the hay that was strewn underneath her as bedding. She would braid some stalks together and throw them in a corner, allowing the mice to take some back to their nests.

There was plenty of cheering and laughter above them, the music echoing through the cavern in a ghostly fashion. Alyx rolled her eyes, she never hated parties until now. Throwing a braid of hay away in annoyance, she heard the door upstairs suddenly opened. She stood up to investigate.

A very drunk guard began to tumble down the steps, laughing on his way down. He took another swig of his drink and coughed. This could be something Alyx could work with. She stuck an arm out to wave the guard down. He looked over at her, scrunching his nose, his blonde beard stained with the alcohol.

"Get back in your cell." he slurred. He took a few steps towards her.

"Oh, but I just couldn't help but stare at you," she started, making her voice sickeningly sweet. Viggo looked at her with bewilderment, his eyes questioning. The guard moved closer to her cell, laying an arm across the bar, alarmingly stone faced for someone so drunk. "You're just so handsome. I've never seen such a man before." she wanted to throw up in her mouth. She felt stupid, he'll never believe it. However, his reaction surprised her. He opened his mouth to say something, struggling with the words, he held up his hand with the bottle of alcohol to point at her as he tried to talk, spilling some of his drink onto the wooden floor.

"That's because you haven't met a man like me. I'm one of the *Kings* guards. Kings, there's two." he said, his eyes slightly crossing as his words slurred. Alyx bit her lip to keep from laughing, this was so ridiculously easy.

"I bet you could show a girl a really good time." she flirted mentally throwing up in her mind. He laughed once and began to fumble with the keys.

"I know I can beautiful," he mumbled as he held up each key to his face and squinted, trying to focus on them. Then he stopped. "Oh shit, by the gods are you trying to trick me?" he began to talk louder. Alyx waved her hands in the air.

"Of course not!" she shouted in protest. He eyed her and drew back. "Oh, for the love of---," and before she realized what she was doing, she reached behind his head, firmly grabbing the back of his neck and pulled him forward causing his face to smack into the cell doors. He swayed a few times but didn't fall right away, so she smacked him against the bars once more, which finally caused him to collapse. "I'm so sick of waiting!" she huffed and squatted down, searching for the keys he had dropped. She grabbed the small chain of keys, trying each one out in the lock until one had worked. As the lock loudly clicked, she pushed the door hard, pushing the guard away as she did. Once she moved to Viggo's cell she almost laughed at his reaction. His mouth was open and his eyes were searching hers for answers.

"By the gods, I didn't think you had it in you." he breathed.

"I know, I'm just full of surprises." she mocked, giving him wide eyes in return and unlocked his door. He pushed his way out as she made her way down the row. She looked into the second to last cell and saw a young man with dark hair and chocolate brown eyes. He had a good bruise on the side of his face but overall, he looked well enough to travel.

"Ezhno?" she questioned, pointing at him. He nodded once and stood up. He was a little taller than her and wore leather pants that had an ornate looking skirt attached around his hips, he was shirtless but had a few bands wrapped around his arms. He had war paint smeared across his face, kind of muting his features, but most of it was disappearing now.

"We don't have time to save him. Let's go!" Viggo spat as he grabbed her arm, pulling her towards the last cell. She pulled against him, glaring.

"I don't like being man handled!" she hissed and turned back to Ezhno. She unlocked his cell and allowed him to push the door open. He stood in front of her, staring her down.

"Thank you." he said and nodded once. He began to jog up the hallway and towards the steps.

Reclaiming her attention, Viggo motioned for her to come over. She looked into the next cell where he was crouched over, staring intently into the dark cell.

Alyx gasped when she saw a girl, who looked very small, lying in a fetal position, her back towards them.

"Fjola?" Viggo called softly. She didn't move. Fear gripped at Alyx's heart.

"Fjola?" She tried. The girl began to slowly stretch out, carefully pulling herself up on an elbow to look behind her.

"Hello?" she mumbled. She seemed so out of it.

"Fjola! Did they hurt you?" Viggo questioned. Alyx was curious to his connection with her, his worried expression was making her feel slightly uncomfortable.

"V-Viggo? Is that you?" she said hoarsely. She tried to get up but swayed.

"By the gods, they drugged you." he said with gritted teeth. Alyx could feel his anger. Looking at Fjola, she looked younger than Alyx, maybe eighteen or so. Even with the bruises on her face and how dirty she was, she looked strikingly like her brother Trygg. Her long dark hair was matted around her.

"I thought you would never come." she tried to joke but began to cough, her whole body shaking.

"Hand me the key, Alyxandra." Viggo demanded and she obeyed. He unlocked the cell and pushed it open. He knelt and scooped her up with ease. Fjola's head swayed back uncontrollably by the force--like a newborn--and her eyes rolled back in her head. She kept mumbling something incoherent.

"We're leaving, now." he said, his face was unreadable. Alyx bit her lip and said no more, following behind him quietly.

They made their way through the hall, briefly pausing in the kitchen, to grab a couple of knives, and traveled up the steps. Now the real question was how the hell they would get out of there unseen. The laughter grew louder as they opened the door. She hadn't seen Ezhno slip out but due to the continued partying from the men, he must not have been seen. She felt relief knowing that he had escaped.

Slowly opening the door, Viggo carefully placed Fjola on her feet.

"I need you to try and walk with me, I'll keep you up." he reassured her. She nodded in a daze but clumsily swung an arm around his neck. He grabbed her by the waist and gave Alyx a nod to begin walking towards the door. She took a step and suddenly felt light headed. She shook her head but her vision became blurry.

"What's wrong?" Viggo whispered to her.

"N-nothing." she lied and pushed herself to keep walking. The door was right there.

Then there was a loud ringing noise in her ears, causing her to clamp her hands over them in pain.

"Alyxandra?" he urged. His voice grew distant as the whole room became inaudible. People's mouths were moving and smiling but she could only hear the loud ringing, it was almost enough to drive her crazy. Then there was a harsh whisper that followed.

"Come find me, little one." it faded on the last word and the ringing subsided. Somehow, her whole being was telling her to find Neena, like some sick game of hide-and-go-seek. Her eyes looked up towards the top of the stairs, which had an ominous dark shadow that sat readily waiting for her to arrive. She swallowed, nervously wondering what she should do. This was obviously a trap, but the knowledge that Neena was so--close--made her impulse so much harder to ignore. She looked back at Viggo who was looking at her like she was crazy. She probably was at this point.

"Go on without me." was all she said, and before Viggo could protest, she began to jog towards the steps, knocking over a few men on her way. She hoped Viggo took that distraction as a means to escape with Fjola but she didn't dare look back. She could only hear the demands and anger of the men as she bounded up the steps, the darkness beginning to greet her.

Just as she busted through the door, everything grew silent. She took a few steps in, scoping out the area which was a long hallway. The door swung shut loudly, causing her to jump and whirl around. She pulled out one of the kitchen knives Viggo had stolen for her, she held it at the ready, hoping that that was going to be enough for whatever she was about to face. Hopefully it was enough to kill Neena and end all of this. Somehow, she didn't quite believe herself.

"Come find me." Neena's voice whispered again through the room.

Alyx slowly walked forward, a strange feeling filled the space, making her skin crawl. The floor was covered in fur rugs and dimly lit torches. She held the blade up defensively as she turned the corner hesitantly. At first, she saw nothing but darkness, there was nothing illuminating the space and then she heard someone or *something* move.

She froze, hearing grotesque sounds and growls.

"H-hello?" she whispered, her voice caught in her throat, her eyes wide with fear.

"I thought you would never come, little one." Neena cooed. She swallowed.

"I thought you didn't have your physical form yet?" she questioned weakly. There was a mocking laugh and two violet eyes appeared through the darkness. No shapes were visible, though the eyes were vibrant, but they reached higher up towards the ceiling at the end of the hallway.

"Is that what my dear old sister told you? Or maybe one of the handsome men in your company that long for my death so?" she asked in a bored tone. Alyx didn't respond, she couldn't move.

"Sonja do something!" she begged in her mind. Another laugh.

"It seems my sister is expending a lot of energy just trying to keep me out of your mind. How cute, she was always the weak one. So caring and compassionate of others." she teased.

"What do you want, Neena?" Alyx demanded, she held the knife up towards Neena. Suddenly, she grew malicious, her violet eyes gleaming as she moved closer to Alyx. More like floated, as Neena cocked her head to the side.

"Something that your family tried to take away from me." she hissed. The shadow grew around Alyx, it was like a thick smoke that billowed around Neena, enveloping everything around the both of them, it seemed almost crushing, threatening to lock Alyx in a dark box, forever alone with her thoughts. That's what scared her the most.

"What did my family do?" she asked, astonished that her family would have anything to do with this monster. Neena laughed again.

"In due time. Instead, enjoy your death by someone you might know." she purred and, in that moment, Eero and Elof stepped out as the shadows subsided. They had stone-cold expressions.

"I don't know them!" she objected, holding her hands up in defense, the knife still pointed at Neena.

"Oh, but you do. The soul is much more familiar than the flesh," the eyes glinted as she looked down at the two brothers. "As both have the same soul so to speak. However, I had to make due by 'borrowing,' for a time, as these two were nothing more than walking bags of meat." Alyx could feel the blood leave her face.

"Wait, you mean, you stole someone's soul to reanimate them?" There was an affirming laugh, bile rose in her throat. It couldn't be who she was thinking, it can't be. "Who?" Alyx demanded and threatened with the blade.

"After your dear old father interfered, I had a certain friend of his take over things. All I had to do was give a little--persuasion." she purred the last word. Alyx looked at Eero and Elof in horror.

"Bradley?" she breathed. She could've sworn she saw an emotion flicker across their faces. Her theory was horribly confirmed.

"In the flesh. So, to speak. Well, more so in two pieces." Neena laughed maniacally.

"You're a sick son of a bitch!" Alyx yelled, she could feel tears sting her eyes. She had known

Bradley since she was little, he was always such a kind person.

"It was rather easy of course, a simple spell to tear apart his soul. I figured, waste not, want not. Although, he was rather handier with a blade than I had previously anticipated." she explained proudly. Alyx bit her lip, trying not to let the tears flow. The men didn't move, they looked like statues. Their eyes glazed over like they were forever frozen in time.

"You forced Bradley to try and kill my dad?" she choked, once the realization hit. Neena tsked.

"Now, technically it was Bradley who did the physical killing," she paused. "But I am *very* good at persuading." she could hear the smile behind her words. Alyx bit back the bile rising in her throat. Persuasion was obviously Neena's specialty.

"How did my father 'get in the way?' We had no idea that you existed until a few months ago!" she pleaded, tears freely pouring down her face now. Neena grew serious.

"It's because of your family that I am without my full power, because of *them*, I am trapped here like an animal," she hissed. "But all of that will

320

change soon." the last word sounded distorted as suddenly her eyes dematerialized.

Then, Eero and Elof began to groan and contort in pain. Alyx took a step back, nervous and disgusted at what was happening before her. Their arms extended forward, but twisted unnaturally with bones jutting out and crunching that made her gag. The torsos began to sink in as they lifted their shirts in shock and released an agonized scream. Ribs began to shift and move underneath the paling skin. They began to lose color and became gaunt. Their own eyeballs rolled back and underneath their sockets turned black.

As the transformation took place in front of her, she couldn't help but see in their eyes the amount of emotional pain they were going through. Who knows what they had seen with those eyes. Somehow, she felt like she could see Bradley through the grotesque creatures they were turning into, or at least fragments of what he used to be.

"Bradley! I know you're in there!" she begged. They just continued to scream. "You're stronger than her! You can fight this!" she kept backing up as they grew in height knowing full well that the knife she held was about as helpful as a daffodil. The men now began to merge together. Their limbs and arms morphing into a creature, no longer human. Towering over her, their four eyes almost touching as it gazed down in a crazed stare, now desperate for blood. Any humanity that was left was now gone as they turned pitch black, Alyx reflected in them as she was targeted.

"A-Alyx!" it managed to make out before its mouth swelled into a toothy grimace. She was so shocked she barely noticed the long fang-like teeth that began to jut out from underneath its lips.

"Bradley!" so he was in there! He was trying to fight through! Maybe she could still save him?

"Alyxandra you need to run! NOW!" Sonja shouted in her head. Alyx looked around noticing that its arms were now reaching towards her, claws glinted from the flames that were almost extinguished. The darkness must have settled like a blanket before she even arrived. The shadow moved around its body like smoke, dancing and thrashing around with each sway of its body. She began to run, turning around, but an arm grabbed a hold of her right leg, causing her to crash to the ground on her back. She could feel the air get knocked out of her once she connected. Gasping, she pulled herself onto her stomach, trying to crawl helplessly from the creature. A distorted laugh echoed through the hallway.

"Try and run, but you will never get away from me, little one. My little mouse." Neena hissed all around her. A screech from the creature behind her made her cover her ears and shut her eyes, waiting for it to all be over.

Like a child.

But as soon as she did so, she heard a yell. Her eyes snapped open and she saw Viggo jumping over her, a unique looking two-handed sword held in his grasp. He swung the one-edged blade at the creature, severing two limbs flailing around them with ease. A black liquid that looked to be ink sprayed onto the ground near her, which instantly began to sizzle.

Its blood is acid! Alyx thought to herself. She pushed herself up onto her feet and began to lean against a wall. They had to get out of there.

"Viggo!" she called to him as he kept cutting down limb after limb until it occurred to Alyx, that it kept regrowing its arms and legs back. The creature reminded her of a Greek monster she had read about, a Hydra. For each head you cut off two more grew back. Each limb he cut off, more and more grew back.

"Stop! You need to run!" she urged, he glanced back at her, worry in his expression as the mass of limbs began to flail around and the creature shrieked in excitement at its new ability. "Come on!" He turned to run towards her, not very eager to run away from a fight, but they both knew this was something he couldn't win. He grabbed her arm and guided her back through the hallway, running across the fur covered path, the door was open at the end, letting in light. She huffed as she still didn't quite have all of her breath back, but pushed herself. The creature knocked over the torches behind them, causing the flames to hungrily reach out and spread. The heat was spreading fast, causing the two to flinch as the fur rugs lit up quickly, the smell of burnt hair was unbearable.

The light from the room in front of them was very much welcomed as Viggo pushed her through with a hard shove, from which she barely kept upright. She began to climb the stairs, not daring to look back at the monster that was probably right at their heels. Viggo huffed behind her, his sword glinting in her peripheral vision. They stopped at the corner once they reached the top of the stairs, the men were waiting with swords and axes drawn.

"You two! Stop!" one of the guards, no longer drunk glared at them. Alyx hesitated but Viggo merely spat at him and pushed her along.

"I said stop!" he shouted again and the sound of a projectile whizzed by their head, barely missing Alyx's right ear. She ducked in shock, but Viggo kept pushing her.

"Keep going, their new *monster-king* will take care of them." he hissed, and as soon as he said that, a roar echoed through the hall. The men behind them began to look around nervously, unaware that their Kings were something much more, and deadlier. Alyx glanced around, slowing her movement. Viggo looked behind them at the stairs, his eyes narrowed.

Like a breath, the creature burst through the small door opening, flames licking around him, the shadow still wafting like an aura. The men let out a terrified scream which distracted the creature, it was now acting upon an insatiable hunger for meat. Viggo pushed her once more causing her to jerk forward, but not before she caught a glimpse of the creature grabbing hold of a man trying to run away and ripping him in two, the sound was gut wrenching and it made the world move from underneath her. Everything slowed down around her, she looked from the monster tearing people apart to the flames that were now crawling up on the walls, scorching the wooden pillars of the gods' totems, a heavy humming echoing in her mind as she made eye contact with the blasphemy. For a brief second, she locked eyes with what she thought was a totem, but squinting into the blaze through the heavy smoke, she swore she saw the shape of a woman perched upon one of the roof beams. She couldn't make out any physical details other than her eyes; bright, icy blue eyes that gleamed through the fire. Eyes that gave such a disdainful look down upon the wreckage and the wailing people. Darkness began to creep around her vision until she couldn't tell what was what within the black smoke rising from the ground. The mead hall was rapidly catching on fire, the creature unaware or merely uninterested in its predicament. With it temporarily distracted, she quickly returned her gaze back up to the roof, the woman had disappeared. It was like finding a spider in your room, and looking away for a split second only to look back and find it missing. Unaware of where it went. Alyx felt an icy chill that clawed its way down her spine.

What had she *really* seen?

Viggo hastily pushed the doors open, with help from the panicked men, not caring anymore about their prisoner, and pulled Alyx with him, her arm going limp as the horror in front of her resumed.

Just as he pulled her into the night, she watched in horror as the creature bit into a man's neck, easily decapitating him and swallowing his flesh rabidly as it turned its attention to the now opened door and right into Alyx's gaze.

CHAPTER 14

ALYX WAS NUMB. Viggo and Alyx ran across the field. Some of the guards were gathering water from a nearby river and dousing the flames. They were like a beacon in the night. The creature had not emerged but she still nervously glanced back up the stone steps leading to the mead hall.

Some people were frantically running for safety while others made their way up, joining the guards, to the burning mead hall to douse the flames with buckets of water. Viggo yanked on her arm, pulling her towards him, her head turning back around to face him. He looked at her with anger. He kept both walking.

"By the gods, what was that?" he demanded as they made their way to the tree line. She looked at him, her eyes narrowing.

"I was trying to end all of this!" she yelled back, fed up with the constant chastising.

"How? By getting yourself killed?" he growled, letting go of her arm once they had the cover of trees behind them. Alyx stopped and threw up her arms.

"I'm so sick of everyone treating me like some sort of child!"

"Then stop acting like one! If you want to be a hero and risk your life, then do that on your own time! You almost got all of us killed in the process!" he whirled around, waving his hands at her in fury. Taken a back, she looked at him, wide-eyed.

"I thought you all made it out by the time I ended up with the brothers," she stated. "I thought everyone was out of harm's way. I just didn't want to leave without facing her, not when she was right there! I could have ended this!" Alyx yelled. Viggo took a few steps towards her, closing in the gap between them.

"I got the others out before I ended up following you." he stated. She drew back, surprised.

"Why *did* you follow me? You could have died Viggo." she asked. This time he paused, drawing back. He looked down, his eyes glinted from the light of the moon. He rubbed the back of his neck nervously. His jaw clenched, not knowing how to react.

"The brothers are not yet destroyed; therefore, we still need you." he said finally. Strange enough, all Alyx felt was disappointment.

"I see." she finalized.

"Come. The others are waiting. I hope Fjola and Ezhno found Trygg alright. They probably think we died in that fire." he said. Alyx nodded slowly and watched as he leads her on. Somehow, all she could think about was how complicated things were getting for her now.

⸻

"Oh, thank the gods!" Kaia shouted as she ran towards her brother. She gave him a firm hug before pulling apart and looking up at him. "You have no right to make me worry like that!" she said, angrily and gave him a soft punch in the arm. He allowed himself to smirk slightly, but nodded. Everyone merely stared at them, surprised that they were still alive, when someone caught her attention. A man locked eyes temporarily with her, he was beaten, a large bruise on the right side of his face, but he was alive. He gave her a slight apologetic nod and kept on walking. Was that Bjorn perhaps?

"I apologize." and he seemed genuine, yet uncomfortable.

"Alyx!" Duncan shouted and jogged over to her. She gave him a quick hug and laughed as he looked her over, making sure she was all in one piece. "Mom would kill me if you were missing a limb, or two." he joked.

"Just a little crispy." she responded and brushed off some ash in her hair. She couldn't help but look at Viggo, who glanced at her while he walked past. Duncan gave her a look and then followed her gaze, with a sigh he looked back at Alyx.

"Seriously?" he groaned. She blinked, looking at Duncan.

"Excuse me?" she questioned.

"Viggo? Really? Of all people you have to like *him*? He hates us. Besides, I don't think you get any points trying to get him killed anyway." Duncan said and began to walk away, throwing his hands up in the air.

"Can you *not*? Why the hell are you being so loud anyway?" she hissed and followed him. Duncan laughed in response and shrugged.

Once they returned to the campsite, they joined Chenoa and Torsten sitting around a fire. He greeted her with a wooden bowl filled with some kind of stew. She took a bite as she wrapped the cloak around herself again. As the three were laughing and talking, all Alyx could pay attention to was Viggo and Kaia sitting at a wooden table across the camp from them, clearly in a heated discussion. She was drawn to him, she didn't know why or how, but she couldn't stop looking at Viggo. The way his eyes looked when he looked at her, the way his lips moved, it was tantalizing. Not to mention he just saved her life. She really did need to thank him for that.

She shook her head and scowled down at her stew. Unfortunately, she wasn't going to get involved with him, she couldn't let him distract her from what she was here to do. Besides, he *did* hate her. He was obvious about his feelings, and she had enough of people hating her. She tucked her hair behind her ear and took another bite of her stew. She could only think about her next move, Trygg was to keep his end of the bargain, she had helped save Fjola, now they would give her the information they needed, and help.

"What did you do to Viggo?" Torsten questioned, catching her attention.

"What? Nothing." she spat. He raised his eyebrows and looked over at Kaia and Viggo. She followed his gaze and saw Viggo sitting alone now, and his eyes were piercing. She felt fire spread across her cheeks as she looked back down at her stew.

"I didn't do anything to him." she spat and stabbed a potato in the bowl.

"I've never seen him like this before." Torsten remarked, still looking at Viggo.

"When is Trygg coming out?" Alyx huffed, wanting to change the subject. She looked over at the tent Trygg was in. "Fjola is with him?" Torsten hesitantly turned his gaze away, but looked at Alyx and nodded.

"How is she?"

"Alive." he stated. Alyx nodded and finished what was in the bowl. Placing it down on the ground she rubbed her hands on her knees, feeling the urge to look back over to Viggo. She allowed her eyes to search for him, hoping to see any form of emotion in his gaze.

He wasn't there.

Disappointed, she sighed and turned back to Duncan, who was in a deep conversation with Chenoa.

"I'm gonna go talk to Trygg." she stated and stood up. Torsten looked up at her, confusion spreading across his face. The others ignored her, like she hadn't even spoken.

"I would not disturb him if I were you." he warned as he scratched his beard, looking bored.

To No End

"I'm not just going sit around and wait for him to decide if he's going to keep his side of our deal." she mumbled and pulled the cloak tighter around herself. The fur was now starting to become too wet to really be functional for her; she made a mental note to replace it. She swung her leg over the log she had used as a chair and marched towards Trygg's tent. She didn't realize how much she huffed now by just walking. She was more exhausted then she thought. Before she entered, she heard hushed voices, they seemed agitated enough, making her pause.

"I don't understand why we can't just kill them. It's not like we need them anymore. They will only get us killed brother." Kaia hissed. Alyx felt her heart drop, holy shit they were talking about her and her brother, no minced words there, and they were talking about *killing* them? She covered her mouth, noticing she was breathing rather loud. There was a moment of silence, then someone cleared their throat.

"Although they did help with my sister's escape, I don't entirely disagree with Kaia, Viggo," Trygg spoke, even though he didn't seem ecstatic about the idea, her anxiety level spiked. "Neena might kill them anyway, it would be a mercy killing."

More silence followed.

After what seemed like decades, Viggo finally spoke.

"No."

She thought her heart was going to give out.

"No? For the love of the gods, why?" Kaia complained.

"Because we are *not* the fool kings. Or more so now the monsters. What have they done to us, but only help." he defended. Kaia scoffed.

"Only because we forced them and threatened their lives if they didn't. That does not exactly give confidence for their loyalty. Or lack thereof. They have no essence for it." she ranted.

"Have you forgotten their loyalty for their father?" he responded calmly. Kaia paused.

"I have not forgotten. That is blood, that is very much different." her response was much softer than before.

"Then we cannot be so quick to assume. We do not know these people." he said. For some reason, it bothered her to be called 'these people.' Was she just another woman to him? Anger filled her, why did it matter? What mainly bothered her was that his opinion seemed to matter so much to her, she did not expect that. Let alone the fact that it was even up for debate on if they should kill Alyx and Duncan in the first place. Even though he voted against it, how did she know that one Kaia or one of the others wouldn't just slit her throat while she was sleeping?

"What does she mean to you exactly brother?" Kaia questioned. She could heart her heartbeat in her ears.

"What are you talking about?" he asked, annoyed.

"Do not try to fool me. I know she means something to you now." she warned. Alyx waited for what seemed like eons for his answer. It was silent.

"I do not see anything in her. She is a helpless child in my eyes. Nothing more. If she died tomorrow, it wouldn't matter, but I would just prefer it not be on our hands." he answered in an almost bored tone. Crimson spreads over her cheeks. Embarrassed, she could feel tears prick at her eyes.

"Are you fucking kidding me?" Alyx hissed. A child? Her? And he didn't care if she lived or died? The fact that she was even hanging on his every word made her want to throw up. The nerve of this guy! Hearing enough, she stormed off, pushing past Torsten on her way.

"Where are you going?" he called after her. She merely gave him a glare, becoming angrier that she was tearing up again as she did so. He gave her a surprised look and glanced back at the tent Viggo was in. She pressed on, looking back in front of her. She just needed some time alone, some time to get away and clear her head.

Once she reached the edge of the campsite, she reached the forest outlining the sea of tents and soldiers.

"Why are you leaving?" Sonja asked weakly, she was barely audible over the pounding of her own heartbeat.

"To get away." she said out loud. She didn't feel like talking, although she knew she should probably ask Sonja at least if she was okay. She hadn't talked to her since they faced Neena and the brothers blob-monster fiasco.

"You must not distance yourself so much from your friends, you are more vulnerable that way---,"

"They are *not* my friends," she hissed, cutting Sonja off, who sighed loudly, clearly too tired to argue. "They would rather murder us in our sleep if it meant Neena would lose. They don't care about me or my brother, and why should I even expect that they would? I don't know these people, and they don't know me. *You* don't know me, even if you are stuck in my mind." After a brief moment, she could feel Sonja leave her mind, relieved at the solitude.

Alyx made her way through the trees, hearing the men laugh and talk behind her. She eventually reached a small grove, the moon piercing through the clouds and gazed down onto the snow, making it sparkle and almost blind her with the brilliance of it. She stopped at a stump seemingly not covered by snow yet. She let out a loud sigh and took slow breathes. She hated feeling this way, she hated thinking about him, she hated how he distracted her from the main reason she was here, even though he was against killing them, he still had no positive feelings towards them. She also hated that he wasn't helping her get any closer to rescuing her dad. However, the main thing she hated was that she didn't hate him at all.

She looked up at the trees, she could hear soft drips from the snow falling off of tree branches in the distance. The overall silence that surrounded her was very much appreciated, considering she hadn't had a moments peace alone to properly think things through. Funny how Sonja just now decided to leave her alone for a bit. Maybe it was because she knew Alyx was in no danger of drinking her problems away, even though a drink did sound really good right about now, mead did not sound very enticing. Alyx made herself comfortable by taking a seat on the stump, grabbing the cloak around herself. The moonlight illuminated the snow, only confirming the deep chill in the breeze that danced around her. She allowed herself to lower her hood, smoothing out her hair which was probably a crazy, dirty mess. Who was she trying to impress anyway? Considering the one person she can't stop thinking about thought she was a child. She let out a loud sigh once again, resting her chin on the palm of her hand, her elbow balanced on her knee.

"Do you do that often?" said a voice warmly. She looked up, meeting an icy gaze.

"Viggo?" she breathed. Was this real? "What are you doing here?" she questioned, her brows furrowed in confusion. He walked towards her, exiting the edge of the forest and into the grove with her.

"Where's your sister?"

"So many questions. However, you ask the wrong questions." he said flatly, continuing to walk towards her.

"What kind of questions should I be asking then?" she drew back a little, narrowing her eyes, hesitant.

"Maybe you should be asking me how I really feel about you." His words caught her off guard, causing her to flush out of embarrassment.

"What?" she breathed, she could barely talk. He stopped a few feet in front of her, his eyes fixed on her. This didn't feel right, she wanted him to notice her, to think of her more than as a child, but not in this way, this way felt--wrong.

"I think about you, a lot. You have gotten under my skin, Alyxandra. I may even be falling for you." he took another step towards her. She stood up, creeping behind the stump now, trying to create distanced between them.

"I don't believe you, Viggo. I want to but I can't," she said, pleading. Viggo stopped, looking at her confused. "I'm appreciative that you saved me earlier and that you aren't allowing anyone to murder us just yet but this isn't real."

"I'm only speaking true."

"Viggo, you just called me a child a second ago." she countered. "And the fact that you didn't care if I lived or died. So sorry if I'm a bit salty." He looked at her surprised.

"I was lying."

"If you were then why should I believe you now?" He didn't respond, seeming at a loss for words, his eyes darting back and forth frantically, as if pleading with her. This wasn't right, even though she had only known him for a few days, she knew that he would have total control of his emotions, and she knew that he would never beg.

"Who are you?" she asked flatly. She clenched her fists, this was an impostor. Viggo's eyes widened in surprise.

"By the gods are you really asking me that?" he whined, which was very unattractive to her. And very unlike him.

"Seriously, give up the bullshit, who are you?" she spat and took a step towards him. There was no readable answer on his face at first, and then slowly a smile began to creep along his mouth, curving up into severe angles, his eyes widened, crazed.

Then, they began to turn a vibrant and terrifying shade of violet.

"Oh, my god." Alyx breathed and doubled back. Viggo seemed to *melt* in front of her, giving a disgusting shrill as his skin bubbled and then steamed into a large puddle of organs, which became a woman emerging from the goo. Long wet black hair stuck to the sides of her tanned face, her widened violet eyes stared up at Alyx as she pulled herself out of the puddle and onto the snow, still soaking with what seemed like waxy skin dripping off her own. Her breathing was loud and labored, and her lungs sounded filled with fluid as she wheezed, but Neena pulled herself up onto her feet.

"Wait, are you really here?" Alyx questioned, the blood leaving her face. Holy shit, how did she release herself from the talisman?

"She, can't be." Sonja said slowly, her voice sounded groggy like she had just been asleep.

Neena looked on, trying to control her own breathing before she sucked in a breath to let out a horrific laugh, shrieking sadistically.

"This bitch is crazy." Alyx commented. Neena stopped and smiled at Alyx.

"You haven't seen crazy yet, little bird. Fortunately for you my power is not yet complete, this is but a shell. I only wanted to send you a little message." she hissed, the bizarre smile widened even more, making her face look like it was going to break from the pressure.

"What message, exactly?" she asked hesitantly. Neena held up her arm and pointed a cracked and twisted finger at her. The Neena-doll cackled.

"Little daddy isn't doing so well, now is he? You are running out of time, tick-tock, little bird. Blood will spill because of you. Run fast, run *fast,* otherwise I will catch you and you will forever

344

be my little bird, caged to die." she hissed. She lifted a crooked, gangly finger and before Alyx could blink, something shot out and she felt a sharp bite on her neck.

With one final shriek, the false-Neena crumbled like ash in front of Alyx. She looked down at her feet, the flicker of violet flashed from her crumbling eyes, glaring up at her. The stinging somewhat subsiding. However, as she dragged her gaze upwards, she saw Ezhno staring at her, shocked. His staff was outstretched, his mouth open slightly. She could only look at him, what would have happened if he hadn't of come and destroyed her? She felt a pang of guilt and some anger as she once again had to be saved. She could feel tears sting her eyes, she glared at him. Since when did she become a freaking damsel in distress?

"Seriously? Who the hell do you think you are?" she hissed at him. He looked at her, confusion filling his features. She felt a slight itch now on her neck, but she ignored it. It would only cause more annoyance.

"What? I just saved you!" he said in defense. She marched towards him.

"I was fine!" she spat and began to walk passed him. She had to get to Duncan and tell him about the message. She refused to acknowledge that Ezhno had saved her, she was done having everyone save her.

"You're welcome!" he called after her, annoyance evident in his voice. She fumed as she made her way back to the camp, vaguely hearing Ezhno follow her, even though he kept a wide birth between them.

Once she got back she saw Duncan with Chenoa, Torsten, Trygg, Viggo, Kaia and Fjola standing in front of the main fire pit, in a rather intense conversation. She glared at Viggo who met her gaze one she appeared. He didn't flinch, but merely looked at her with a bored expression, only increasing her frustration. Duncan looked up, clearly feeling the tension.

"Where have you been?" he questioned.

"Does it matter? Although I have something to tell you." she motioned for him to follow her. He nodded and stood up, walking towards her. They walked a few feet away from the others who watched them curiously, but didn't bother to butt-in.

She itched the back of her neck, it was starting to get intolerable.

"What is it, Alyx?" Duncan asked, crossing his arms.

"I saw Neena."

"Wait, what? You saw her? I thought she was still trapped!" he said a little too loudly. She hushed him.

"Not to the world please! She wasn't exactly alive and kicking, it was more like a doll. She animated a clay doll."

"Like a golem?" he responded. Even Duncan listened to their dad's stories from time to time, learning different legends played a significant role in the McOwen household, even if they didn't listen to them half the time.

"Exactly. She had a message to give me," she paused, making him urge her more. "She said that we haven't got much time to save dad. The poisons getting to him, he's dying, and fast."

"Why would she want to warn us? To push us to save him faster?" he gave her a look. She shrugged. She really wished Sonja would talk right about now, she felt so confused, and surprisingly, lonely.

"She has something planned, I just know it." she stated. Duncan narrowed his eyebrows and nodded.

"We've got to talk to Viggo's mom. Now. I've been asking them to take us to her but they keep ignoring me." he said with gritted teeth. Alyx narrowed her eyes and sneered over at Viggo, of course his expression was blank.

"I've got this." she hissed and marched over to the group who all greeted her with a surprised look, Duncan close behind.

"Okay, so I am *so* done with asking nicely. I don't give a flying fuck who you all think you are. My brother and I helped you get your sister back so I think it's time that you help us in return. My patience is growing very thin. Where is your mom?" she spat and folded her arms. The breeze picked up slightly around them as small specks of snow began to fall. Kaia fumed as she stomped closer to Alyx getting ready to say something. She didn't back down, she vowed she would never be afraid of intimidation tactics ever again.

"Calm down, bitch," Alyx held out a hand and dramatically rolled her eyes. Kaia stopped and looked at her shocked by her reaction. She looked down at Alyx's outstretched hand, not knowing how to respond. "You can try beating me to death but I will not submit to you. Ever." she glared at Kaia. Kaia took a step towards Alyx, her fist clenched. Alyx wouldn't forget how quickly Kaia jumped to the decision on trying to kill them. Viggo stepped forward and grabbed his sister by the arm, stopping her.

"There's no need for blood, sister." he said softly. Alyx glared up at him as Viggo stood in front of Kaia, who was now raging behind him. Torsten pulled her away from the group. He looked down at her, his expression composed but she could tell his serenity was cracking from anger. She glanced around at the others, Trygg was merely giving an intrigued smirk while Fjola looked at her curiously in wonder. Chenoa of course looked bored as usual. her two-colored eyes focused on Duncan.

"What the hell do you *want*, Viggo?" Alyx almost begged. She pleaded him silently, her hands palm up and outstretched, urging him to explain.

"I'm tired of these games. Where is your mom?" He looked down at her, his eyes piercing.

"We will allow you to speak to her." he stated after a few moments. She stopped, taken a back.

"Wait, you will?" she asked, surprised.

"Unless you have changed your mind?" he began.

"You're done," she cut him off. "Where is she?" she finalized, holding up a hand in front of him.

"This way." he nodded his head back, motioning for her to follow him. Alyx looked back at Duncan and waved for him to follow.

The group made their way through the camp, dodging flicking horse tails and already drunk soldiers, who behaved as soon as Trygg gave them a look. They soon came to a relatively isolated tent on the border of the camp, two soldiers standing outside.

"She's inside, she only wished to speak to you two." he said. Duncan gave him a look.

"Why are you just now bringing us to her when I have been asking you for the past half-hour?" he grumbled. Viggo raised his eyebrows.

"We were waiting for your sister to show up again. She disappeared so quickly before." he responded and shrugged. He gave Alyx a parting glance and walked through the group, whom all stared at him as he passed. They stood and waited outside as Alyx and Duncan slowly made their way inside.

Once they entered they were hit by a strong smell of herbs and some spices. A bird was singing in a rather large cage that hung on a wooden pole that kept the tent up. There was a woman softly humming to herself as she mashed what looked like a strange paste into a clay bowl. She had her back to them, but she was a rather petite woman with long dark hair braided down her back.

"Um, hello?" Alyx asked softly.

"So, you both have finally come to see me?" the woman asked, not turning around. Instead she reached over and grabbed a small bottle, shaking the remnants inside, into the bowl. She continued to hum to herself as she continued crushing the herbs.

"Finally? We weren't allowed to see you. Thank your kids for that." Alyx responded curtly. She snorted and shook her head, laying the stone mixture down as she did. She rubbed her hands together as she turned around. She had a kind face with soft green eyes and laugh lines. Everything about her read joy. She was very lovely and looked almost too young to be their mom.

"You're Viggo and Kaia's mother." Duncan stated. She nodded and gave a slight bow.

"That I am. And you two must be the ones that witch and the false brother kings are after. Pity. I am Malena." she rubbed her hands on the front of her skirts. She walked over and poked the fire that was steadily dying.

"Then you must know why we are here." Alyx said. Malena nodded.

"Young Fjola had told me all I needed to know. There is very little that I can help you with unfortunately." she took a seat in front of the fire, gathering her skirts as she did. She held out a hand towards the two vacant chairs on the other side of her. They took their seats and looked at her with confusion.

"We were told that you know all about antidotes for poisons and other ailments." Duncan said. Malena nodded and looked at them softly.

"I do, but that is only half of your troubles." her voice was full of pity.

"What you two must face on your own, I am unable to assist with. I can tell you what you need and how to prepare it but I do not have what you seek to save your father," They slumped back, disappointed. "You do not have much time. The poison is a rather aggressive hybrid. A concoction of that horrible shaman-woman."

"Shaman?" Alyx questioned in her own mind.

"She is talking about Neena." Sonja spoke up quietly. Alyx jumped slightly at Sonja's quick response.

"You okay?"

"Is that even a question?" she spat. Good point. She refocused on Malena who once again poked the fire, who was intently listening without facing them at all.

"What do we need to do, Malena?" Duncan asked. She looked at him solemnly. Alyx fought the urge to scratch viciously at the back of her neck.

"My child, it will not be easy. You will face much peril, and may even lose your sanity." she said ominously. Alyx felt a chill crawl up her spine. She was so matter-of-fact about it.

"Please, explain to us." she urged. Malena sighed.

"You both love your father very much," she started, deep in thought for a moment. "Very well, first, you will need a White-Root from a Weeping Birch. You will need to dig it up and cut it out of the tree. Keep in mind that you will have to dig it out of the ground. That can only be found in the Forbidden Valley. That lies a little West from here. That place, not very many venture. It is filled with traps and other terrors you cannot imagine. Neena has her own manner of dark creatures that she keeps locked away inside so no one would be able to make the antidote in the first place. We had lost men who tried to obtain it. It was Neena's main hold for her rituals. She was the Shaman of the village after all."

"Probably why it's called the Forbidden Valley." Alyx bit her lip.

"Really?" Duncan whispered and shot her a look. Malena looked at Alyx.

"Good to know that children still have attitudes." she commented. Alyx gave her an apologetic look, and allowed herself to scratch her neck.

"Nice going." Sonja mumbled.

"Sometimes the sarcasm just slips." Alyx spat in her mind.

"Anyway, how do we get inside the valley?" Duncan asked.

"There is a blood payment. A stone entrance." Malena said, waving a hand in the air.

"What's the second thing?" Alyx questioned. Duncan gave her a disbelieving look, as to why the news of a blood payment didn't faze her. She continued to ignore him.

"You will also need Fairy Moss. It is very rare and difficult to find since it is only found underwater, or more specifically in the Red Depths. A lake just north from here. It is very old, grown by the faeries themselves, since the beginning of time," she looked off into space, deep in thought. "I would very much like to see it for myself someday." She mentioned softly.

"How do we mix these up?" Duncan asked. Malena looked at him, coming back.

"With the White-Root you must crush and grind it up into a fine powder. Mixing the Fairy Moss's liquid that is in its casing with the powder. Your father must ingest it all for it to fully cure him."

Feeling a sense of joy, Alyx stood up, anxious to go fetch the ingredients. Malena stopped her.

"In order to obtain the Fairy Moss, you must swim down to the very bottom of the lake. It is very dark and very cold. Also, it has been guarded by a certain creature for centuries. They will not appreciate you taking something they have worked hard to protect." She warned.

"What are they?" Alyx asked. Malena gave her a slight grin, testing her reaction.

"fiskr fljóð." Fish woman.

CHAPTER 15

"SERIOUSLY? A *FISH WOMAN*? Are you talking about mermaids?" Alyx raised her eyebrows. Sonja scoffed at her.

"Really? After everything you just witnessed you still choose to deny things exist such as mermaids?" she was probably shaking her head. "Maybe I will never understand you, Alyxandra."

"There are worse horrors to worry about in the Forbidden Valley if *fiskr fljóð* do not concern you or what you call *mermaids*," Malena cautioned. "But just know, they are very old creatures, born from the gods' will. They are not to be trifled with."

"I'm sure. How far away is the Forbidden Valley from here?" she questioned, trying to change the subject. Something about mermaids made her worried, but she pressed on.

"It is about a two-day journey from here. Travel West and you will pass through a small village on your way. They should have accommodations for you," she paused for a moment. "Do you and your brother plan on journeying alone?"

"Yeah."

"That is not a safe decision. If Neena's creatures do not get you, robbers surely will. There are very unkind people in this world, you do not want to seek them out."

"I don't know who else would go with us." Alyx responded. Malena looked at her, knowing that that wasn't a lie.

"Hoping you make it out of the Forbidden Valley alive, you will then travel East to the Red Depths, a lake that is centered in a grove near a very isolated village named Fjoll. It is known to exist in The Withered Highlands, that's not too far from the Valley."

"Convenient that Neena kept both of the antidote ingredients near each other."

"Not as convenient as you would think. You best pray to the gods now, children." she said and stood up, returning to crushing the herbs in the bowl.

"Ominous." Alyx said to Sonja. Sonja gave a soft chuckle.

"She isn't wrong about Neena, I'm sure she has more than enough creatures to keep 'thieves' at bay." Sonja stated.

Duncan stood up, looking down at Alyx.

"So, when should we leave?" he looked at her expectantly. Alyx blinked, she hadn't quite got that far.

"If it's a two-day journey we will need to prepare." she wasn't quite sure how they would get there in one piece, they didn't even have any weapons. This was going to be a lot more difficult than she realized. Standing up she ran a hand through her matted hair, she really needed a brush.

"Well, we better plan something out then." Duncan finalized and turned to leave. She gave him a look.

"Okay?" she turned to follow him but stopped, looking back at Malena.

"You have something more to ask?" Malena asked without turning around. Alyx bit her lip.

"It's just," she paused, "nothing. It's nothing." she finalized. What could she ask her? Hey what happened to your family? Why are your kids the way they are? Why is Viggo such an ass to her? She decided the questions she wanted to ask weren't as important now. Shaking her head, she gave Malena an apologetic smile and exited.

"It's probably smart to not get involved." Sonja interjected. Alyx merely nodded. She joined Duncan who was talking once again with Chenoa, causing a sliver of annoyance to wedge itself in Alyx's mind. She didn't quite understand why she felt that way, maybe it was because she felt completely alone here, in this world. She kept getting her emotions and responsibilities mixed up. Viggo's eyes were haunting to her, she couldn't shake him for some reason. Which was ridiculous seeing as he hated her.

Once she joined the two she heard someone coming towards them. Looking around she saw

Fjola, her hood down and her hair in disarray. Even though she was out of breath, she was all cleaned up which Alyx now could see her innocent giant brown eyes more clearly, since she was no longer filthy and drugged up anymore. She was exasperated as she pushed past Duncan who gave her a surprised look. She tucked a strand of her dark chocolate brown hair behind her ear as she tried to catch her breath. She had a kind face which made her look younger than she was, but when she talked, she seemed older and more mature. Alyx reached out and laid a hand on her shoulder, she was much shorter than her, which maybe made her feel more protective of her. Strange, since she didn't really know much about this girl, yet she felt a deep connection to her.

"What's wrong?" Alyx asked, judging by the look on Fjola's face, something was very wrong. Fjola looked up at her, her eyebrows raised in worry as she breathed heavily.

"I saw how you and your brother will go home." she stated. Alyx met Duncan's gaze, both of their mouths flew open in shock.

"Wait, you did?" Duncan pressed her. Fjola nodded.

"It will be very dangerous, if not impossible, but it is the only way," she paused, her breathing slowed. She closed her eyes momentarily, recounting what she had just seen. "You will need to find the Serpentine Crystal. It is a pouring pot of some kind." she stopped, struggling with what she was seeing.

"Like a pitcher or a decanter of some sort?" Alyx looked at Duncan who shrugged.

"Perhaps, as long as a *pitcher* is something that pours the tears of lost souls. Tears of the dead." she said opening her eyes. The colors in her eyes danced, creating a galaxy effect, that floated slowly, lazily with all the knowledge of the world, safe in their keeping among the stars.

"Where is this pitcher?" Alyx questioned. Fjola blinked, causing her eyes to shift again.

"It is in the Forbidden Valley. However, it is hidden from view."

"Immensely helpful." Sonja grumbled. Alyx crinkled her brow.

"I need you to focus, Fjola. Where do you see it?" Fjola looked off into space, ironically and figuratively, her eyes shifted, searching the galaxy for answers. The snow started to fall around them in silence as she focused her energy. Finally, her eyes returned to normal, rather abruptly, causing her to blink rapidly.

"I'm sorry, that is all I can see for now." she looked disappointed. Alyx softened, giving her a small grin. She rubbed her shoulder, trying to console her.

"That was more than enough help, thank you." she nodded. Fjola responded with a hopeful smile in return.

"There is one thing to worry about though," her smile slowly vanishing. "I have heard of this crystal vessel, and it is nothing but evil. No one can use it without consequence, Alyxandra. Many have gone insane because of it." she urged, looking worried. Alyx wondered why this girl she had just met felt so concerned about her safety. It gave her a glimmer of hope that maybe she wasn't so alone after all.

"When we get there, or better, if we get there, then we will definitely be careful." Alyx assured her. Fjola nodded once. Alyx gave her a weak smile and started to scratch at her neck again.

She caught Fjola's reaction, which looked troubled, and lowered her hand.

"I also wanted to thank you for saving me. I know you went through great trouble because of it. Viggo told me what you did." she said, trying to keep her gaze elsewhere.

"It's okay. I'm just glad you're safe now." and she genuinely was. She felt like she had known this girl for years. Such a strange connection.

The more she thought about it, the more depressed she grew. This place, these people, she didn't really understand what she was hoping to feel, but felt disappointed at the outcome none the less. Maybe it was seeing her brother with Chenoa, and Kaia and Viggo always together, and even Torsten with the rest of the men, but she felt so alone. She didn't have her friends or her family, so what now? She came to save her father, but she felt like she might lose herself in the process.

She excused herself from Fjola, who looked after her with worry, and wandered off. She knew better this time than to leave the encampment but needed the space. She felt so selfish, wanting someone who hated her, wanting to feel accepted and wanted. Why is it that she so desperately wanted this place, this time to be it? She found a bare stump on the edge, a few men leaving once she appeared like she was evil incarnate. She sighed and sat down, wrapping the fur cloak around herself. The snow continuing to fall around her, like it seemed to do rather frequently here. She looked up, allowing her hood to slip off, the breeze was almost welcomed as she could feel the heat from her annoyance and sadness radiate up and disappear into the night sky. The moon seemed brighter than before, but it was needed--very much needed.

"If I come sit next to you, are you going to get up and leave?" asked a voice suddenly making her jump. She stood up and turned around, surprised to see Ezhno. She visibly relaxed and shook her head.

"No. I'm sorry about that earlier." she said feeling guilty. She felt so stupid about how she treated him. He did save her life after all. Resuming her seat, she watched Ezhno take his place on the snowy earth, laying his staff beside him. There was a moment of comfortable silence between them as they just watched the moon, as they did so she noticed that his rather long, dark brown hair was now braided down his back and was adorned with a few feathers. No longer in disarray and dirty. He was handsome. She was just grateful for his kindness. She sorely needed it.

"Ezhno? Can I ask you something?" she questioned. His eyes studied her for a moment, but nodded.

"Why did you follow me earlier?" He paused, not knowing what to say at first.

"I had been meaning to find you, and thank you for saving me from that horrible place. I saw you walk out of the camp by yourself and knew something was wrong. So, I followed," he shrugged. "I didn't realize that that evil woman would be there trying to kill you."

"You only saw Neena?" she pushed. He nodded again. She felt relief knowing that he hadn't seen her take the form of Viggo before, trying to tempt her into false pretenses. She didn't want anyone to know that he tempted her at all.

"Well, thank you again." she said and gave him a soft smile. He returned with a genuine grin, a single dimple showing itself.

"You're a lot prettier when you smile you know that?" he stated, causing her face to burn. That was out of nowhere. He laughed and looked back up at the moon.

"Uh, well, I would smile more if I knew what my brother and I were going to do next. We have no supplies, no weapons, nothing. How are we ever going to save my dad now? The Forbidden Valley is miles from here." she rambled. She looked at him, realizing that he probably has no idea what she was talking about. She gave him a guilty look.

"Sorry, long story."

"Fjola had told me about your problem." he stated nonchalantly. Her eyebrows raised.

"Oh? What did she say?" He glanced at her.

"Everything, about your father--and your destiny." Alyx rolled her eyes.

"There goes that word again: destiny. People seem to think that some prophecy will be fulfilled because of us. We're only here for my dad, that's it. Case closed. We're not involved in this war, just because my ancestor royally screwed up doesn't mean we have to fix it." she spat and folded her arms underneath her cloak. Her neck was itching again.

"You're acting like a child, maybe Viggo *was* right about you." Sonja murmured, causing a flare of anger to claw its way through Alyx's heart. She unfolded her arms and sighed, regaining composure. Ezhno was too busy gazing up at the moon to notice. Why was Sonja acting like such a bitch? More than usual at least.

"There are many things that are thrown our way, Alyxandra. Many things that we do not wish to do, but when faced with the decision, would you make the right choice? Or would you run?" he didn't look at her. She bit her lip, not knowing what to say. Would she stay and fight? Or would she be the child everyone thought she was.

"I--I guess I don't know." she stated, and it was true. She had never stared death in the face before, would it snuff her out, or show her mercy was the real question.

"I'm afraid that the time will come soon for you. I hope you will know by then," he rubbed the side of his face and yawned. "It is late. It is time for us to rest for now." he stood up, brushing some of the snow off of his leather clothing and grabbed his staff. He offered her a hand and she accepted it with a friendly smile.

They walked back together, causing people to stare warily in their direction. She wasn't sure if the men were warier of her or of Ezhno, knowing the history between Vikings and Native Americans. Neither were probably welcomed.

"You'd think with me being 'destined' I would get a little more respect around here." she stated, rolling her eyes. Ezhno looked at her in wonder.

"Don't you think they have had enough of people demanding respect from them?" he asked. Alyx sighed.

"Ezhno, I understand what you're saying--," she started.

He cut her off. "No, I don't think you do," he shook his head. "They all have been through hell. Things that you cannot even imagine." he whispered.

They found Duncan and Chenoa talking with Torsten and Kaia, which was strange to see Kaia without her brother. Alyx couldn't help but search the crowd around her for Viggo, but she couldn't find him anywhere. Her heart began to pound, but she ignored it and took her place next to Duncan who was in deep conversation with Torsten about which route to go and what help or aid to seek out. Alyx tried to focus on the information, but she couldn't, so many things had happened, so many questions she had yet no one to answer them. The itching was unbearable again, only raising the agitation within her. Sonja was in and out which was odd, she was nowhere close to saving her dad, she had miles to travel and she still had no idea on how to get back. The stress was eating away at her and she felt like shutting down. She never wanted a drink so badly in her life before now.

She also had been scratching so much at the back of her neck that it was almost raw. Alyx silently thanked herself for growing her hair out long so it could hide the evidence.

"Alyx? Where you listening?" Duncan interjected.

"Hmm?" she said dumbly. He sighed and rubbed the back of his neck.

"Where do you go all the damn time?" he mumbled, trying to keep his voice down as he moved closer to her. She shrugged and stared around, lost in her thoughts. Duncan grumbled and shook her shoulder.

"Hey seriously, ever since you got back from the mead hall you have been acting crazier than usual. What happened back there? Did Viggo do something to you? What happened when you went missing earlier? You came back with Ezhno?" he questioned, eyeing her suspiciously.

"What? No!" Alyx hissed meeting his gaze. "He saved my life! I would have been eaten alive if it wasn't for him! And he and I were just talking, nothing more. Way to think so highly of me." He hushed her and tried to gather his words.

"I'm just saying, I need you to be fully focused, dad needs us and we're wasting time. Now is not the time to have a crush. You're letting yourself get to distracted."

"You're one to talk!" she whispered harshly. He looked taken a back.

"What are you talking about?"

"Oh, don't play dumb, Duncan. You and Chenoa have gotten awfully close haven't you. It's only been a couple of days. Don't be a hypocrite!"

she gritted her teeth. He couldn't say anything to her. He didn't deny it.

"She is a good person, and she knows a lot about this land. I've learned a lot from her. More than you've been trying to do. All you do is run away and blame others for shit that happens to you." he growled, no longer trying to hide their conversation. He stood up, causing the others to break the conversation. He stomped off, moving past Chenoa, who looked from him, to Alyx and gave her a look which infuriated her.

"Don't try and make me feel guilty. He's *my* family!" she spat and stood up, she turned and walked away before she could see the reaction Chenoa might have had.

"How dare he!" she hissed in her mind. Hoping Sonja would say something, anything. Nothing. Not even a sarcastic comment from her anymore. Only on Sonja's terms it seems.
She incessantly tore at the back of her neck, only causing her skin to catch on fire. She even started to think of them as friends.

"I'm going fucking crazy here," she said out loud, grabbing a strand of her hair and rubbing it between her fingers as she shoved past some rather irritated Vikings. She was losing her mind. "And it won't stop *itching*!" she snarled.

"Alyxandra?" his voice was like butter, which seemed to coax her for a minute. She stopped and turned to see Viggo looking at her questionably. She was hesitant, not knowing if this was another trick or not.

"Are you really him this time?" she spat. He looked taken a back.

"As far as I know, I am me. What is wrong with you?" he looked at her like she belonged in a mental hospital. Maybe she did. Then she began to cry, it was an unbelievable force she couldn't control. She began to sob and ugly cry like she had never done before. She felt erratic and unpredictable. She was just so glad to see that he was real and in front of her, she had no idea why she was so relieved, but he was the one she truly wanted to see. She did something she never thought she would do.

She collapsed in his arms.

He didn't know what to do at first, but then he wrapped his arms around her, strong yet gentle.

He smelled of the earth and something she couldn't put her finger on, his natural musk screaming protection, power, and---love?

She felt protected for the first time in a long time. She didn't feel so alone. The itching subsided a bit, allowing her to relax. She was about to say something when she suddenly felt a hard smack across her head, causing her vision to go blurry.

Then she blacked out.

She heard frantic voices as she came too, the world was swaying as she began to open her eyes again. Then she flinched, an unbelievable pain spread through the back of her neck just then. She reached back to feel fabric, like gauze wrapped around her now exposed neck, her breath sucking between her teeth.

"What the hell?" she muttered unintelligibly and tried to sit up.

"Slow down." said a familiar voice. She turned her head back and saw Duncan and Viggo sitting in chairs nearby, she was lying on a makeshift cot in a tent, probably still in the encampment. Her heart skipped a little when her eyes met Viggo's, not forgetting how he held her, even if it was fleeting.

"What's going on?" she demanded. Duncan glanced at Viggo.

"Okay, don't freak because I know how you feel about these kinds of things," her brother began. Her eyes widened.

"What?"

"You had a parasite in you. I don't know how you got it, but Viggo thinks it may have happened when you disappeared earlier. When Ezhno brought you back. You've been out for a while. Viggo has already questioned him. He didn't do it." Duncan explained slowly. Alyx could feel the blood leave her face, and she could feel her skin crawl.

"A, parasite...?" she whispered. She had had a major fear of anything parasitic since she was little. Ever since she got a leech stuck on her ankle when her family went boating out on the lake one year when she was about thirteen, she was officially traumatized by it ever since.

"You can thank my mother for getting it out. It wasn't easy. You have been asleep for a couple of days now. We don't know what it may have been poisoned with just yet."

The room was spinning, a couple of days? She had wasted that much time? Also, she had been poisoned? Was she going to die?

"That explains the strange behavior from you." Duncan commented. This whole time, she had some blood sucking parasite attached to the back of her neck?

"Did you know about this?" Alyx practically roared in her mind. She could feel Sonja's presence.

"If I was strong enough I would have sensed it easily, but sadly, no, I didn't know. But I think the little bastard was behind my energy drain. I just don't know how long it had been there," she hissed. "It's not a normal parasite either I'm afraid. It was siphoning my spells which has Neena written all over it," she spat. "Do not worry, the poison is not fatal. It was merely to drain." Sonja quickly added. Alyx relaxed a little.

"That explains your complete absence," Alyx stated. "Sonja? W-What would have happened if that *thing* stayed in me longer?" She was terrified of the answer.

"I'm not for certain, but my guess is that it was placed within you, to kill me. Which means you would have to die."

Alyx felt light headed. She looked desperately around the room.

"Where is it?" she asked aloud. Duncan hesitated, probably knowing her reaction. She looked him square in the eye. "Show me." she hissed. He opened his mouth to say something but stopped. He looked back at Viggo and nodded his head slowly. Viggo glanced over at Alyx, but nodded and turned around to grab a wooden box. He stood up and walked over to her, carefully taking the lid off. She pushed herself up as best she could, allowing herself to look. She gasped at the sight of it.

It was barely breathing, or more so--*pulsing*. It looked like a spider mostly, with its multiple legs spread out on the bottom. It also had around six or seven tiny beady eyes that looked weakly up at Alyx. Its body however, was long and skinny, shaped like a mosquito with vibrant shades of greens and purples mixed, and it had two claws, half the size of its own body. She bit back the vomit that was making its way up her throat.

"Oh my god. This *thing* was inside of me?" she looked desperately at Duncan, who answered her with a nod. "Where?" she pushed. He squinted slightly, pointing to the back of his neck.

"It was almost fully burrowed inside the back of your neck." Viggo said unflinchingly. Duncan looked at him in annoyance.

"Seriously? That's not how you tell people shit like that." Duncan scoffed, holding his arms up.

"You cannot hide that from her," he stated and closed the lid. He tossed it on the table nearby and folded his arms, looking down at her. "You still think that you are not a part of this war, and yet the war has been inside of you this whole time." he muttered. Her eyes widened, she opened her mouth to say something but was at a loss for words. Viggo turned to leave but she held up a hand.

"No wait," he looked at her, his face unreadable.

"I don't know what else to do. All I ask is for your help. I don't know what I can do to stop this war, but all I really know is that I can't do this alone. So, I'm willing to try if you are." she stated, choosing her words carefully. For once, Viggo was left speechless, his eyebrows lifted. After a few moments passed, he spoke.

"Very well then. By the gods, let us fight this war. And end this." For the first time since she arrived, she saw something in Viggo that she didn't see in herself. His eyes started to glow within a low, embered fire.

Hope.

CHAPTER 16

BY MIDAFTERNOON Alyx had something to eat and drink, and felt rested enough to begin packing for their journey. As she laid in the cot, the others had come in for a short meeting. Viggo enlisted of course his most trusted companions which included, much to Alyx's dismay, Kaia, then the ones she wasn't disappointed in having, Torsten and Chenoa who gladly agreed to accompany them. Trygg, wanting trusted eyes as they traveled, sent his cousin Bjorn and Svein, his best spy. Alyx gave Bjorn a shy wave in greeting, who merely gave her a slight nod in return, just like before. His face still bruised, but visibly healing well.

To No End

As Alyx saddled her horse, she looked over at the two who would accompany them. Bjorn was tall with light, sandy-colored hair that was pulled back in a tight bun though the sides were shaved. He had kind eyes, but something about his expression always seemed sad to her, like he had gone through too much far too young. Then again, most of the men had that air about them. Probably things that Alyx would never understand. Next to him, Svein, she thought, was a very handsome man who had wandering eyes, yet somehow, she would always see him look back at Fjola. He had light hazel eyes and strawberry blonde hair that was braided back like most of the other men. She was still getting used to the culture and the way they dressed. Most of it was braids and tattoos but there was also a deep sense of religion and faith in the gods that just emanated throughout the camp. There was such a deep-rooted sense of respect for the gods that made her curious to learn more. She knew very little about the Viking ways but wondered, were they so different from the Native Americans? She looked over at Chenoa and thought about the passion she had about the earth and the different spirits that balanced throughout the world.

Then something came to her.

"Sonja? How close were you with Neena's mother?"

"The Shaman woman? Very, she taught me and Neena all we know about magic and using the earths energy." Sonja said fondly, she had a hint of sadness in her tone, probably thinking back on old memories.

"So, did she ever talk about the balance of the spirits in this world and the next?"

"Of course, there are many gods that keep this earth thriving. Why do you ask?"

"I have this feeling--there seems to be so much more to Neena than just mere siphoning magic, don't you think? If she's able to do more than you--have more power--then what exactly is she feeding off of? Just look around us, the earth feels like it's slowly dying. There can't be enough for her to feed off of constantly. Even the earth has limitations." Alyx stated. Sonja didn't respond at first.

"Are you saying there might be gods involved?"

"Are you going to rule that out? At this point, I feel like anything could be on the table." Sonja gave a disbelieving scoff.

"By the gods, you might just be right." she breathed.

"There's just no way it could be all Neena's doing. Besides, how she's always decaying or never really in full form whenever she tried to approach me, made me feel like she was still limited. When she came to see me back at home, nothing was dying around her. She wasn't siphoning, so where was she getting the energy from?" she questioned. She could tell Sonja was impressed.

"Alyxandra, I can't believe I'm saying this, but you are very surprising. I never know what you will do or say next."

"Some call that spontaneity." Alyx said in her mind, smug. She finished tying off the fur saddle and tightened the cloak around her.

"Or insanity."

"Call it what you like." Alyx shrugged and went off to find Viggo through the soldiers bustling around her.

———⋘◈⋙———

After asking Torsten for Viggo's whereabouts, she made her way to Malena's tent. Walking through the entrance after greeting the guards she very soon found that she was interrupting a rather intense conversation.

"Sorry, should I have knocked?" Alyx gritted her teeth, embarrassed. Malena looked at Viggo, her eyebrows narrowed.

"No. My son was just leaving. Do you need something?" she asked. Alyx nodded.

"I need to talk to him actually. There's something I need to tell you." Viggo looked at her questioning. He nodded and gave Malena a glance before following Alyx out the entrance.

"What is it?" he asked once they were far enough away.

"I think Neena might be teaming up with a god." she said in a rush. Viggo looked genuinely surprised.

"A god? Really? Which one?" he blurted. She looked apologetic.

"I don't know." She forgot the many gods the Vikings worshipped.

"Well, how do you know this?"

"Mainly just a feeling I have."

"That's it? A feeling? That is not much to go off of." his said as his shoulders visibly fell in disappointment.

"Hey, I know it's not much to go off of, but it makes sense! How else could she never possibly run out of energy? Doesn't the earth feel like it's dying around us and she keeps getting stronger? That smells like total bullshit to me." he looked down, contemplating her words. He placed a hand on his hip and rubbed his face, his eyebrows drawn.

"I guess we cannot exactly rule that out. I feel like we should bring this up to the others, get their take on it as well," he met her gaze. "Thank you. At least it's something we can consider further." She felt like she was going to faint, he thanked her? That was unbelievable.

Almost.

———◈———

Once she finished helping the others by gathering the necessities, she joined Duncan and Torsten who were sitting by a fire, trying to warm up before they set off.

"Once we get to the Forbidden Valley, then what?" Torsten questioned. Alyx chewed on her bottom lip.

"The goal is to find the ingredients that we need to save our dad. Hopefully we can find something there that can also take down Neena and the brothers. Or brother-monster-duo-blob-thing," she said, talking to no one in particular. "There has to be." she said deep in thought now. She heard a gruff scoff. Blinking, she turned to look at Duncan who had a grin on his face.

"What?"

"Oh nothing. It's just, you're different. A good different. Something about you is changing. Ever since we got that thing out of you, you're more focused, more motivated." he laughed with a wide toothy smile which made her smile in return. She couldn't help it; the positive energy was contagious. She play-punched him in the arm.

"And here I thought I was perfect this whole time." she joked. Torsten joined in the laughter. She *did* feel different, she couldn't quite explain it, but she felt almost lighter, airier. She didn't feel bogged down by depression or self-doubt. As she looked around the camp, somehow everything was in distinct color, even the snow had a certain hue to it that she couldn't quite pinpoint. The world was sparkling again. Her life made sense again, and whether it had to do with the parasite, or it was her own negative energy being blown up by Neena, it felt good to finally have some control again. She felt a sense of peace and meaning that was carrying her now. She felt like now she could take on Neena, she could finally save her dad, and she had the drive to accomplish it. She also felt a sense of relief because she knew she wouldn't be doing it alone.

She scanned once more over the men and her gaze fell onto Viggo who was studying her like he had done the first moment they met. It had been a week since then, and she felt a budding connection with him. He didn't hate her, but he maybe wasn't exactly warming up to her quite yet either. She looked at him and felt mainly a feeling of being immensely grateful. She gave him a curt nod and a slight grin, trying to silently communicate. His mouth parted slightly, and there was something that flickered in his eyes but she couldn't quite make out what it was. Shutting his mouth, he gave her a nod back and pulled his gaze away. She sighed, maybe one of these days she would understand him. But until then, she knew she wouldn't be alone. Maybe this world would open her eyes and answer the questions she so desperately asked herself.

"When do we go?" she asked Duncan enthusiastically, tucking a strand of hair behind her ear. She rocked on her heels, causing the snow from underneath her to crunch loudly.

"Actually, there is a slight errand to do before we leave." Torsten said, weighing his words carefully. Alyx stopped.

"An errand? You can't be serious--now?" she
scoffed. Torsten nodded and waved for them to
follow. He motioned to Viggo who quickly joined
them. If Viggo was involved then it was an
important errand.

Alyx and Duncan followed Torsten and Viggo
towards a nearby tent, its opening flapping from a
gust of chilled wind. There was the loud clanging of
metal on an anvil being pounded into shape. Alyx
ducked under and into the small space. She was
quickly greeted by the smell of sulfur and burnt
metal. In front of them stood a rather large, and old
looking man who was swinging a hammer down on a
piece of glowing metal, banging it into position and
folding it to his will. He had his back turned to them,
but all Alyx was focused on was the large mural
tattoo that exposed itself slightly on the back of his
neck. It looked like runes along with glowing
objects, or shapes. She couldn't quite tell. Viggo
cleared his throat, not bothering to speak. The
blacksmith stopped swinging at the sound and
sighed, agitation arising.

"I already told ye, I am not joining your little
'cause,' now leave me be. I agreed to show the

blacksmith you already have how it's done." he said with a gruff and tossed the hammer down onto the ground. He turned around, grabbing a water pouch and unstoppered it, taking a long swig before pausing and focusing on Alyx. She looked down uncomfortable. He had a very intense gaze which only fueled the intimidation. She could still feel his eyes on her, causing her to peak up at him. He was now a few feet away from her which made her take a step back in surprise. He didn't seem to notice her meekness and gave Viggo a glance, his brows rising.

"Where is the blacksmith by the way?" Torsten mentioned. Without looking away, this blacksmith smacked his lips.

"I sent him to go fetch some ore," he said in a bored tone. "So, this is the girl that Fjola saw, eh?" he scoffed. Viggo nodded and folded his arms. The blacksmith rubbed his bearded chin. He was bald, but his scalp was completely adorned with tattoos. He was the most decorated old man Alyx had ever seen. "And I am guessing you expect me to agree now that you have proof." he asked. Viggo shrugged. Alyx grinned at how nonchalant he is.

"Is it working?" Torsten commented.

"Immensely. How do I know she's willing to fight and actually win?" he added. Viggo took a step forward.

"With your weaponry expertise of course. Teaching a blacksmith isn't enough, we *need* you. You are the best chance we have." It was odd to see Viggo try and reason, instead of order. Something had told her that he probably felt the same way. There was a pause as the blacksmith studied him. Finally, he let out a boisterous laugh and clapped Viggo on the shoulder, making him jerk forward, his brows raised in surprise.

"Well, I never thought I would see the day the son of Atle the mighty begging me for help." he chuckled and tugged on his long beard. Viggo looked embarrassed.

"I never beg. I persuade." he mumbled. Alyx giggled, he looked more like a boy which was refreshing.

"Alright. Whatever you tell yourself. But I will help ye. You should consider yourselves lucky, I turned the fool kings down. They considered that a mighty treason," he turned to stoke the fire more.

"Had to go into hiding for it. Luckily, Trygg found me, otherwise I would've been in a mighty tough spot." he gave Alyx a wink.

"Excuse me, but who are you?" Alyx asked hesitantly. The blacksmith took another swig from the water pouch.

"I am called many names--but, I prefer to go by Øystæin Ragisson." he declared and took a seat on a wooden chair adorned with animal rugs. He motioned for them to sit and they obeyed, all taking a spot either on the floor or in a nearby chair.

"Øystæin, do you know anything about a weapon that can destroy Neena?" Duncan questioned immediately. He looked at Alyx's brother and smirked.

"Of course," he said smugly. "However, it doesn't just happen overnight. The weapon you require takes at least a month. I need to have the right material, and it will take me a bit to siphon up enough energy to imbue it, of course. Most likely will need some assistance with that part." he said nonchalantly. Alyx blinked.

"Wait, imbue? Are you like Neena?" she questioned. He laughed once.

"Neena isn't the only one who can learn to siphon the world's energy. But no, I am not. For one I have decency. Also, I have learned that ability far before she was even a thought."

"Where did you learn?" Duncan asked.

"From the ancients," he waited for their reactions. He grinned, a deep rumble of laughter emanated from his chest. "Yes, I am older than I look."

"I guess I don't follow. Who are the ancients?" Alyx responded, trying to meet anyone's gaze for answers.

"They are from the very beginning, my girl. The first Shamans. I was here long before the fool kings led their army into this territory. I learned many things from the oldest tribe."

"Tribe? They were Native American?"

He scoffed. "Is that what you call them where you are from? But yes, the Crimson Mountain tribe. They dwelled in the mountains West from here. It is a very holy place. Unfortunately, most of them are gone," he said solemnly. "It was because of them that the fool kings found this land in the first place. Of course, not knowing what would become of them, they were far too kind. I was out hunting when those two deranged imbeciles arrived. They demanded respect and immediate hospitality," he spat venomously. "It made me sick. Then, as time wore on, there were whispers of a nameless threat. Something that the shamans of old did not foresee."

"You are talking about the dark spirit are you not?" Viggo said. Øystæin nodded, his brows furrowed. "Even my people fear it." he added.

"Dark spirit?" Alyx questioned, her brows knitting together.

"You see, there are things in this world that connect us to the beyond. There's Valhalla, and then there are other realms. Ones we do not know about. But the ancients have seen it. There were gateways created long before their time. The dark spirit must have sensed the fool kings and relished in their power-hungry egos."

"Negativity breeds negativity." Alyx muttered. Øystæin held out a hand, agreeing.

"The ancients proceeded to close the gateways, not knowing that the dark spirit had planted a very dangerous seed. You see, it had already helped the fool kings travel to this land."

To No End

"That's why they traveled so far inland! They went through the gateways." Duncan guessed.

"The ancients ended up closing the gateways, sealing them off so the dark spirit could not reach for human life. If it did, who knows what it could unleash." Then it clicked for Alyx.

"What if it got out?" she asked. Everyone looked at her, their eyes wide. "Seriously, what if that's how Neena is siphoning so much energy?" she said in a rush. Viggo looked at Torsten.

"That could very well be, but if that theory is indeed true, then we might as well pray to the gods because Helheim is going to be unleashed." Øystæin whistled. Duncan stood first, Alyx looked at him questioningly.

"Well, are we going to go then? Øystæin needs a month to make the weapon, and we must find the antidotes. We don't have much time so we can't waste anymore of it." he stated. Alyx nodded and stood up as well. As everyone began to walk out, Øystæin gently grabbed her arm. She stopped and looked at him curiously. He waited for everyone to walk away before he looked at her gravely.

"Beware that Neena is always hunting you. If what you say is true, then you all are fighting against something that isn't human. The woman may be trapped, but she will eventually get out. Are you ready to face her when the time comes?" he warned. Alyx's lips flattened into a straight line.

"With your help and that weapon, I stand a better chance than without," she stated. Øystæin searched her eyes once more before letting go. Hesitating she decided to ask: "Why didn't you stop the kings? I'm sure your more powerful than you look." He snorted, but his eyes fell and sorrow filled them.

"I was young and a fool. That was back when I feared death and darkness. Fear makes you do terrible, and cowardly things."

She nodded her head, understanding and decided she didn't want details. He gave her a soft grin and a wave of dismissal. She turned back, leaving the tent as she did so.

"Alyx? Let's go. We're moving out." Duncan said as he and Torsten made their way towards their horses.

"Coming." she said and followed.

"Let's do this." Sonja said making Alyx grin.

"As you wish." she responded in her mind. She pulled herself onto her horse and clicked her tongue, following the line of procession of horses. Duncan caught her eye, he gave her a goofy grin. She laughed once, meeting his gaze.

"What?" she insisted. He shook his head, the grin remained.

"Nothing, it's just you're not obsessed with that necklace anymore. I haven't see you touch it in a while is all." and with that he proceeded forward, keeping up with the others.

She looked down, uncovering it from underneath her cloak and holding the necklace out in front of her. It gleamed from the faint sunlight dimly poking through the hazy clouds. He was right, she hadn't really thought of it all since they arrived. Curious, perhaps it was because she no longer feared Sonja? Or that her erratic emotions didn't seem to affect the necklace anymore either.

"I fear it may have to do with how weak I am getting." Sonja interjected. Alyx blinked.

"Weak?" Alyx responded in her mind.

"Yes, Neena is siphoning everything. It is getting much harder to obtain consciousness because of it." she whispered. Not wanting to force Sonja to use up any more energy, Alyx dropped the discussion for now. She would need Sonja when it came down to it.

Alyx glanced back at the men and hoped that she would make a big enough difference for their lives. It wasn't just about saving one man anymore it seemed, she now felt the responsibility of saving thousands. Looking forward, she saw the sun was burning high in the sky and felt hope that because the sun would rise tomorrow, she had a chance of fighting back.

Alyx tightened her cloak around her more and got ready to travel through the night as they headed West.

Gaebrielle Wieck is a fantasy writer who currently resides in Omaha, Nebraska with her husband and their little Corgi-potato, Pippen. She's obsessed with all things to do with movies, video games and reading. Her true passions reside within fantasy, science fiction and young adult to new adult fiction. *To No End* is the first book in her new adult fantasy series, The Skorravik Trilogy, and her debut novel. She is the founder of Wandering Hope Publication, LLC.

CONNECT WITH GABBIE AT:

www.gaebriellewieckbooks.com
www.wanderinghopepublicationllc.com
www.facebook.com/authorgabbiewieck/
Instagram @yurfutureauthor68
Twitter @GabbieGabbieILW

<u>Acknowledgments</u>

I wanted to give thanks to all the people who have been there for me since day one, and I apologize ahead of time, it's quite a list!

Seeing as it's my first book I felt it necessary to make such a list.

I don't believe we thank all the people in our lives properly as much as we should sometimes. For me personally, I believe everyone that has come into our lives, good or bad, is a gift and fate bring those who are needed at that time. I wanted to say thank you to everyone that I am friends with now, or have been, because you have all impacted my life in a big way. I am the person today because of all of you. You have made me stronger and witnessed that true humanity is about treating other people reflects on how you feel about yourself. I have grown up--at least to my knowledge--and have learned that even in defeat, you can thrive, and that everyone that's in your life is there for a reason. You should always embrace the good and the bad because we learn from every mistake and imperfection that we have or have made. I wanted Alyx to be very human even if she wasn't always the most likable of person sometimes. I have also learned that you should never take anyone for granted because you never know when you may lose them. Live for today, and thank all of those who matter. So, on behalf of that, Thank you!

First, I wanted to say thank you to my parents Amy and Chris because they have *always* pushed me to be the very best that I can be, and have supported me with anything that I wanted to do, foolish or realistic. My dad has fed my love of fantasy since I was small and ever since he read me my first 'real' book, it changed everything. You changed everything for me, just by being the best dad anyone could ask for. Also, for my mom's unfailing patience even when I came up with the most ridiculous ideas.

Second, my sister Arianne, even if we never really see eye to eye, you still supported my love of writing and wanted me to be myself always. You also wanted me to be wise and kind, even when that wasn't always my strong suit. I appreciate your sensitivity and your passion.

To my Oma, who is just as stubborn as I am which allowed me to never give up on fulfilling my dream of becoming a writer, and dedicated to my Opa, who had never given up on me, and always supported the big dreams I had, whether I wanted to be a writer or a movie star you would always oblige and cheer me on. You both are an immense blessing in my life and I have become such a stronger person because you believe in me and have taught me so many things that only you two can do.

To my grandparents Annette and William, who show me the real joy in life and to always keep a positive attitude, and that family is a very important thing. They have given me the inspiration that explains why Alyx is so family oriented and that no matter what happens, the people that really matter are the ones who have never left your side.

To Justin, my incredibly patient and supportive husband, who no matter what we have been through, we have been through it together. I thank you for everything you have done for me and you mean the absolute world, and no matter what will happen in the remainder of our lives, good or bad, you are still number one, and will continue to hold my heart.

To Chris, Brent and Kyle, you all are equally important in my life because you have been my second family and have shown me to stay positive as well and have helped me through a lot and have always cheered me on with anything and everything that I have wanted to do, and continue to do so with an open mind.

To Cheryl Golden, for having our Border

Bookstore days where we could sit and write/ read for hours at a time. You helped fuel my passion for literature. Thank you for sharing your love of books and your support for my crazy ideas and story lines.

To Karen Grinberg, because you have pushed me to embrace perfection and push myself continuously because you knew that I could be and do more. Thank you for pushing my realization further that writing is my absolute purpose in life, and that I do in fact need this to feel fulfilled.

To Sarah, Taylor S, and Mariah, because no matter what good or bad we have always remained friends, you all have been there when others haven't and have supported and defended me when others wouldn't dare of doing. You have risked your reputation by being my friend and have embraced my nerdyness. I love our long talks about boys, clothes, college, and the future and I hope we will always remain as close. You girls have made me stronger as a person, even if you had never realized that.

To Taylor H, who will always be my potato in crime and my constant cheerleader, I have learned so much from you over the years and your humor never fails to make me smile even when I just want to cry.

To Sue, who helped me with frustrating titles and allowed me to push through my writer's block, your support is unwavering.

To Jake, I owe a lot to you because without our brainstorming sessions, this book probably would not have been seen through to the end. Thank you so much for your unwavering support and sharing your love of mythology as well as your knowledge of the unknown with me. Editing was a lot less daunting and frustrating because of you.

To Kristen Martin, Jenna Moreci, Natalia Leigh, and Vivien Reis, for guiding me on this crazy journey. Without any of you, my favorite YouTubers/ Vloggers and writer guru's, To No End would never have seen fruition. I will never be able to thank you all enough. Being a writer can be very challenging and overwhelming, you all helped ease that path with much less difficulty.

And a special thanks to all the readers of course, without you, Alyx wouldn't have the support to reach the end. You are all amazing!

Thank you again to everyone, you all have made such an impact in my life. I can never say thank you enough to truly have you all to understand how grateful I am.

DON'T MISS OUT ON THE EXCITING
SEQUEL IN THE SKORRAVIK TRILOGY:

FORBIDDEN GUIDES

Coming soon!

To No End

28091038R00239

Printed in Great Britain
by Amazon